MW00713507

Blessings,
Carol Taraff

The Christmas Baby

A Windmill Gardens Novel

By

Carol Ann Tardiff

Copyright © 2005 by Carol Ann Tardiff

All rights reserved. No part of this book shall be reproduced or transmitted in any form or by any means, electronic, mechanical, magnetic, photographic including photocopying, recording or by any information storage and retrieval system, without prior written permission of the publisher. No patent liability is assumed with respect to the use of the information contained herein. Although every precaution has been taken in the preparation of this book, the publisher and author assume no responsibility for errors or omissions. Neither is any liability assumed for damages resulting from the use of the information contained herein.

This is a work of fiction. Names, characters, places, and incidents either are the product of the author's imagination or are used fictitiously. Any resemblance to actual events or locales or persons, living or dead, is entirely coincidental.

ISBN 0-7414-2734-6

Cover credit: Katie Tardiff

Editing credit: Eleanor Burley

Scripture quotations are taken from the King James version of the Bible

Published by:

INFI∞ITY
PUBLISHING.COM

1094 New DeHaven Street, Suite 100
West Conshohocken, PA 19428-2713
Info@buybooksontheweb.com
www.buybooksontheweb.com
Toll-free (877) BUY BOOK
Local Phone (610) 941-9999
Fax (610) 941-9959

Printed in the United States of America
Printed on Recycled Paper
Published September 2005

Consecrated to:

Jesus Christ – my Lord, my God and my All –
and to Mother Mary

Dedicated to:

Mom and Dad Tardiff, who have modeled
for over fifty years
the joys and sacrifices of Christ-like married love;

and to Aunt Becky, whose heart has always been
for the babies

*Note: In order not to disrupt the continuity of the story, there are no
footnotes; however, additional information for particular chapters
is given at the end of the book*

1

The Waiting Begins

The moonlight poured like liquid silver through a slim crack where the ceiling of the humble resting place joined the back wall. It lay as a shimmering pool on the straw-strewn floor, its cool luminescence in contrast to the softer radiance of a low fire in the center of the area. From the flickering flames a wisp of smoke rose lazily upwards.

A sudden movement drew attention to the presence of a man standing near the fire. The yellow light glowed on his weathered face as he peered over the top of a dark robe he was holding up to the heat. Every so often the man would run a hand over the fabric to feel if it was warm enough.

Finally he seemed satisfied and, gathering the garment close to his body, he stepped around the fire to the other side. A slight figure seated on a short wooden stool turned and smiled at him as he draped the robe around her shoulders. He arranged it so it wouldn't slip off, then the trailing end he pulled over a wooden feedbox next to her. After tucking the edges carefully into the closest corners of the box, he paused for a moment gazing down at it before returning to the fire. As he held his hands toward the flames in an attempt to gather some warmth in that dismal place, there was a shuffling noise behind him and the bleating complaint of a ram was heard.

At the sound, the robe in the feedbox unexpectedly moved as a tiny foot kicked outwards in a gesture reminiscent of every newborn child. The woman smiled and, laying a hand gently on the makeshift blanket, beckoned to the man with her other hand. At the gesture, he left his comfortable place at the fire to peer more closely at the baby lying in the manger...

"Dr. Greenwald, you have a call on line three. Dr. Greenwald, line three."

The intrusive sound of the intercom cut like a knife through the dream-like images running through the woman's mind. She shook her head to clear the thoughts which had taken her far from this brightly-lit room. She'd been staring at a small nativity set which had been set up on a large end table in the hospital's waiting area. Under the soft lighting of a table lamp stood not only the nativity scene, but also a stuffed snowman and several figures of rather ugly children on sleds which were carved, none too skillfully, out of balsa wood.

The woman leaned closer to touch the manger scene, wondering that it was here at all, given the animosity with which most public institutions treated the religious side of Christmas.

And anyone could walk off with these pieces... Then she realized that everything had been glued to a piece of plywood carefully camouflaged with cotton snow. *Just look at those tacky sparkles sprinkled on top!*

The woman sighed to herself, thinking, *Maybe, when no one's looking, I could loosen those ugly sledders. Then some kid might come along and play with them – and accidentally lose them.* However, that thought was quickly forgotten as she saw the familiar figure of her neighbor open the door of the waiting room and hurry over to her.

"How are you doing, Del? You look awfully tired."

The newly-arrived woman perched on the arm of a nearby chair. She absentmindedly removed her headband and repositioned it in her wavy auburn hair, her eyes filled with concern.

Del took off her glasses and laid them in her lap, rubbing a hand across her weary face. She attempted to smooth the short flyaway strands of salt-and-pepper hair around her face into the longer hair coiled neatly at the back of her neck.

Replacing her glasses, she replied, "I'm fine, Ann." She nodded gratefully at the younger woman and patted her arm while asking, "Were you able to find out anything?"

"Well, I'm doing everything I can. Being a nurse doesn't mean I'm privy to everything going on, especially since I haven't worked here since before my kids were born. But I'm listening closely and trying to hang around the appropriate doors. And I know a few of the other nurses. Even though they're not allowed to give out confidential information, I'm trying to pick up what I can. No one else has arrived yet?"

When Del shook her head Ann got up to leave.

"Don't worry, Del – I'm sure everything will be fine. I'll let you know as soon as I hear any news. Why don't you go down to the cafeteria and get something to eat?"

Del thanked her neighbor, saying that maybe she'd do that. She watched as Ann held the door for several others before disappearing down the hospital corridor. With additional people coming in all the time, there was ever more commotion in the waiting room. Men and women sat in little knots, some leafing aimlessly through magazines and others talking among themselves. A rather large, newly-arrived group had requisitioned a corner for themselves and seemed to be making no attempt to keep the noise down. A short while before it had been quiet enough in the room that Del was able to keep her mind occupied by focusing on the nativity scene. Earnest prayer had tumbled from her heart to the Christ Child represented in the manger, the One Lord who heard all prayer and held all petitions close to him.

It's too soon, Lord! It's just too soon, she found herself saying over and over again. *Please, don't let it be now.* She knew that he knew the same things that she knew, but that didn't stop Del from telling him anyway. She did have a tendency to speak to God as if she was on familiar terms with him.

Loud laughter burst from the corner party, and Del glared at them.

It's no use trying to pray in this place! Maybe I should go get something to eat, as Ann says. Or I could head on down to the chapel where it'd be quieter.

Yet Del didn't move. She knew that prayer would be difficult no matter where she was, as worries and troublesome thoughts kept running over and over through her mind. So she settled herself more firmly into the uncomfortable hospital chair, determined to stay where she was until she found out some news. Prayers and anxieties swirled about in her head and, before long, Del found herself pondering all that had been going on lately. How strangely everything had turned out!

As her eyes refocused on the small crèche in front of her, for the first time she noticed a tiny wooden ladder leaning against the side of the stable. Upon seeing it her thoughts were instantly drawn back to the beginning of October.

2

The Autumn Garden

It was a pleasant fall morning. The sun shone brightly and there was a bit of a nip in the air, just enough to remind one that winter was waiting in the wings. Del was in her large backyard garden, seeing what kind of havoc the previous night's frost had wreaked. She carried a plastic bucket in one hand and a pair of garden shears in the other. As she wandered up and down the wood-chipped paths, she stopped here and there to snip off the top of this plant, or cut that plant entirely down to its roots. Into the bucket went wilted or frost-damaged foliage and flowers. Even at this time of year Del liked to keep a neat garden.

She stopped to admire the still-bright chrysanthemums, thanking the Creator for these lingering spots of color in the quickly browning landscape. Then she moved on, working her way along the winding center path until she reached the very end of the garden where her husband's old workshop stood. There she paused for a minute, stretching her aching back and sweeping her gaze over her entire yard. From here the house looked so small, dwarfed by the tall, steel windmill which stood by a corner of the garage. The blades of the windmill, silhouetted against the blue sky, were barely moving in the light breeze. As Del began working her way back along one of the side paths, she heard her name being called.

A man was up on a ladder which leaned against her one-story house. He was attempting to repair a portion of the gutter which had come loose and was hanging at an angle. When Del approached, the man explained to her that the old gutter had twisted so much that it was going to be difficult to nail it back on.

"I really think you'd be better off just replacing this whole run," he said, gesturing with his hand to the length of the house.

"I don't know," replied Del doubtfully. "Won't that be rather expensive?"

"Not too bad. I can pick up the gutter for probably around fifty to sixty dollars. 'Course you'll also need hangers and nails and that'd be extra."

Her forehead wrinkled in thought, Del stood there for a moment trying to decide what to do. She hadn't planned on the extra expense right now, and yet the old gutter *was* starting to look pretty beaten up. The aluminum was dented and the color was peeling here and there. She pictured how much nicer it would look to have a new gutter, as she always hung baskets of beautiful flowers under the roof edge every summer.

"All right, Lamont," she finally responded. "Could you go ahead and do that for me? It would make the backyard look so much prettier for all those garden ladies who come every summer for a tour of my garden. Say, I guess you won't need to remove the leaves from the gutter if you're going to take it down anyway. So do I get a discount for that?" she teased.

The man grinned. Del asked if he'd like a drink of water and trotted into the house to get it. She reflected on how grateful she was that Lamont Tierney and his son Steven had come to help with the fall cleanup. After her husband had died she had managed on her own for a few years, but lately it seemed easier to pay someone to do the heavier chores.

Right now seventeen-year-old Steven was hard at work in the back corner of the garden, raking leaves under the far-reaching limbs of a maple tree. Del waved to him as she returned carrying a glass of water for his father.

"Much obliged," said Lamont, draining the glass. After he handed it back to her, he hesitated. Repositioning the old baseball cap on his head, he cleared his throat, saying, "Uh, Del?"

When he had her attention he began again.

"Um – I've been meaning to ask you." He stopped and frowned to himself before continuing.

"I've been meaning to ask you – well – it's just, uh – what do you know about that girl Mara Ramsey?"

Del caught her breath. The question, coming out of nowhere, caught her off guard. Not knowing exactly how to answer, the woman asked a noncommittal question in return.

"What do you mean, 'know about her'?"

"Well, I know that you know who I mean," replied the man. "I've seen the two of you around town together."

"That's true. Mara and I are friends. But why are you asking me about her?"

The man glanced over at his son working diligently in the far corner.

"Well, it's just Steven. I think he has a crush on this girl. Ever since she arrived new at the high school this year, Steven's been moonin' around, talking about her all the time. She's a senior and he's only a junior, but I guess they might have some classes together."

Del didn't say anything so Lamont went on.

"Now, Del, my son ain't too bright. Oh, I don't mean academically. He does okay in that regards. I mean socially. He don't always pick up on things that are obvious to everyone else."

Lamont stopped, waiting futilely for her to answer, then in a frustrated tone of voice burst out, "Come on, Del! Stop making this so hard – you know what I mean! It's obvious to everyone, except my backward son, that this girl is pregnant!"

Del shifted uncomfortably on her feet. She stared at the middle-aged man who was just a bit younger than herself. She could see the resemblance between him and Steven in their lanky hair, light brown eyes and a certain stubborn set to the chin. She didn't actually know this man all that well, since the boy usually came by himself to help her with chores. She had had Lamont out only once or twice before when she needed some repair work done. He seemed to be a nice enough fellow, but she certainly didn't know him well enough to share confidences with him.

"Well," she answered at last, seeing his growing impatience. "I guess it's no secret any longer. But I'm not exactly in a position to speak for the girl."

When he saw that Del wasn't going to be drawn out any further, Lamont shrugged his shoulders and began to climb the ladder. As he put his foot on the bottom rung, he had one more thing to say.

"She'd better stay away from my son. I don't want him getting mixed up with a girl like that."

Del narrowed her eyes. "You needn't worry about that," she replied acidly without thinking. "She already has a boyfriend."

6

The man started up the ladder but threw down his parting shot.

"Yep," he said in a steely voice. "That's plain to see. Yes, ma'am, that's real plain to see."

Del spun on her heel and marched through the back door into the kitchen. She was angry and knew if she stayed outside she'd probably say something she'd regret.

The nerve of that man! she fumed, throwing the morning's dirty dishes into the sink and running water over them. She scrubbed the dishes furiously. *Where does he get off being Mara's judge and jury?*

Then Del took several deep breaths to calm down. *After all,* she tried reminding herself, *on the surface it would certainly appear that Mara is 'a girl like that.' But it's not up to me to tell him the whole story.*

Her hands still buried in the dishwater, she bent her head and wiped her watering eyes on her shirt sleeve. *Oh, Lord,* she prayed in her distress. *Mara has such a long and tough road ahead of her. Could you please help her in all of this? Help people to be understanding and compassionate. Give her the strength to do what's right in your eyes. In the long run, only that is going to be best for her.*

Suddenly Del remembered that Mara had phoned earlier to say that she'd stop by the next day. *Thank goodness she didn't come today. I'd hate to have her be exposed to that man's meanness.*

Yet even as she thought it, she knew deep inside that Lamont was not really mean. He just didn't understand and, naturally, wanted to protect his son.

But, anyway, he doesn't have to worry about that! I'm sure that Mara hasn't done anything other than talk friendly-like to Steven. She's cute enough, with her long blond hair and blue eyes. It's no wonder he has an interest in her. But I can guarantee Lamont that Mara has no interest in his son.

Del was a generally a kind, gentle person, but now as she heard the sound of the gutter being ripped from the edge of the roof, she had a barely-suppressed desire to run outside and shake the ladder. Hard.

3

Two For Lunch

Since the sun was hiding behind the clouds the next morning, Del pulled on an old sweatshirt against the chill in the air. Even this late in the season there was always something that needed to be done in the garden. She was shivering a little but stalwartly began to clear a patch of soil under the large maple in order to set some bulbs of wood hyacinth. She could hardly wait to see their delicate blossoms of Wedgewood blue, creamy white and cotton-candy pink light up the shade beneath the tree next spring.

Suddenly she heard a voice calling her.

Mara! she thought with delight, and rose as quickly as she could. She brushed off her knees and, pulling off her gardening gloves, hurried back to the corner of the garden nearest the house. There her visitor stood holding the hand of a small child.

"Oh, it's so good to see you, Mara!" Del exclaimed, giving the tall teenage girl a quick hug. "And who's this you've brought with you today?"

Now Del knew quite well who the little girl was next to Mara, but she always got a kick out of hearing the two-year-old proclaim in her small breathless voice, "I'm Stephie!"

They both smiled at the golden-haired toddler. Now that Stephie had made her bold pronouncement, she had a sudden attack of shyness and hid behind Mara's leg. Del bent down to ask her, "Did you come to help your sister and me work in the garden?"

The tiny girl nodded and the three of them set about finishing the planting. Even Stephie helped, as Del dug the holes and showed her how to place the bulbs pointy end up. Mara took over shoveling the soil back over the bulbs and her little sister was delighted to tromp it firmly with her feet.

The gardening task accomplished, they went into the house to wash up for lunch. Stephie headed right for the cardboard box under the kitchen table where she knew she'd find Mama Cat curled up with her kitten, Coco. After waking them rather rudely by patting their backs with enthusiasm, Stephie minded Del's exhortation, "Be gentle!" Obediently, the child settled back on her knees to wait for the cats to emerge from their comfortable nest and stretch themselves. Coco yawned widely then bounded over to Stephie, ready and willing to play.

As soon as the meal was ready, the three of them settled around the roomy kitchen table where Del said grace.

"Bless us, O Lord, and these Thy gifts, which we are about to receive from Thy bounty, through Christ our Lord. Amen."

Mara knew Del so well that she didn't even raise her head at the "Amen," but kept it down for more prayer which was sure to follow.

"And thank you, Lord, for blessing this food and for blessing us. Thank you for Mara and Stephie visiting today. Keep them and their mom safe in your care. Amen."

Mara still didn't raise her head, as Del could be as voluble in prayer as she was in regular conversation. However, since Stephie was wiggling in her seat, perhaps the woman thought it best to cut it short today. Passing around the fruit and sandwiches, she helped the little girl with her food.

As they ate, Stephie warmed to the occasion and began talking silly. Del smiled and listened to the child's chatter while she reflected on Mara. She thought back to yesterday's troubling conversation with Lamont. As upset as she was with the fellow, she had to agree with him that Mara's condition was obvious in spite of her penchant for wearing large, loose shirts. Being five months pregnant was becoming increasingly difficult to hide, especially on such a slender frame.

After Stephie finished her lunch and went to play with the kitten again, Del asked, "So how's school going?"

"All right, I guess."

Mara wasn't much of a talker at the best of times. Del was sometimes able to draw her out with questions, but she always refrained from pushing her too much. Now she just waited quietly for further information.

After a moment, Mara looked up from her plate.

"It's a much smaller school than my old one in the city was. The classes are okay and the teachers are pretty nice. But the other kids..." She trailed off and fell silent.

Del felt she understood what remained unspoken. She could well imagine how difficult it was to be the new kid in town, coming from a totally different background. And being pregnant on top of it all – well, it would be surprising if Mara *didn't* feel out of step with everyone else.

Mara's mother, Alyssa, had decided to move her family here to this small town at the beginning of the school year. She said that there was nothing left for them in the city except a ton of bad memories. Even her daughter's best friend, Peter, having gone away to college, was no longer there. Knowing that Mara had made a few friends in this rural community made it logical for Alyssa to settle here. She had rented a small apartment in town where it was easy for Mara to walk to school, and Alyssa had quickly found a waitressing job. Mara watched her little sister after school and on weekends while their mom worked. When Mara couldn't do it, a young mother in a nearby apartment would trade off baby-sitting with them. Sometimes, like today, the girl would drive her mother to work and then bring Stephie out for a visit with Del.

Choosing this area was sensible from another standpoint. Mara was receiving counseling from a crisis pregnancy center in a nearby town. When Alyssa realized that the counseling sessions were free – and that the center had offered to cover some of the medical expenses for Mara – she figured it wouldn't make much sense to move elsewhere.

In her heart, Del felt that the only place Mara felt really comfortable and accepted was here at her place. It was Del who had taken her in this summer when the girl was a runaway, and it was she who had poured out unconditional love on the confused and lonely teenager. Even her garden, as the two of them worked together in it this past summer, had had a place in helping the girl to find a measure of peace in her life.

"Mom can't take me to my appointment on Wednesday. She has to work." Interrupting Del's thoughts, Mara's voice sounded strained.

"What time's it at?"

"Four o'clock. I can have our neighbor watch Stephie."

"Okay. I'll pick you up at three-thirty."

Del was thankful that Mara and her mother were still going to the counseling appointments. *They have a long and rocky road ahead of them,* Del reflected. *You can sense the tension between them – understandable given the circumstances...*

On Wednesday in the center's waiting room, Del tried concentrating on an article in a magazine. She lost interest quickly and finally pulled out a rosary from her pocket. Just holding the set of beads always helped her, even when her mind was distracted, to slide more easily into prayer. The repetition of familiar words helped to calm her and slow her breathing. As she prayed she felt more able to lay her anxieties, once again, at the feet of her beloved Lord.

She was just finishing when Mara opened the inner office door and emerged, followed by a tall, striking woman. The woman's dark, wavy hair was in a short, attractive cut and her hazel eyes were direct and friendly. She smiled broadly when she saw Del and came over to give her a warm hug.

"Hi, stranger, long time no see!" she declared.

"Crying out loud, Eva, I was here just a couple months ago! But you needn't be a stranger – there's always the phone, you know."

Del, too, was smiling, clearly pleased to see the other woman. She had gotten to know Eva years ago when they met at a series of prayer vigils outside an abortion clinic. They had quickly become friends. The two women enjoyed carrying on long conversations and met regularly for lunch until they had both gotten too busy. When Del had first brought Mara to the crisis pregnancy center in August, she'd been surprised to discover that Eva was a volunteer there.

But why should I have been surprised? she had asked herself afterward. *I knew that she had a degree in counseling. She hadn't worked in the field after her younger kids were born, but I can't think of anyone who could do this kind of work better.*

Eva was speaking to her.

"Please make sure," she asked Del, "that Mara gets to her next checkup. Dr. Walkerman has offered her services free to all our clients, but it won't do any good if a person doesn't go."

Eva turned to Mara, laying her hand on the girl's shoulder.

"Okay, Mara?" she asked. "It's very important that you keep seeing the doctor. You seem to be doing well and you want to keep it that way. And, sweetheart," she continued kindly, "I know how tough this is for you. Just keep taking it one day at a time. God has a plan for you. Trust in him. I've given you my home phone number, which I don't do with everyone. But I want you to call me anytime, day or night, if you need anything. All right?"

The girl nodded, her expression guarded. Inwardly Del sighed, knowing that the poor child had a hard time trusting anyone, no matter how well-meaning they were.

"Del," Eva was speaking now to her, "we really must have lunch together. It's been too long. Why not this Friday? I'm not scheduled here on that day. We could meet at Tony's Deli like we used to and catch up on our lives."

Del was more than willing, and waved goodbye to her old friend as the two of them left. When Del stopped the car in front of Mara's apartment, the girl thanked her, adding, "I'd rather go with you than my mother, anyway."

Del's eyebrows rose.

"Still problems, huh?"

A disgusted look flashed across Mara's features.

"Nothing new. She's just mad at me all the time."

"Is that right?" Del sympathized.

The girl stared out the window for a moment. When she turned back to Del her face was set and there was anger in her voice.

"I really think she wishes I had gotten an abortion. Of course," she added sarcastically, "she never comes right out and says so! She keeps saying it's up to me to decide, yet she manages to get in little digs all the time. But I don't care what my mother thinks!"

Mara climbed out of the car and slammed the door. She poked her head back in the open window.

"It's my baby – and I'm keeping it!"

4

Jelly and Deli

Engrossed in her task of jelly-making, Del examined the crabapples bobbing in her kitchen sink. Cutting the small fruits in half, she tossed them into a large pot to simmer while setting up the equipment to extract their juice. Next she washed and sterilized the canning jars. When the juice was ready she added the proper amount of sugar and boiled it until the jelly mixture sheeted off a large metal spoon. Of all the jellies she made, crabapple was one of her favorites because it was so simple. The fruit had its own natural pectin, so no messy store-bought pectin was needed. *Saves on costs, too,* reflected Del, always one to appreciate the value of a dollar saved.

Several hours of work were rewarded by seeing fifteen jars of crabapple jelly lined up to cool on the kitchen counter. They would be added to the growing collection of jellies and jams in her pantry. Her current inventory included the usual favorites like cherry, strawberry, peach and raspberry. However, there were also wild blackberry, elderberry and mulberry jellies, with other varieties soon to come. Earlier this fall, to her delight, Del had discovered a large patch of ground cherries in an open field. She had pulled up dozens of the weedy plants by their roots and hung them upside down in the garage until the fruit ripened. Now hundreds of orange-colored cherries, enclosed in papery lantern-like husks, were ready to use.

Won't get a lot of jam from those little things, but every year someone is sure to ask for it.

Del's jellies and jams were a popular item in the city where she and her neighbor Richard Spencer rented a booth at the farmers' market. Richard sold farm products, his wife Ann sold handmade crafts and Del took in a few dollars from her preserves. Her customers had come to expect some unusual varieties from this woman who knew the woods like the back of her hand.

"Yep," she said out loud. "Some of them return every fall to see if I have ground cherry or May-apple jam. And, of course, they fight over my corncob jelly!"

Looking at the clock she realized she'd need to stop admiring her labors in order to meet Eva for lunch at their favorite deli. It was seldom crowded at this hour of the day, which gave them time to relax and visit with each other.

Eva, already there when Del arrived, waved her down from a corner booth.

"It's great to see you, Del!" she exclaimed, and Del smiled, thinking to herself that Eva always greeted her exuberantly whether they'd just seen each other or not.

The woman stood up and kissed Del on the cheek, and before they could even slide into their seats the waitress brought the menus. Del knew right away what she wanted, ordering a grilled cheese sandwich and a bowl of vegetable soup.

"Del," Eva teased, "don't you know that you Catholics can eat meat now on Fridays?"

Del chuckled. This was an old joke between them. They were of different faiths but had established an easy camaraderie over the years. They didn't gloss over their differences, yet found a lot of common ground in their mutual love for the Lord.

"Eva, for heaven's sakes, haven't we've been through this before? The rule about abstaining from meat may have been relaxed, but it wasn't thrown out!"

"I know – you've told me," Eva replied, a twinkle in her eye. "You said you're still supposed to practice some type of self-denial on Fridays to help commemorate the day of Christ's death. So what kind of penance is eating lobster or shrimp, like some people do?"

"It would be for *me,* since I can't stand either!" Del declared, grimacing. "But, seriously, I do think that some of us had forgotten the reason behind the rule. Perhaps giving up meat isn't mandatory any more, but it's still recommended. Jesus did say that some things can only be accomplished by prayer and fasting. Maybe there's some evil spirits somewhere I'll be needing to cast out!"

The women laughed easily together and then got down to the serious business of eating while catching up on their lives. It wasn't long before the topic turned to Mara.

Del asked Eva, "Has Mara told you what she wants to do about the baby?"

"I can't tell you what she's told me in confidence. You know that, Del."

"I understand," answered Del. "But she's told me several times that she plans to keep the baby. That poor girl! She's in such a crazy, mixed-up situation! And I have the feeling it's going to get worse before it gets better."

She laid her half-eaten sandwich on the plate and looked out the large window. The view encompassed little except a parking lot, but Del didn't notice it anyway.

"You know as well as I do, Eva," she continued in a quieter voice, "of the circumstances surrounding the baby's conception. Tom, her mother's boyfriend – drunk and abusive – and Mara running away and ending up at my place. And when she realized she was pregnant, she tried to get an abortion."

"I know," interrupted Eva, just as quietly. "The only thing that stopped her was that she didn't have the money. But, Del, surely you're aware that she still could have gotten an abortion even after she returned home to her mother's."

Del nodded. She and Eva both knew that abortion is legal in the United States even through the ninth month of pregnancy. *If people only realized,* she thought. *So many people still think that abortions can only be obtained in the first couple months.* The mental image of a tiny but fully formed baby being killed by gruesome dismemberment or caustic chemicals shot through her mind. She felt queasy.

Taking a deep breath, she turned back to the conversation at hand.

"Anyway, she knows how dead-set I am against killing a baby to solve your problems. Mara seems to respect my opinion and that may be the only reason she finally opted not to get an abortion. But I'm not sure. I'm beginning to think she might also be trying to get back at her mother."

"Del," said Eva, taking a bite of her chicken salad, "as I do with all the girls I counsel, I have discussed her options with her, including adoption. Omigosh, can you even imagine her raising the child herself? She's still in high school, she has to babysit for

15

her little sister – whose father, by the way, is the same man who got *her* pregnant! – and there's loads of stress between her and her mom." Eva shook her head slowly. "It wouldn't be easy – to put it mildly."

Del played with her sandwich for a few moments before taking another bite.

"I've spent a lot of time thinking about it," she replied. "The bottom line may be that Mara is looking for someone to love who will love her back. She's such a needy child. You know how her father left town after the divorce and only contacted her a couple times before dropping out of sight. She's had no idea where he's been for nearly four years now. It's understandable that her head's a little mixed up."

Eva nodded. "I've come to similar conclusions. Given the circumstances, I don't think trying to raise the baby herself is the best choice for either her or the baby. But I won't tell her what to do. My job at the center is to give the girls the information they need and help them discern which option is best for them. Ultimately, all I can do in the end is to let them go – and pray like crazy!"

Del agreed, adding, "Well, anyway, the baby's not due until February. There's still time for her to change her mind. The most important thing is to let her know that we care and will be there for her no matter what."

They finished their lunch and hugged goodbye. Del had a lot to think about on her way home. She was still deep in thought when she walked into her house and saw the "Message" button flashing on the phone. She punched it absentmindedly but came to full attention when she heard the distraught voice of Mara's mother.

"Del, can you call me back as soon as you can? Please hurry! I need to talk to you before Mara gets home from school!"

5

Alyssa's Place

As she drove to the apartment complex in town, Del had a jumble of thoughts going through her mind.

What's going on now? Why am I the person she called? She really doesn't know me all that well. Doesn't she have any other friends? Maybe not – she doesn't have time for much besides work. Maybe I was the first person to come to mind.

Del remembered the first time she had met Mara's mother, when Alyssa had come to pick up her runaway daughter from Windmill Gardens. Del could see the resemblance immediately. They were both slender, although Mara was taller. Both had blond hair – Mara's natural and her mom's highlighted. The daughter's hair was long, usually pulled back in a ponytail, and the mother wore hers in a short, sleek cut. Mara's blue eyes, nearly identical in shade to her mom's, were usually lowered in shyness around people while Alyssa's were more friendly and outgoing.

She remembered how grateful Alyssa had been for the safe refuge which Del had given to Mara. The woman couldn't thank her enough. Although there was so much that remained unsaid at that first meeting, Del didn't press the issue.

Sometimes, she figured, *it's better to say less and pray more.*

Ever since they had subsequently moved to her town, there were several occasions when Del and Alyssa had had a chance to talk. Alyssa wasn't hesitant about sharing her problems. Sometimes Del felt a little overwhelmed, and she wasn't exactly sure what to expect today. The younger woman had sounded stressed when Del returned her call.

"Oh, Lord!" Alyssa had moaned. "Can you believe this? Scott called!"

Scott? Then Del remembered that was the name of Mara's father. *After all these years? Where's he been?*

Del tried to calm Alyssa and promised to drive right over. Now, as she pushed the outside buzzer and was let in, she found herself dreading to hear what was likely to be a whole new set of problems. A door opened at the top of the inside stairs.

"Del? Is that you? Please come up!"

Del climbed the steps as quickly as the arthritis in her knees would allow her and closed the apartment door behind her.

"Where's Stephie?" she inquired.

"I put her down for a nap." Alyssa talked rapidly but quietly. "Let me just check and see if she's asleep. Have a seat."

Del stooped down to pet Pepper, Mara's black kitten. Then she settled herself on the old sofa and looked around with interest. The last time she had been in the apartment, there were packing boxes everywhere. Now everything was fairly neat. A giant TV screen dominated the living room in between several very large bookcases filled with paperbacks.

Good! It seems we have one thing in common – we both like to read.

Del had stacks of books everywhere at her house. She usually had several books going at one time, depending upon the mood she was in. During the winter, having fewer outside chores, she would spend hours most evenings curled up with a book. Her favorites were religious books, nature topics, travelogues and, of course, gardening. Sometimes she enjoyed a good novel.

Maybe we can discuss books sometime in the future. I'd like that. But I don't think now's the time...

Alyssa closed the bedroom door quietly and returned to the living room where she plopped down on an overgrown beanbag. She buried her head in her hands.

After a moment, when there seemed to be nothing forthcoming from the woman, Del tentatively prodded, "So – your former husband called you?"

Alyssa raised her head. She had a strained look on her face.

"Yeah! Just out of the blue. Can you imagine that?"

She hesitated, then came a rush of words. "I can hardly believe it! He walks out on us five years ago, files for divorce and then drops off the end of the earth!"

Del remembered Mara saying she had received letters from her dad for awhile. She asked Alyssa about it.

"Oh, yes," she answered, bitterness in her voice. "Two or three letters! And maybe a couple phone calls. Then nothing. My daughter was crushed. What was I supposed to tell her? That her dad didn't care about her any more? The jerk! He simply didn't care about what happened to his kid!"

From the few facts she knew, Del herself wasn't too crazy about the man. But then again, Alyssa hadn't done right by her daughter, either. Just look what had happened to Mara because of her mother's poor decisions. However, Del kept silent, waiting for Alyssa to continue.

Anger was written in every gesture as the woman pushed her hair back from her pinched face.

"Just what does he want from us? I can't even imagine!"

Del tentatively asked, "Did he say why he was calling?"

"He said he wanted to talk to me."

Del frowned, thinking out loud.

"You've just moved here. I wonder how he knew where you were."

"That's what I wanted to know. He said he went to the house where we used to live. And when he found out we weren't there anymore, he went down the street to talk to Gayle."

Del already knew from previous conversations with Mara that Gayle was a long-time neighbor of theirs in the city. She and Alyssa had known each other for ages and one would have to assume that Scott was well-known to Gayle also.

"It's hard to believe that Gayle would give out information about you."

"It sure is, isn't it?" Alyssa sounded resentful. "What kind of friend is that?"

She continued, "But then again, she always liked Scott. She was really upset about our divorce. Anyway, he said he went there several times pleading with her before she finally gave in and gave him my phone number. Isn't that something? But I'm sure he sweet-talked her into it by saying how much he wanted to see his little girl."

Del shook her head slowly, then asked, "So, are you going to see him?"

Alyssa lowered her head and rubbed her forehead and eyes, before looking up at Del with tiredness awash across her features.

"I don't know," she said wearily. "Del, I'm so confused. I was hoping you could help me sort through all this."

19

Del blinked in surprise. *What am I supposed to say?* Before anything came to mind, Alyssa continued.

"He says he'd like to see me, but realizes I might not feel too friendly about him right now. Boy, that's an understatement! He doesn't want to be 'pushy,' he says. He's gonna call back in a few days to check with me again."

Alyssa shook her head. "I don't really care if I ever see him again! But, of course, there's Mara. He *is* her father. At least he had the decency to talk to me first before trying to contact her.

"And, I suppose," she rambled on, "that I should at least talk to him. I have to admit I'm curious about what kind of excuses he'll come up with. But…he wants to meet with me in person, not just talk on the phone. I don't know about that."

"Well," interjected Del, "I don't know if that's a good idea. I mean, I don't know much about him, but you don't want to meet him where no one else is around, do you? Is there a chance he might get violent?"

"Oh, no," said Alyssa quickly. "He never hit me or anything like that, even when we were arguing. And I have to admit he was a good father. At least in the beginning…"

She trailed off, her thoughts fastened on memories somewhere from the past. Then she returned to Del, picking up the thread of the conversation.

"I think you're right, though, about not seeing him in private. If I do decide to meet with him, is there any place you could suggest?"

Del thought for a moment. "Well, there's the town park. It's out on Hill Street, not far from here. It has a small lake with benches by it. Maybe that would be a good place to talk. There would be people around, but it's not what you'd call crowded."

She looked at Alyssa and offered, "And if you need someone to watch Stephie for you, let me know. Uh…did you happen to mention anything about Stephie to him?"

Alyssa looked worried and a guilty look crossed her face. "No. And that's another problem. How am I supposed to bring up *that* subject? 'Oh, Scott, by the way, after you left I found myself a boyfriend – and now I have another kid!'"

Then she shook her head angrily. "Wait a minute! I don't have to explain myself to him! He was the one who walked out! Not me!"

She glanced at Stephie's bedroom door and lowered her voice. She was on a roll now, spewing out more information than Del would ever have asked for.

"You have to understand, Del, Tom wasn't always so bad. After Scott left, I found work at a restaurant and Tom would come in to eat all the time. He treated me so nice, joking with me and lifting my spirits when I was down."

There were tears in Alyssa's eyes as she continued. "After awhile he started bringing me flowers – something Scott never did! – and he was always talking sweet to me. It was fun having another adult to laugh and talk with! I was lonely and one thing led to another. Cross my heart, Del, I had no idea that he had a drinking problem. After we'd been together for awhile he started drinking more openly and he'd get so awful when he was drunk. I was afraid of him, but by then I had the two kids and didn't know if I could make it on my own." She sighed. "Not that he was much help."

She compressed her lips and tears shone in her eyes. Del shifted uncomfortably on the sofa.

"But, anyway," Alyssa continued, looking away from Del. "You have to believe me, if I'd known he was abusing my daughter…"

She tried to tell you, thought Del, but she merely said, "The past can't be changed, Alyssa. What's done is done. You have to leave it in God's hands and decide what to do about your present problem. Mara will be home soon, and you need to get yourself together before she gets here."

At that moment the door opened and Mara walked in.

6

A Not-So-Dreary Day

On this day the weather didn't look as if it was going to cooperate. The sky was leaden and a chilly wind had picked up during the night. Del finished her morning prayers and spent a little time sitting at her table, gazing thoughtfully out at the garden. Even now, with most of the flowers gone, her backyard was attractive. The maple tree, dressed in translucent yellow, looked striking next to the flaming orange viburnum. The smokebush was clothed in maroon, its feathery plumes faded from their red summer hues to a misty-looking pink. Flaming crimson robed the sweetspire, and the large flowerheads of the hydrangeas had exchanged their vivid summer blues for a softer mix of violet and burgundy.

Del had originally planned to go out in the woods this day to look for the wild grapevines which twined their way through bushes and tree branches. If the grapes were decent, with a rich fragrant aroma, she would pick them for jelly. But even if they weren't worthwhile she would still cut some of the vines. After stripping them of leaves, she'd take them down the road for Ann to weave into wreaths.

However, it was looking like rain might begin any minute, so Del simply changed her plans. Each moment of every day is in God's hands, she believed, and if she couldn't do one thing, well, then it was meant for her to do something else. She thought of all the jars of jelly which were waiting to be labeled. That would be her first order of business. Mara had printed some nice labels on the computer which were much more attractive than the pieces of masking tape she had stuck on the jars.

Thinking of the girl, Del's mind returned to the previous day when Mara had arrived home from school. Alyssa was still wiping her eyes when her daughter came in, but she jumped up, saying brightly, "Hi, honey! Del and I were just having a nice visit! How 'bout if I get you something to eat? How was school today?"

Alyssa quickly set about rustling up a snack in the kitchen. Mara sat down cross-legged on the living room floor and picked up Pepper to cuddle. She looked quizzically at Del, who smiled kindly at her but said nothing. Del didn't know how Alyssa was going to tell her daughter that her father had returned, but she was certain that it wasn't her place to let the cat out of the bag. As a small, singsong voice began to call, "Mama! Mawa!" from the bedroom, Del used the opportunity to bid them farewell.

After saying a prayer for them, her thoughts returned to her jelly. She made many trips back and forth from the pantry, bringing out all the jars to set on the table before trotting off to get dressed. After putting on her work clothes she picked up her scapular, looking at it thoughtfully. It occurred to her that some people might consider the small devotional item she held in her hand an odd-looking thing.

It consisted of a couple of small squares of brown felt with two narrow ribbons connecting them. On one of the squares was a picture of Jesus and on the other a picture of Mary. Many centuries ago, a scapular was a much larger piece of fabric, worn over the shoulders by those in the Carmelite religious order.

It sure has shrunk in size over the years, Del mused, *which is a good thing, since a bigger one would look a bit funny with my blue jeans!* Yet for Del and the millions of others who wore a scapular, it still served as an outward sign and reminder that, like Mary, they had given everything in their lives over to God.

As Del put the scapular over her head and tucked it beneath her clothing, she prayed, "Jesus, my Shepherd, before me, to lead me where I should go, and Mary, my mother, behind me – to give me a little push!"

It didn't take long for Del to label the jelly and then she busied herself with her normal routine of chores. Eventually she took another look at her preserves. The light from the large window behind the jars, even on this dismal day, was bright enough to set the transparent colors to sparkling. Del's eyes sparkled, too, as a new thought hit her.

She trotted once again to her bedroom and searched through her closet until she found some attractive gingham material. Grabbing her sewing shears, she cut squares of the fabric and tied them over the canning lids with some gaily-colored yarn. Then she stepped back to admire them.

I do think, she decided, *they look nice enough that I could charge an extra dollar each!* True, a dollar wasn't much, but Del depended on the money she brought in from the market to help supplement her husband's social security check. *This year my customers will really be impressed!*

Del was humming to herself as she returned to her regular housework. In spite of the dreary weather the day flew by quickly and it was soon time for choir practice. After an early supper she was on her way.

As she barreled toward town in her ancient green car, she chuckled at the novel idea of her – Del! – being in the church choir. How her dear husband would have chortled if she'd said she was going to join a choir. *I always told Joey that I don't sing good but I do sing loud!* In all truth, she felt she could carry a tune well enough, even if her family *had* been fond of teasing her that they'd be grateful if she'd carry it somewhere else.

However, Del, having a generous heart, wanted to support the newly-formed choir. Six weeks ago the long time organist at their church had died. Few in the congregation tried to sing along when the woman had played, as the notes rushed by at the speed of a 747. With her passing, a younger woman with musical background had offered to pull together a choir. Some of the parishioners had volunteered and Del decided to join them.

She parked in the church's small lot and hurried into St. Bernard's. First she went through the vestibule into the church, where she genuflected and greeted her Lord. Then she scurried up the carpeted steps and into the brightly-lit choir loft, almost colliding with a tall man. When she glanced up to apologize, a blush spread over her face.

"Why...why, George!" she exclaimed, flustered. "What are *you* doing here?"

7

Choir Rehearsal

The handsome, silver-haired man laughed.

"Well, hello yourself!" he said in a pleasant bass voice. "I've decided to join the choir. That *is* okay, isn't it?"

"Well, of course!" Del huffed, a bit embarrassed. "I didn't mean it that way! I was just surprised, that's all."

Del scooted around him, picked up her music and quickly found her chair. The others were milling around talking, but good-naturedly took their seats when the choir director, Laurie, tapped her podium. Del glanced around at the others. Even with the addition of George there were less than a dozen people.

Lord, help us! It's going to take a real miracle to get this together by Christmas.

Laurie didn't seem to share Del's unspoken pessimism. With enthusiasm she seated herself at the old piano and ran through the warm-ups. The choir then practiced their music for the upcoming Sunday's Mass before taking a look at the more difficult selections for Christmas. Del made every attempt to tone down her volume, knowing that she certainly wasn't the best vocalist in the crowd.

Maybe we don't sound too bad, she was beginning to think. Just then Ernestine, their most senior member, hit a shrill high note. Del tried not to wince, realizing that she was hardly one to judge. She tried valiantly to follow the unfamiliar music. Others were stumbling along also, and giggles were heard during some of the more confusing sections. Mae Beth Cranston, a quiet, rather plump woman in her twenties, blushed crimson when her voice went somewhere no one else's had ever gone before. Laurie charitably pointed out that this was their first run-through of the music, after all, and she was certain with time and practice they would rival the Mormon Tabernacle Choir.

Laughing and shaking their heads, everyone returned the octavos to the music shelf and milled around for what was fast becoming their favorite part of choir practice – catching up on everyone else's business. Del was tired and still needed to pop into the grocery store down the street for a few things, but Joe Nagley cornered her before she got very far.

"Hey, Del," he said, "I haven't had a chance to tell you how much Nicki likes your black raspberry jam."

Del, puzzled, stopped and looked at the young man.

"Nicki?"

"My wife. Don't you remember her?"

"Oh, yes," Del replied. "That's right. I met her at the kickoff potluck when we started the choir. Hey, what happened to her, anyway? Wasn't she going to join us?"

Joe grinned. "What's happened to her is morning sickness. Why they call it 'morning' I don't know. She feels sick from the time she gets up in the morning until the time she goes to bed."

Del smiled at him. He seemed to be such a nice young man.

"Well, don't worry," she replied. "It might take nine months, but it does go away. And by the way, congratulations!"

"Thanks. But the reason I mentioned the jam is because Nicki had some at the potluck, and now she's developed a craving for it! Told me tonight to be sure to ask you for a jar."

Del chuckled. "Well, there's worse things to crave. Just be glad she doesn't want oysters on the half-shell or anything like that! Sure, Joe, I'll bring you the jam next time."

Del rummaged through her purse for a piece of paper and a pen. She knew she'd never remember if it wasn't written down. Then she tucked the note to herself into a jacket pocket. Many months would pass before she would finally come across that scribbled note, and then a puzzled expression would engulf her face as she'd try to decipher her writing.

Now why did I write that down? She'd frown at it for several long seconds before turning the paper upside-down. *No, that doesn't make any sense either!* For some time she'd ponder what strange impulse would cause her to write "TOE JAM" on a piece of paper and stuff it into her pocket. Finally, Del would shrug her shoulders, crumple the paper and throw it away. Perhaps Joe was too embarrassed to ask a second time for a jar of black raspberry

26

jam or maybe his wife developed a different craving. In any case, he never did mention it again.

After speaking to Joe that evening in the choir loft, Del tried once more to slip away. However, George caught her at the top of the staircase.

"Del, where're you going so fast? I haven't talked to you for quite awhile."

Del turned to face him with a smile that felt a bit forced. It wasn't that she didn't want to talk to George. It was just that she wasn't sure how she felt about him. He was certainly nice to look at, with his silvery hair and winsome smile. He, too, had lost his spouse to cancer, and in recent years he and Del had spent a bit of time together. She always had a good time with him as they'd gotten to know each other better.

But I'm just not interested in being anything other than friends. I'm not quite sure what George expects.

They chatted for a few minutes before Del claimed that she really was tired and needed to do a few things before getting home. George seemed reluctant to let her go.

"I wanted to invite you to go to the cider mill with me on Friday. The weather is supposed to clear up and they're predicting a near-perfect day. What do you say?"

Del considered the offer for a moment. She'd always loved making an annual autumn visit to the cider mill. It had become a ritual not to miss ever since her children were young. This year, so far, she'd been too busy. Yet, it did sound appealing to spend time enjoying the beautiful fall woods surrounding the mill and drinking ice-cold cider. The anticipation of biting into a crisp and juicy caramel apple finally convinced her.

"Okay, some fresh air does sound pretty good right now."

Actually, now that I think about it, spending time with George doesn't sound so bad, either.

8

More Questions Than Answers

On Thursday morning Del was up early. She headed to the large freezer in her back room and pulled out bags and bags of frozen tomatoes. All of her surplus summer crop was here, and today was as good as any to make tomato sauce. Del sold most of her jellies and jams at the farmers' market, but tomatoes were another story. The sauce she put up in the fall would last her most of the winter.

She rounded up as many large pots and pans as she could find and dumped the frozen tomatoes, which clunked out like hard red balls, into them. Next she checked her canning supplies to make sure she had enough lids on hand.

Before long she was interrupted by the ring of the telephone. It was Alyssa calling to say that she and Scott had set up a meeting.

"When?"

Del was surprised to hear, "Today."

Alyssa went on to explain, "He wants to see me as soon as possible. I didn't have to work today so he said he'd take a day off his job and drive here. We're going to meet in the park at ten."

"Where's he coming from?" asked Del.

"Says he's here in Michigan. Didn't tell me anything other than that. I know it's short notice, but could you watch Stephie?"

Del promised to be there at nine-thirty and hurried through her breakfast. She looked with dismay at the pans of thawing tomatoes sitting around her kitchen. Should she put them back in the freezer?

But babysitting shouldn't take too long, right? she convinced herself. She decided to leave things as they were, with hopes of getting back to the canning later. Before leaving the house, she paused briefly in front of the crucifix on her living room wall to pray for Alyssa. Del gathered up her prayers and thoughts in a large mental sack and laid it at the feet of her crucified Lord.

I don't know where this all is leading, Lord, but I believe you love all of them. I pray only that your will be done in their lives. And please, help Mara deal with whatever happens. She's already borne so much in her short life.

Ever since the girl had arrived at Windmill Gardens – by the grace of God, Del felt – she had held a special place in Del's heart.

I just want to protect her from any more heartaches.

Alyssa, acting more than a little nervous, clicked off the TV set when Del arrived. She hurried out the door, leaving Del playing hide-and-seek with Stephie in the small apartment. The woman squeezed her bulk into closets to hide from the little girl, chuckling at the shrieks of delight from the child when she was discovered. When Stephie would "hide," Del would pretend not to see her, looking under pillows and lamps and books until there were giggles coming from some obvious hideaway. Next they read books together and played tea party with stuffed animals. Finally Del glanced at the clock. Realizing that a couple hours had passed, she got a little nervous. What could be taking Alyssa so long?

She found the fixings for peanut butter and jelly sandwiches and made lunch. By that time the little girl was rubbing her eyes. After reading one more book, Del tucked her in bed for a nap. Within minutes the youngster was asleep.

Well, that was easy enough. I wish my own kids had been so cooperative!

Wearily, Del sank onto the sofa, but the nearby bookshelves caught her eye. Rolling off her seat and crouching on the floor, she perused them, pulling out several and reading their covers. She replaced them and quickly scanned other titles. *The Restless Heart, Flames of Passion, Hot Tamale, The Secret Admirer*...

After some time, Del returned to the sofa and stayed there deep in thought until she heard a key turn in the door lock. Alyssa breezed in, dumped her jacket and purse and threw herself backwards onto the beanbag chair. She wiped her arm across her forehead in an exaggerated gesture before addressing Del.

"Is Stephie in bed?"

Del nodded. She was dying to ask how it had gone, but decided to wait for the woman to speak first.

Alyssa settled back, combing her hair back with her fingers, and stared into space for a few minutes.

"Well, that was most interesting!" she finally declared.

Del's eyebrows shot up like question marks, but she remained silent.

Alyssa brought her gaze back to Del.

"I got some answers, but there's still a lot more questions."

She dropped her voice and heaved a big sigh.

"Turns out he's been in jail."

"What?" exclaimed Del involuntarily.

"That's what he told me." Now that Alyssa had started telling the tale, she talked in a tumble of words. "He apparently stayed in our part of Ohio only a short while after the divorce, then found what he thought would be a better job in Michigan. He got involved with a new group of people, and before long there was some monkey business going on with drugs. He didn't do anything wrong but he was hanging around with some guys who got him into trouble."

She narrowed her eyes.

"At least that's what he claims."

Del shook her head, her lips set in a grim line.

Great! Now Mara gets to deal with the delightful fact that her father's a jailbird. Dear Lord, what else can happen?

Alyssa went on, "Said he stopped writing to his daughter because he was ashamed to let her know he was in prison. He was in jail for fourteen months and now's been out for awhile."

"So why hasn't he tried to contact her since he got out?"

"Says he started to write her several times and each time threw the letter away. He kept thinking that maybe she'd be better off if he'd stay out of her life. Can you imagine?" she ended with a scowl.

They sat in silence for some time, each lost in thought.

Finally Del asked, "Well, what changed his mind?"

"Del, I don't know how much of what he says I can believe. He's lied to me before. This is what he told me and, I have to tell you, I take it with a grain of salt. He says while he was in jail, there were some visitors who came from the local church. They did Bible studies with the prisoners and Scott claims he had a conversion experience."

Alyssa sounded as if she did not believe him.

I don't blame her, thought Del. *People claim all kinds of things.* Nevertheless, she kept her thoughts to herself.

"And?" she prodded.

The other woman clambered out of the low chair, went into the kitchen and came back with an apple.

"Sorry," she said. "I'm starving. I was too keyed up to eat breakfast after he called this morning." She took a big bite and sank back down onto the beanbag.

She continued her tale, chewing while she talked.

"He tells me he had a lot of time to think while in jail. He got to know one of the visitors pretty well, a man named Marshall. Apparently this Marshall has been mentoring him, even now that he's out. He speaks highly of this guy and says he's been going to church with him."

She finished the apple and tossed the core into a nearby wastebasket. She sat pondering for awhile before picking up her train of thought again.

"You know," she said quietly, "we went to church all the time after we got married and when Mara was young. We were in a Bible fellowship group. I don't know if Mara told you but she asked to be baptized when she was ten."

Del nodded and Alyssa went on. "Somewhere along the line, though, we got too busy and would miss here and there. Then we drifted away from it altogether. There was a lot of tension in our marriage and that didn't help," she said, but didn't explain further.

"Anyway, it was this Marshall who finally convinced him to contact Mara. The first year he was out he couldn't go very far under the terms of his release, but as soon as he could he tried to see us. Of course, we were gone by that time."

"What are you going to do now?" asked Del.

"Don't know yet. He does seem different. I got…well…I got a little upset with him today as we talked. And he didn't shout back. Unlike before," she said, rolling her eyes. "Anyway, he said he'll call again and we'll talk some more."

"Uh, did you happen to bring up Stephie?"

Alyssa glanced at Del with an inscrutable expression on her face.

"Didn't have to. He already knew. Gayle apparently told him about Stephie – and Tom."

"About Tom? About what he did to Mara?"

Alyssa shook her head. "No. Gayle doesn't know about that. Remember, Mara was back home only a short time before we decided to move here."

She leaned back wearily in the beanbag chair, closed her eyes and sighed heavily before saying, "I don't know, Del. Just don't know. Do I trust him or not? And anyway, how am I going to tell him that his little girl's pregnant?"

9

Fruits and Nuts

As the weatherman had promised, Friday was looking to be a mighty fine day. But Del wasn't admiring the morning's blue sky. The day before she'd had just enough time to get the tomato sauce cooked. She had left it simmering overnight to thicken and now she was faced with the task of ladling it into the canning jars in order to process it.

She also tried to process the thoughts which were still going through her mind from yesterday.

A conversion experience, eh? Well, time will tell. 'By their fruits you shall know them,' the Bible says. Maybe Scott's so-called conversion will bear fruit and maybe it won't.

Del was not exactly what one would call a cynical person. However, she *was* blessed with a lot of common sense. "Wait and see" was generally the attitude she adopted when things took unexpected turns. As she continued with her canning she prayed that Mara wouldn't be hurt any further.

Several hours later she was finished and the hot jars were resting atop a folded towel on the countertop. She hadn't forgotten that George was taking her to the cider mill today, but the time had gotten away from her and she was alarmed when she glanced at the clock.

Oh, no! He'll be here in a few minutes!

Del scrutinized her clothes to see if what she was wearing was presentable. There was no tomato sauce on her, but she decided that the old grass-stained jeans had to go. She scurried into her bedroom for a quick change. Being in a hurry, she left her shoes on. However, she failed to reckon with their thick rubber soles. She tried pulling a pant leg over one shoe, but it stuck tightly. By wiggling it back and forth and pulling determinedly on the sturdy fabric, she finally yanked it free and began to slip the other leg off.

This time the shoe-pant leg combination did not cooperate at all. The thick hem of the denim jeans bound up securely in the middle of her shoe, and pulling downwards just seemed to wedge it more tightly. After tugging with all her strength to get it off, she decided to try pulling the pant leg back on.

"It's stuck that way, too!" she complained out loud after several fruitless tugs. "I don't have time for this!"

She twisted and pulled every which way, but her fingers just didn't have the strength they used to. The pants were stuck fast, and Del glared angrily at them as if they had made the decision to make her life more difficult.

Okay, then! Since you're so stubborn, I'll take a pair of scissors to you!

She found her sewing box in the closet and hunted through it for her fabric shears.

Where could they have gone? Del tried to think quickly. *Oh, for crying out loud! I probably stuck them in the kitchen drawer after I cut up that fabric the other day.*

Del hobbled to her bedroom door, opened it a crack and listened carefully for any sound of George's car.

Good! He's not here yet.

She trotted awkwardly, trailing the pants around one ankle, as fast as she could to the kitchen. She yanked out the drawer where she kept kitchen utensils and pawed through it. Just as she spotted the scissors and grabbed hold of them, she froze. A knocking was heard at the front door and, in what seemed like only a microsecond, the door creaked open and a male voice called, "Hello! Del?"

Darn! she scolded herself. *Why do I always forget to lock that door?*

George pushed the door open wider and entered the house. He glanced around the empty living room and then proceeded directly to the kitchen.

"Where could she be?" he mumbled to himself when the kitchen proved to be unoccupied also. He looked out the big window, his eyes sweeping over the forlorn garden. What a contrast to how it looked in the summer! Now there were no glorious blooms, no vistas of softly waving greenery nor luscious-looking fruit hanging, just begging to be picked, from the peach and cherry trees.

There was also no Del to be seen. He scanned the entire backyard before concluding that she wasn't out there.

"My goodness, she wouldn't have gone out in the woods, leaving her front door unlocked, would she?" George said to himself. "Anyway, I'm sure I told her I'd be here at eleven to pick her up."

He stepped away from the window and, for the first time, noticed the door leading from the utility room to the garage.

"Well, it's worth a try," he declared, turning the knob. Pushing the door open and squinting in the dim light, he stepped down into the garage and came to an abrupt halt. There was Del, sitting behind the steering wheel in her car with the window rolled down. She stuck her head out and looked at him with surprise written all over her face.

"Why, George!" she exclaimed. "What are you doing here?"

George rubbed his chin and said slowly, "Well, um...uh, didn't I tell you that I'd be here at eleven to pick you up?" He frowned in confusion. "What are you doing in your car?"

"Oh, you did?" Del replied. "Oh, yes, you did! I remember now. But didn't I say that I would drive?" she went on, an innocent expression written all across her face.

George's face was looking more puzzled by the minute. Del's mouth twitched a little but she managed to smile sweetly at him when he finally answered.

"Well...actually...no," he said slowly, trying to feel his way cautiously through this strange conversation. "I'm sure I told you that I would drive. I know you don't like to drive this old car any great distance."

"Well, then, that's no problem at all!" Del replied, beaming. "It's all settled. I'll be most happy to let you drive. Why don't you go on out to your car and I'll join you there? I just have to make a quick change into something decent. Won't take but a minute."

After a prolonged pause, George nodded hesitantly. He headed back into the house, but not before turning around one last time to glance quizzically at the pant leg hanging out the bottom of Del's car door.

10

The Spencers

Saturday also proved to be a lovely day, a perfect afternoon for Del to head to the woods. She followed the trails that she knew so well until she came to a familiar thicket. Here were a variety of trees and bushes covered with the wild grape vines that she sought. She looked them over well, selecting a few grapes at random to pop into her mouth. She made a face and spit them out.

Whoa, a bit sour. I think I'll forget making that jelly.

Del was looking over the tangle of vines to select the best for cutting, when suddenly another thought occurred to her.

Butternuts!

She turned on her heel and retraced her steps, then struck off at a different angle. After a long walk she came to a dense, rich part of the woods. Hardwood trees grew here in thick profusion, their crowns high in the sky and their slender, almost limbless trunks covered with yellowing poison ivy. Del circled around them and the patches of dying thistle, until she came to an area where the woods thinned a bit.

There she found what she sought – her treasured butternut trees. She knew that it was considered unusual to find them growing in this part of the country, but she didn't waste any time pondering how they had gotten there.

Thank you, birds, squirrels, or whatever humans might have dropped a few nuts many years ago. Now I get to reap the harvest.

Although butternuts were related to walnuts, they were seldom sold commercially. Because of that, Del had been delighted when she had discovered these trees years ago. She loved butternuts.

I'm surprised the squirrels left me any. There must have been a bountiful harvest this year.

She pulled a few paper bags from her dilapidated backpack and scooped handfuls of the large oblong nuts into them. She didn't even mind that they would likely leave her hands stained in shades of grey.

After stowing several bulging sacks of nuts in her pack, Del contentedly retraced her steps to cut the grapevines. Upon returning home, she sorted the nuts and tossed the good ones in a roasting pan to dry at low heat in the oven. Then the woman turned her attention to stripping the vines of their leaves and rolling them into large, loose coils.

After dinner that evening, Del drove to the Spencers' small dairy farm just down the road. In the driveway, she beeped the horn lightly and from the farmhouse bounded the two Spencer children. Del clambered from the car while Sean, a tall pre-teenager, retrieved the large plastic bags filled with grapevines from the car trunk. Six-year-old Abby latched onto Del's hand and skipped along, pulling her toward the house.

Ann was cleaning up the kitchen while keeping an eye on baby Jacob. The infant was lying in a playpen, looking around with bright eyes. When Del leaned over to talk to him, he stared fixedly at her. Then just a hint of a smile trembled on his tiny lips.

"He's learning a new trick – how to smile!" declared Abby as she leaned over the crib edge, eager to show off her baby brother.

"Hey, Del, what's up?"

The deep voice coming from behind startled Del, and she turned to see Richard striding into the kitchen. He was a big, broad-shouldered man with dark hair and a perpetual grin on his face. Del smiled back at him, feeling blessed to have this likable couple as neighbors.

"Not much," she replied. "I just brought some grapevines for Ann. Though I don't know how she'll find the time to make wreaths. I imagine this crew keeps her pretty busy!"

Richard chuckled. "She manages – somehow. Hey, son," he went on, turning to the boy, "I need your help out in the barn."

Sean made a face but went to get his jacket. Then Richard bent down to talk to his daughter.

"And you, little miss, didn't finish stackin' those egg cartons in the cardboard boxes like I asked you to. I suggest you do that right now."

"Oh, Daddy!" Abby whined, scowling. "Do I hafta?"

Her dad folded his arms and stared at her until she finally turned and stomped none too graciously into the utility room. Richard glanced at Del with a grimace, saying, "See ya later," before following Sean outside.

Ann finished her work in the kitchen and scooped up the baby who was starting to whimper. She beckoned Del to follow her into the living room where they settled comfortably on the overstuffed couch. While Ann nursed the child, it was a perfect time to catch up on their visiting.

Del told her about the butternuts and promised to share some of the bounty. Then the conversation drifted to the beautiful fall colors. Del mentioned that the cider mill had the most gorgeous scenery, and that led to telling Ann about the pants episode the day before. By the time she was finished with the story they were both laughing so hard that the baby started to cry. Ann had to rock him to calm him down.

"And George?" she questioned, smiling at Del. "Anything new happening with George?"

"What do you mean, 'anything new?'" asked Del.

"Well, it certainly must be clear to you, as it is to the rest of us, that he likes you."

"And?"

"Oh, for heaven's sake, Del! Hasn't he asked you to marry him yet?"

"Marry him! Good grief, Ann, that's the last thing on my mind!" Del protested.

Ann laughed. "But I don't think it's the last thing on *his* mind, is it?"

Del sighed. "You're probably right. He's been dropping some pretty broad hints lately. Like yesterday at the cider mill."

"So what did you say?"

Del shook her head and grinned. "I kept changing the subject."

"But, Del, I know that you like him. He's a good, kind man. And he certainly isn't bad to look at! You know, there's some other ladies in town who'd love to steal him away from you!"

"I suppose that's true. But all those reasons aren't enough to marry him." Del looked imploringly at Ann.

"Joey and I had a wonderful marriage. We had a lot of struggles in the beginning, but with God's help we came through them. A good marriage takes more than liking each other. It even takes more than love, if love is based only on feelings."

She paused before continuing, "As you know, I don't try to make important decisions on my own. I've prayed about it, but just don't have the sense that God is calling me to get married again. Who knows," she shrugged, "maybe in the future. But not right now."

"Did you tell George that?"

Del looked a little sheepish. "Not exactly. I guess I chickened out. It was easier to keep dancing around the issue!"

Ann laughed again and changed the subject.

"And how's Mara doing?" She put the sleepy baby on her shoulder and patted his back.

"Well, she still sees a counselor every other week. Usually her mother goes with her. They both have a lot to work through."

"That awful man!" declared Ann, remembering Tom and how he had abused the girl. "I'm glad he's dead!"

Del rubbed her eyes wearily, saying, "But the problems keep on coming. Did you know that Mara's father is trying to see her?" The Spencers had befriended the girl while she was staying at Windmill Gardens, so Del knew that Ann was concerned.

"Her father?" Ann asked in surprise. "I thought they didn't know where he was!"

"They didn't. But out of the blue he called Alyssa. Earlier this week she met with him to talk things over, and last night Alyssa called to tell me that he was coming again today."

"To see Mara?"

"No. Scott – that's her dad – is just talking to Alyssa for now. Mara doesn't know anything about it yet. Alyssa told Mara to babysit Stephie today so she could 'run a few errands,' she said. She was meeting Scott out at the park on Hill Street."

The younger woman frowned, asking, "Do you think this is a good thing?"

Del shook her head slowly. "I just don't know, Ann. I'm worried about Mara, that she's going to get her heart broken again. And then there's the business of her being pregnant. I'm afraid what Scott will do when he finds out his daughter was raped."

Her voice sank to a whisper.

"Lord help them – what a mess!"

11

Eva's Place

On Sunday morning Mara called to ask if Del could pick her up and take her to Mass with her. The girl and her mother occasionally attended a small non-denominational church since they had moved to town. But Mara told Del over the phone that her mother had a headache this morning.

Del was most happy to pick her up for church. *She's still searching,* thought Del, *which is certainly a good sign. There are people with fewer problems who simply give up on God.*

In the car Del inquired how her mom was doing. The girl shrugged.

"It's just a headache. She gets them sometimes. Maybe it has something to do with yesterday."

"Yesterday?" Del approached the matter-of-fact statement cautiously. "What happened yesterday?"

"Dunno. For some reason when she got back from her errands she was in a terrible mood, worse than usual. Seemed I couldn't do anything right the rest of the day. I'm glad to get out of the apartment."

Mara had her head turned away, but Del could imagine the look on her face. She had seen it many times before. It was as if a door would suddenly slam shut in the girl's emotions and a wall would come up to block out everyone. Del was aware of the vulnerability of this poor child and didn't try to push past it. She simply listened to and loved her.

"Well," said Del, changing the subject, "this works out fine. Since you and I were going to Eva's for lunch today, I was planning to pick you up after church anyway." Mara's mother had given permission for the girl to go as long as she was home in time to babysit. "What time does she have to work?"

"Not 'til six."

From her place in the choir loft, Del watched parishioners file in. Halfway down the left side she saw the Spencer family. Mara had taken a seat next to Ann.

Good choice, reflected Del. *Ann isn't Catholic, either, so Mara won't feel out of place sitting by herself when everyone else goes to Communion.* She found herself wondering what had happened the day before between Mara's parents that had put Alyssa in such a bad mood.

I suppose I'll find out soon enough.

Del shook her head sadly and picked up her hymnal as Mass began. She noticed that there seemed to be some dissonance in the music this day at Mass, something slightly off key. She dropped her voice to an inaudible level in order to hear better.

Well, it's not me, she thought with some relief, *but I can't tell who it is.*

It turned out that it wasn't a *who* after all, but rather a *what.* As soon as Mass ended the complaints started.

"That old piano!" declared Harriet O'Meir, whose keen sense of hearing was always able to pinpoint problems. Except, of course, when she herself was the problem. "How long has it been since it was tuned?"

"I just had it done a few weeks ago," protested Laurie. "But it's just too old. The piano tuner said he spent a lot time pounding in the tuning pegs because the soundboard is aging. He said we'd be better off getting a new piano. I've already talked to Father Mike about it."

"What'd he say?" they all wanted to know.

"Just what you'd expect. There's no money in the budget for a new piano."

The choir stood around debating the situation. Del knew Mara was probably waiting for her but she was never one to leave in the middle of a good discussion. Their church, being in a rural area and with few families, didn't have the amenities one could expect in a larger parish. When it had been built, money was tight and plans had to be scrapped to purchase a pipe organ. They had gotten by for all this time with just a small electronic organ and the piano. Laurie preferred the more mellow sound of the piano, but it did seem as if its useful life was coming to an end.

41

"Well," somebody finally threw out, "why don't we have a fundraiser to buy a new piano?" Everyone quickly seconded the proposal and ideas were bandied back and forth. Most were totally impractical, some were nigh impossible, but a few reasonable ones emerged. In the end, the one idea which came out on top was that of a choir cookbook.

"Great idea!" they all concurred. "Everyone go home and write down your best recipes!"

Mara had come up to the choir loft to see what was taking Del so long, just in time to hear George say, "We'll have to put a few of Del's recipes in the book – using dandelions or some other weeds!"

Everyone laughed. Del glared at him before motioning to Mara and leading the way down the stairs.

"If they only knew," she confided earnestly to the girl once they were out in the sunshine, "how nutritious those wild foods really are!"

Mara didn't say anything, trying to suppress a grin. She had heard it all before.

Eva lived a ways out in the country in a comfortable house on several acres of land. Her husband had built a small barn, and their menagerie of animals – besides the dogs, guinea pigs and rabbits they had owned previously – had grown to include a sheep named Woolly and some chickens. She had asked them to come to lunch this day to meet their latest acquisition – a pony, bequeathed to them by a neighbor who had moved away.

Pulling into the driveway, they were met by Eva's and Kirk's three children who still lived at home. The youngsters swarmed around Mara, urging her to come out to the barn. Del, following them, squinted when she first stepped into the barn's darkness. When her eyes adjusted, she saw the piebald patches of a large brown and white pony. He stood patiently allowing everyone to pet him. Del cupped her hand around his muzzle and rubbed behind his ears, delighted at the softness of his coat.

A clanging bell was heard coming from the direction of the house.

"What's that?" asked Mara.

"Oh, that's just Mom," laughed fifteen-year-old Risa, "calling us to lunch."

At the meal that day there was much bantering going on between members of Eva's family. Her husband was an affable man, and it was hard to decide who would win a prize for the corniest jokes – Kirk or one of the kids. Lunch was over in a jiffy and the young people poured back outside. A cart had come with the pony and they were hitching it up to get ready to go.

Del and Eva joined the boisterous party, sitting on lawn chairs in the warm sunshine and watching Kirk help the four children find seats in the cart.

"Is it safe?" worried Del.

"Oh, perfectly," reassured Eva. "They've taken the pony out lots of times. He's really gentle and nothing ever spooks him. The family that owned him had a whole passel of young'uns," she laughed, "so he's probably used to anything. Kirk and the kids have cleared all the debris from the path. The pony knows his way well – down the lane, through the path in the woods, then back through the meadow."

The reins were taken up by thirteen-year-old Megan, and her younger brother Dylan sat beside her. Behind them were Risa and Mara. Kirk slapped the pony's flank before heading into the barn. His daughter shook the reins.

"Giddyup, Old Paint."

Smiling, Del watched them leave before turning to Eva.

"I'm glad your daughters have been so nice to Mara. She could use some friends right now."

"Well, they like her and so do I. She's a real sweet girl."

Eva paused for a moment, reflecting, then continued, "Besides, Del, I owe you."

"Owe me?" Del asked. Her eyes widened in surprise.

"Yes," said Eva, turning sideways to look directly at her friend. "If it weren't for you, I wouldn't have those three wonderful kids."

12

Whoever Welcomes the Least of These

At that Del chuckled, having an idea where this conversation was going. When she and Eva had first met, the younger mother had two children and was planning to return to her job as a counselor as soon as possible. As they progressed in friendship they discussed many topics, including the meaning of marriage and God's plan for families. It was because of their praying together outside the abortion clinic that a lengthy discussion ensued concerning the link between abortion and contraception.

Del declared that such a connection made a lot of sense.

"After all," she maintained to Eva, "if a baby can be prevented by using what's called 'birth control,' why can't you end the life of your child by aborting it? That's birth control, too."

"Well, it's not the same thing," Eva argued. "You're not taking the life of an already-existing child when you use contraception. You're just preventing it from ever getting started."

"Oh, really? And what about the birth-control pill? I've heard you say that you believe human life begins at conception. Don't you know that some of the time the pill acts as an abortifacient? It prevents the implanting of the fertilized egg in the womb of the mother."

Eva's brow furrowed.

"That can't be true or I would've heard about it."

Del urged her to look into it. Several weeks passed before they were in touch with each other again. Eva admitted that Del had been right, as she had done extensive research and had come up with the same information.

"But I also asked my pastor about it and he said that using contraception is a way to exercise responsible parenthood. After all, who'd have the time or money to raise a dozen kids or more?"

With a smile, Del quoted Scripture, "Children are a heritage from the Lord; blessed the man whose quiver is full of them."

She continued, "But seriously, there's no saying how many children anyone will have. Some have large families, true. But some are only given one or two, or no children at all. Let me ask you, Eva – do you believe that a true Christian marriage involves three persons?"

"Of course," answered Eva promptly. "A man, a woman and God."

"If that's the case, then why not leave the question of how many children to have to the smartest of the three?"

Eva laughed a little but shook her head.

"Del, you're just spouting the Catholic line. The rest of the Christian world has other ways to look at it."

Del wasn't deterred. "But didn't you know that up until the year 1930 all Christian churches, Catholic and Protestant alike, had always condemned the use of artificial birth control? In fact Luther, Calvin and Wesley were unwavering in their opposition to both abortion *and* contraception. And after the Protestant churches gave way on this issue, it wasn't long before many of them were allowing abortion, too."

It was clear that the younger woman didn't believe her and their get-together that day had ended on a strained note. Yet Eva, a woman of great faith, was also a lover of the truth. In spite of her feelings, she believed that truth needed to be pursued wherever it might lead. On her own she delved into the questions that the other woman had raised. She read books, contacted people she knew, asked questions and spent time in prayer over it.

It was months before she ran into Del again and, without any preamble, blurted out, "Okay, are you happy now that you've turned my life upside-down?"

Del, surprised, asked her what she was talking about.

"All that stuff you told me about contraception! After talking it over with my husband, we decided that we were going to prove you wrong. He did his research and I did mine – and we've come to the conclusion that we've been sold a bill of goods on this issue."

Since they happened to be at a shopping mall, Del suggested they find a more private place where they could talk. They seated themselves in a nearly-empty restaurant and ordered something to drink. Then Del asked Eva, "So, what now?"

Eva looked down into her cup, swirling the coffee around. "I'm still trying to process everything I read. I came across some books that talked about marriage in such a beautiful way. Stuff I'd never thought about before. One spoke about how we carry in our own bodies the divine image of God. It explained how God in his very nature is both unitive and creative, and that he created marriage to reflect both of those attributes. Just as we can't divide God's oneness from his creativity, in marriage we can't separate the unitive from the creative aspect."

She paused and Del waited quietly for her to continue.

After a moment Eva went on, "Another book said that marriage is meant to mirror Christ's union with his church. Spousal love is meant to be absolutely self-giving, the way Christ gave himself entirely, withholding nothing – even his very life – out of love for his 'bride.' When we use contraception during the marriage act we are actually withholding a part of ourselves – our fertility – from our spouse. And that means that we are really telling a lie with our bodies."

She placed an elbow on the table and rested her chin on her hand. "You know, Del, before this I never spent much time thinking about the meaning of marriage. But now I'm finally finding out what God's plan for marriage is. It seems that what it really comes down to is that we have a choice between *selfishness* and *selflessness*. I really didn't realize how selfish Kirk and I had become in our day-to-day life. It's always been all about *us*. And whether *we* wanted children."

She looked over at Del. "It's funny, isn't it? It never even occurred to us to ask God to help us be open to *his* plan for marriage. We prayed about everything else, but ..." She stopped abruptly and looked over at her friend with a question in her eyes.

"But, Del, don't you think that this is too hard a teaching to follow? I mean, how could anyone be expected to do this, especially in this day and age?"

Del reached over and touched the other woman's arm.

"God always wants the absolute best for us in everything. What he has in mind for us is better than anything we could think up on our own. You're absolutely right – this is a hard teaching.

But if it was easy, then we wouldn't need to depend on God's help, would we?"

She continued gently, "Children are meant to be a blessing from God. Each new child has something to teach us, and every child is a challenge for us to grow in patience, generosity and love. You could say that children are our personal holiness trainers! And besides, every baby brings into our home a new guardian angel, and we can always use another angel around."

Eva had to leave then, but Del was not too surprised when she received an excited phone call from her a few months later announcing that she and Kirk were expecting another baby. And in their newfound openness to life, two more children eventually arrived.

In the meantime, Eva became a teacher for natural family planning. In her research, she had been thrilled to discover that fertility awareness was very empowering for women.

"And did you know," she declared in one phone conversation with Del, "that this method is as reliable as taking the pill? And it doesn't have any of the side effects, either! It's true, it requires more sacrifice on our part – but it's certainly made our marriage stronger."

Del already knew the benefits of natural family planning. She just cautioned Eva that even with all its benefits, it, too, could be used selfishly to thwart God's ultimate and best plan for their family.

"I know," responded Eva, "and that's how I present it when I teach it. You know, Del, one of the very first things I tell women is that pregnancy is not a disease. The contraceptive mentality treats fertility like a disorder to be fixed and children as burdens. Now I see children as the gifts from God they actually are."

After that phone call, a long time passed until Del met up with Eva at the crisis pregnancy center. And now here they were, picking up the same thread of their conversation as naturally as if there were no intervening years.

Eva stated resolutely, "I don't know if I ever thanked you properly. It's only on looking back that I can really see how much closer my husband and I became once we started following God's plan for our marriage. We developed a special strength that helped get us through the hard times."

She sighed and fell silent but Del knew what she was referring to. Years ago she had heard that Eva's eldest daughter had been in a terrible traffic accident shortly after she was married.

"And how is Patricia doing these days?" Del asked solicitously.

"Oh, thank God, she's doing better now. And what a blessing our son-in-law has been! He was at her side night and day. It was really touch-and-go for awhile. He's such a great young man. Did you ever meet him?"

Del shook her head. "I'd like to, sometime. And how is your son doing at college?"

"Oh, just great! I don't know if he's going to..."

Eva stopped talking, hearing the faint ring of the phone inside the house. She excused herself, hustling over to the screen door and letting it bang closed behind her. She was gone only a minute when she burst outside again and ran towards the barn, shouting, "Kirk! Kirk! The center's on fire!"

13

The Singer

A crowd had assembled in the street near the pregnancy center. Fire trucks lined the sidewalk with their lights flashing and cutting through even the brightness of the afternoon. The fire was nearly out and smoke no longer poured from the shattered windows.

Del stood with Mara and the other onlookers. After the phone call, she had told Eva and Kirk to go on ahead and that she would wait for the kids to come back to tell them what was happening.

"Make them stay here!" yelled Eva over her shoulder as her husband quickly backed the car out of the garage and she jumped in. "Don't let them come with you!"

Now, standing anxiously in the street, Del finally spotted Eva where she was talking with a yellow-coated firefighter. She and Mara wended their way through the crowd. As they approached, Eva turned to them and the man returned to his duties.

"Do they know what happened?" asked Del.

"Not yet. It's going to take days to sort through the mess and figure it out. Actually, the building itself sustained little damage. But the contents will be ruined by the smoke and water."

Eva looked as if she was near tears.

"Oh, Del!" she cried. "Our files! And all those things that have been donated to help the women and their babies! All gone!"

Del hugged her but couldn't offer much by way of comfort. She realized that she needed to be getting Mara home, so asked Eva to let her know if she could do anything. Eva nodded wordlessly and went off to find her husband.

The ride back to Mara's place was quiet as both were lost in thought. After dropping off the girl, Del turned onto the road leading home to Windmill Gardens. Just at that moment her old car sputtered to a stop.

Del cranked the engine over and over again to no avail. Finally, she slammed the car door and walked to the nearest house to call a tow truck. When it eventually arrived the mechanic poked around under the hood for awhile. He looked up at Del with a grim face.

"Sorry, Del," he began. The random thought occurred to her that it probably wasn't a good thing when your auto mechanic knows you well enough to be on a first-name basis with you. "It looks like it might be the fuel pump. I'll know for sure after I get it back to the shop."

Using hooks and chains he winched the old car onto the truck bed. With Del in the cab, he started back to town.

"Lucky for you I was in today. Don't usually work on Sundays but my wife's car needed some work done and I haven't had time to get to it. If you can wait for an hour or so 'til I'm finished with her car, I'll give you a lift home."

Del was tired but there didn't seem to be any other choice. She was starting to resign herself to the long wait when she suddenly thought, *The auto shop is only a short distance from church. Why don't I go and pray?* She asked the man to drive over and honk the horn when he was ready, and she trudged to the church.

Del unlocked the heavy wooden doors of St. Bernard's. The late afternoon sun was pouring through the dancing colored flames of the yellow and orange stained glass windows. Del had plenty of illumination as she walked wearily down the carpeted aisle and sank heavily onto the kneeler before the tabernacle.

Lord, why? she found herself asking in prayer. She wasn't thinking of her own difficulties, but of the fire at the center. *They are trying to help your hurting people. So much good is coming out of that place. Why do they have to go through all this? And who's going to help those poor women now?* She thought of Mara, and how Eva and the others had been there to aid the girl in her time of need. *Why, Lord, why?*

In the silence she stretched out her arms before her with hands clasped and rested her weary head on them. In spite of everything, she knew that here in the presence of Jesus she could have a few minutes' respite. Even though there seemed to be no immediate answers forthcoming from her Lord, she knew beyond a shadow of a doubt that he heard her and that she needn't carry her burdens by herself.

Some time passed. Evening began to set in and everything in the church faded into shadows. As the windows were still bright from the rays of the low-hanging sun, Del didn't bother to switch on the lights. With her head bent and her mind occupied in prayer, the slight sound of the front door of the church being opened and closed softly did not even enter into her consciousness. A moment later, when the first strains of a hymn sung in a lovely soprano voice floated down lightly from the choir loft, Del did not raise her head. Perhaps she was too engrossed in prayer to hear.

It took a little time, and the swelling boldness of the voice in the quiet church, to register with Del. As the voice grew in volume, she raised her head slowly and listened with quickening heart to the most astonishing performance she could ever imagine. At first she tried to understand the words, but came to the realization that they were in Latin. Anyway, the words diminished in importance as the clear voice rose and fell, catching her up in a spectacular, haunting melody she could not remember ever hearing before. The dark stillness of the church became alive with graceful notes and exquisite runs of pure golden splendor. It almost seemed like the base things of earth had disappeared and heaven was beginning to manifest itself right there at that moment in time.

As if caught up in a dream, the woman knelt there unmoving and, in fact, barely breathing, unwilling to break the spell of the ethereal music as it glided and soared and floated gently to earth. A single-voice symphony, it played impenitently with the emotions. It made one feel like breaking into sobs and, alternately, laughing out loud in sheer joy. It was wondrous, it was breathtaking – and it was over all too quickly. After the hymn's final crystal notes faded from gleaming to shimmering and then into silence, Del turned around to look with awe into the choir loft at the back. She wouldn't have been a bit surprised if she saw a dazzling angel standing there, because she was sure that only a celestial being could have sung in such a manner.

Her movement must have startled whoever it was. She caught just a glimpse of a head, black-shadowed against the brightly illuminated window behind, before it suddenly dipped and disappeared. A bumped-into chair skidded on the wooden choir loft floor and it wasn't but a moment before Del heard the church door clunk noisily shut.

Oh! marveled Del to herself. *I've never heard anything so beautiful in my life! Who was that?*

She thought of each and every woman who was in the church choir and eliminated all of them. *Absolutely no one in our choir can sing like that. Most of them – most of US,* she corrected charitably – *don't even come close.*

She turned back to prayer in wonderment, thinking about the power of beauty to lay hold of our souls. Reflecting on all that had happened earlier that day, the frustrating as well as the tragic, she admired the graciousness of God who would weave a shining thread of unexpected pleasure through it.

Oh, Creator of the beautiful, I thank you.

Hearing the beep of a horn outside, she glanced one more time at the now-empty choir loft before leaving. Her thoughts, though, remained transfixed on that stirring, grace-filled voice for a long while afterwards.

14

Riddles

A few days passed before Del heard any more from Alyssa. Del had been taking advantage of the continuing warm weather to finish putting her perennials to bed for the winter. Some she covered with leaves and others she left bare, depending on their hardiness. Any remaining annuals she pulled out, saving the seeds to start new plants next spring.

Out in the woods she searched for roses, looking for the ones which had the biggest hips – *one instance when large hips are to be desired!* she chuckled – and gathered the red berries to make her popular rosehip jelly. On her foray this day she cut wild plants which would make nice additions to flower arrangements. She added them to her growing collection of dried flowers and herbs in the garage.

On one of the nicer afternoons, Sean helped her haul armloads of the now-brown bulrushes from streams in the woods. She intended to tie together bunches of these tall grass-like plants and sell them at the farmers' market.

It's just amazing what city folk will buy, thought Del.

It was Wednesday morning when Alyssa finally called, ready to talk about what had happened with Scott the previous Saturday.

"It was the pits, Del," she said. "A real bummer. In the beginning he was in a pretty good mood and we talked for a while friendly-like. But when he started asking if he could see Mara, I knew I couldn't put it off any longer. There was nothing to do but jump in and blurt out all the bad news."

Del grimaced. Knowing how blunt Alyssa could be at times, she could just imagine the scene.

"Lord, Del, he just exploded! He got so angry! Anyway, that's nothing new with him. But I stayed calm. I just sat there and let him yell. 'Course, I had to remind him that if he hadn't walked out, then all of this might not have happened."

Of course, thought Del. *She would have to remind him of that.*

"Well, after a while I started to get pretty ticked, too, and told him a thing or two. He was not a happy camper by the time he left. He just jumped in his car and took off."

Del cradled the receiver in her hand. She shook her head sadly and said, "I'm sorry."

But Alyssa was still talking. "Now this is the really weird part. Yesterday he calls and apologizes! I don't get it! Is this the Scott I remember? He said he was sorry for yelling, that he had no right to be mad at me, that he took full responsibility for anything that had happened. He also told me – now listen to this – that he thought I was doing a good job as a mother! Can you believe it? I was shocked."

Del was surprised but skeptical. "What do you think he wants?"

"Uh…I'm not really sure. What he *says* he wants is just one thing – to see Mara."

"Did you agree to that?"

"I'm not sure I have a choice. Mara has a right to see him. After she turns seventeen in a few weeks I'll have no say in the matter anyway. But I still haven't told her about her dad yet. Del, I don't know if I trust him."

Del wasn't sure if she would, either. She urged Alyssa to pray for guidance before doing anything and they hung up. Her heart was uneasy as she went back to her work.

That evening, Richard dropped Del off in town to pick up her repaired car. She got to church a bit early for choir rehearsal that night, but didn't mind as it gave her a few minutes to sit in the church and pray.

Father, that whole family has so many problems! I know that you know all about them and I certainly don't need to tell you. But, naturally, Del did anyway. She just talked to God as she would to an old friend.

Where is this going, Lord? Please help this to work out the best for all of them, especially Mara. She's your child and I believe she's trying to draw closer to you. But it's so difficult for her right now. Help her to trust you – help us all to trust you.

As the other choir members arrived she joined them. It was difficult to get practice started, however, as some of the ladies were all excited about the choir cookbook. They had been back and forth on the phone with one another during the week and now presented their plans to Laurie.

"We found out that we can use the copy machine here at church. That will save us a ton of money from having to hire a printer!" bubbled Mae Beth.

Laurie was dubious. "Don't you think that's a lot of work to be doing yourselves?"

"How hard can it be to print and assemble five hundred copies or so?" asked Harriet. "Also, Joe's wife used to work at the school. She said we can probably borrow the tool needed to punch the holes and insert the plastic spine. Right, Joe?"

Joe nodded and Laurie gave up. "Okay, you guys seem to have things under control. Now, what about the recipes?"

"Oh, we've got an article going into the church bulletin this Sunday asking parishioners to drop off their favorite recipes. We'll put a box in the vestibule to collect them," said Ernestine.

"And don't forget," she added imperiously, "all you choir people bring in several, in case we don't get enough!"

George, with an impish grin on his face, started to say something – most likely about Del's recipes. But when she glanced sideways at him, he changed his mind and rehearsal got underway. Afterwards Del asked the group, "Do any of you know a person who can sing like an angel?"

They all looked at each other, then back at Del.

"Huh?" muttered Ernestine.

"I mean someone, a girl, who has a voice so beautiful that…well, if you heard it you'd never forget it."

"I've heard a few unforgettable voices, right here in our choir," drawled Franklin Samuelson, who didn't speak a lot but fancied himself a bit of a wit. After a few snickers and a couple of frosty stares, he amended, "I mean, we *do* have some pretty good singers. But…well, perhaps not any angels."

"Del, what are you talking about?" demanded George. "You're not making any sense."

Del smiled and shook her head, falling silent. Obviously the answer to the riddle didn't lie here.

15

Interlude

By the next afternoon it had warmed up enough that Del needed to don only a light jacket before heading out to the woods. She walked and walked, finding her way along the unmarked trail she had come to know so well over the years. How she treasured being out where there was only silence, except for cries of birds and rustling of leaves, all around her.

Oh, it wasn't that she didn't love her home. After all, it was where her children had grown up and she and her husband had enjoyed many happy years until he passed away. But with every fiber of her being Del longed to be, as much as possible, out in the wild. Her Algonquin mother had understood much about the woods and instilled in her daughter a passionate love for nature.

Right now the woman was intent on reaching her favorite destination. Each October she looked forward to this, biding her time and watching and waiting until the most perfect day would arrive. It would be after the first frost, when cool nights and daytime sunshine combined to produce the finest palette of autumn colors. The perfect day had to be cloudless, with perhaps just a faint breeze to stir the air. When the first light this morning had promised just such a day, Del found her anticipation growing as each hour passed.

Even her daily prayer break, which she was accustomed to take after lunch, was cut short by her decision to head out to the woods. *I can finish my Rosary while walking,* she decided with joyful anticipation, *and surely God won't mind too much if I admire all the beauty he created while I'm doing it.*

For several hours she traveled, going much further than on her everyday jaunts. Every so often she'd take a short break, find a seat on a fallen tree and drink from a bottle of water she had stashed in her old backpack. On one such break she found herself close to a patch of thistle, with cottony silk puffing out from each flowerhead. A goldfinch darted from a bush and settled on the dried thistle, pulling out the seeds with its beak before flying off. Another finch came and then two more, and Del's eyes followed with delight their short swooping flights to a nearby tree. The males had already molted their bright yellow plumage for a duller green-gold and now it was difficult to tell them apart from their mates, who were always dressed less conspicuously.

In the woods, Del noticed everything. She would admire the way black-eyed Susans, bereft of their vivid petals, had their dark seeds arranged geometrically in a spiral. The fluff of cattails she'd pluck and distribute on the ground for mice to carry off to their winter nests. Coming across peppergrass, she would never fail to pop a few of the pungent seeds into her mouth.

Yet Del was a woman on a mission today and didn't tarry long at any of these other distractions, delightful though they were. As she drew nearer to her destination her expectancy grew, until at last she sighted a massive stand of spruce that marked the edge of her special meadow. With great anticipation she followed the familiar path through the evergreens and emerged into an open field.

Her breath caught in her throat. There they were! Across the clearing, almost glowing in the bright sunshine, were a multitude of paper-white birches. Del never failed to be astonished at the trees' brilliancy against the azure October sky. With their bright trunks and peeling bark, they stood in enchanting contrast to other trees around them. Every birch blazed like white and gold fire as its clear yellow leaves lit up by the sun trembled and shimmered in the gentle breeze.

Del had first come across this remarkable sight many years ago and never failed to be moved by it. She knew that other people might think it quite foolish to be awestruck over such a simple thing as trees standing in a field. And to walk half a day just to see them! But Del had a large capacity for wonder, a hollow place in the middle of her being which longed to be filled with the beautiful.

What did Dostoyevsky say about beauty being the only thing that is absolutely indispensable? He said that, without it, there's nothing in the world worth doing. Del reflected for a moment about how that which is beautiful – whether exquisite music or stunning scenery – stirs up a yearning in our hearts for the transcendent. Because of that yearning, she knew, our desire for beauty will never be totally satisfied by anything here on earth.

As a backdrop to the yellow and white birches, the reds and oranges of other deciduous trees added their own glorious mix of color. And hanging from branches just over her head the scarlet leaves of Virginia creeper vine swayed gently in the light breeze. *It's as if Paradise itself has descended to earth in this little forsaken spot,* she thought, settling herself on a large rock positioned almost like a seat at the edge of the woods.

After a while she managed to take her gaze off the scenery, noticing the antics of the little cottontails who bounded by. They'd stop suddenly and sit up on their haunches to peer at her over the long grasses and weeds. Finding no reason to be alarmed, they'd simply go back about their business. There were also fat brown squirrels scurrying up and down trees and over the ground with nuts in their mouths. Busily they buried their winter food supply, placing each nut in a separate hole.

How many trees, it occurred to Del, *must have sprung up through the ages from squirrels' forgotten treasures!*

High up in a maple were a pair of turtledoves, their mournful cooing the first indication of their presence. On an oak branch two argumentative blue jays quarreled in a petty disagreement, and a flash of red was seen as a cardinal whisked by. Del glimpsed a slight movement on a nearby trunk. She turned her head just enough to see a brown creeper searching in the bark with its long beak. Just at that moment, a shadow passed overhead. Del glanced up in time to see a hawk circling lazily in the sky. The little creeper must have seen it, too, for it flattened itself against the tree trunk, unmoving and nearly unnoticeable.

Don't worry, little friend, she smiled. *I won't let that hawk get you while I'm here.*

Del could have spent many more hours simply enjoying the beauty of God's earth. But eventually a glance at the sun as it sank lower in the sky reminded her that she needed to get back. Reluctantly she stood and swept her eyes across the panorama, trying to fill up until next year with everything she had seen. On the coldest days of winter she would take out these mental snapshots, dust off the memories and fondly revisit the beauty the Lord had blessed her with this day.

16

Daddy's Little Girl

On Saturday afternoon Mara unexpectedly arrived at Del's with Stephie in tow. The child ran right to the kitchen and scooted under the table to play with the kitten. Del took one look at Mara's face and knew immediately that something had happened. She invited her to sit in the living room and asked if she could get anything for her. Mara shook her head. Before Del could say anything else, she noticed tears trickling down the girl's face.

"I saw my dad last night," Mara said without preamble.

The woman brought a box of tissues for the girl and sat near her on the couch. The girl dried her face before continuing.

"Mom told me on Wednesday that she'd heard from my dad and that he wanted to see me."

She sniffed and took a deep breath. Del asked, "Did she tell you anything else?"

The girl shook her head. "No, just that he wanted to see me and that he'd explain everything. He called Thursday and said he'd meet me the next night at McDonald's. Del," she said looking up with anguish written all over her face, "I was so scared, sitting there last night waiting for him. What if he didn't show up? And all I could think about was – where's he been all this time?"

She gulped, trying to get her ragged emotions under control. Del waited silently for her to continue.

"When he walked in, my heart just jumped," Mara said with fresh tears. "And…and when he saw me, his face…well, he looked so happy to see me! He came over and hugged me and he actually had tears in his eyes! I don't remember my dad ever crying before."

Now Del had tears in her own eyes. "Then what happened?" she prodded.

"Well, he asked me what I wanted to eat and I said I wasn't really very hungry and he said he wasn't either. So we went out and sat in his car where it was more private. And then he really started to cry. He kept saying, 'I'm sorry, baby. I am so sorry.'"

The girl sobbed softly, but otherwise there was silence in the living room. They could hear the little voice of Stephie as she talked to the cats in the kitchen. It took a minute before Mara was able to continue.

"He told me he got mixed up with a bad crowd and was sent to jail for awhile. That's why I didn't hear from him for a long time. Then he couldn't find us because we moved. He wants to start seeing me again, if I want to."

"What did you say?" questioned Del, although already sure she knew the answer.

"Of course I want to see him!" Mara lowered her eyes and dropped her voice to a whisper.

"He knows about Tom – and the baby and everything." She looked at Del, her face filled with pain.

"He said it was all his fault – that if he hadn't left, none of this would have happened. He asked if I could ever forgive him. When I nodded, he just hugged me and cried for a long time."

Again she stopped and wiped her face. Stephie came wandering into the living room and, totally oblivious to anything going on, threw herself onto the easy chair and declared that she was bored. Del went into one of the unused bedrooms and emerged with a cardboard box of toys.

"Here you go!" she said, setting it down on the rug. "These are some toys I have for my grandchildren when they come to visit."

Stephie immediately dumped all the toys out and climbed into the box. Through her tears, Del had to smile at the child's antics before she turned again to listen to Mara.

"My dad asked if we could start over."

Del was surprised. She asked, "Does he mean him and your mom?"

Mara shook her head. "No – him and me. He wants to start seeing me again on a regular basis. He said if it's okay with Mom, he can come on Saturdays to see me and we can do stuff together. He gave me his phone number and asked me to call him."

She fell silent except for a few sniffles. Del sat thinking quietly, asking finally, "Did you talk to your mom about it when you got home?"

The girl nodded. "She didn't say much, but she told me to be careful and not let him disappoint me again. She started to say something else – I think it was probably something bad about him – but she stopped and just turned away. I'm glad. I don't need them putting each other down." She sighed. "Like they used to."

Del went into the kitchen to pour them some cider, and the girls joined her at the kitchen table. There didn't seem to be much else to say, and besides, Stephie filled the silence with her chatter. When it was time for them to leave, Del stood by the front door and helped the little child zip up her jacket, then laid a hand on Mara's arm.

"Don't forget I'm always here if you need anything. I'm glad your dad is back, but your mom is right. Give yourself time to get to know each other again. Take it slow, okay? And let me know how things are going."

Mara nodded without saying a word, took Stephie by the hand and left. Del, her mind running in all directions, stood in the doorway and waved as they drove off. She wasn't sure what to think about this turn of events. She didn't much like this Scott. He had left without a word once before. Who's to say it wouldn't happen again?

17

To Have and To Hold

That Sunday after Mass the choir members made a point of greeting parishioners in the vestibule. They pointed out to everyone the article in the bulletin requesting recipes. If a person was known for an exceptionally tasty dish, then a special request was made for the recipe – with a little flattery thrown in for good measure.

Del left them to their devices and returned to the sanctuary, waiting for Father Mike to finish what he was doing. Eventually he emerged from the sacristy with a pyx in his hand. He opened the tabernacle doors, placed several consecrated hosts in the pyx and gave it to Del, and she left the church to make her rounds.

Some of the St. Bernard parishioners had volunteered to bring Holy Communion to shut-ins on a rotating basis. Today was Del's turn, and on this chilly autumn day the visits seemed to go quickly. Before she knew it, she was at the last house on her list. She always looked forward to visiting this particular couple, Jacob and Una Sigorski, and they in turn were delighted to see her.

She rang the doorbell and waited patiently for Jacob to shuffle his way to the door. Finally it swung open and she could see the slight, bent-over figure of the elderly man in the dimly-lit entrance hall.

"Welcome!" he exclaimed, a big smile lighting up his face. "Thank you for coming!"

He was dressed in brown polyester pants held by suspenders, with a wrinkled white shirt under an ancient hound's-tooth sports coat. A bow tie at the neck completed the attire. For many years he had dressed like this for Mass and now wouldn't dream of receiving Holy Communion in anything less than his Sunday best.

"Una!" he called in a loud, slightly wheezy voice. "Del is here and she brought us Jesus."

He said the same thing every time Del came, even though his wife couldn't hear it. Physically, he was surely the healthier of the two of them as Una had been bedridden for quite a while. But Jacob believed staunchly that he also had much better hearing than his wife. Del, having known them for quite some time, doubted that.

She followed Jacob down the hallway and through a doorway into a dimly-lit bedroom. Heavy yellowing lace curtains hung at the single window, casting long shadows from the afternoon sun onto the old-fashioned flowered wallpaper.

Suddenly Jacob stopped right in front of Del. She stepped to the side in order to see the slight figure in bed propped up with several pillows. It was obvious that Una had not heard her husband's call as her head was lolled back in a sleeping position. As Del glanced at Jacob, curious as to why he had stopped, she saw that he was gazing at his wife with barely-concealed delight.

"Isn't she beautiful?" He breathed the words quietly, a gentle look in his rheumy eyes.

Del looked again at Una. Her mouth was open slightly as she snored softly and short white hair stood up in tangled strands on her head. Del wondered what there was about the woman which occasioned such a remark from her husband. Maybe he was remembering her as she once was, as she appeared in the portrait which stood on their bureau – a golden-haired beauty, svelte in figure, with gorgeous limpid eyes.

But on the other hand, reflected Del as the gentleman moved to his wife's side and bent over to gently awaken her, *maybe he sees her exactly as she is now and that's why he loves her so much.*

Del knew something of this couple's story. She had heard about the difficult time they had had in their native Poland after World War II broke out, about their narrow escape, about their emigrating to this country where they eked out a living in Detroit before moving to a farm – *in fact,* Del remembered, *this very place* – to raise a family. Life had been harsh for them, with several of their children dying at a young age. They had been through a lot together but, instead of hardship pulling them apart, it just seemed to draw them closer together. Now here they were in the twilight of their lives, still depending on each other. Jacob had often been urged by well-meaning friends to put his wife in a nursing home, but he adamantly refused. He would ask those folks what he could be doing that would be as important as taking care of his Una. And he did as well as anyone could expect under the circumstances.

Their closeness was obvious as she awoke with a slight start and smiled up at Jacob. Del greeted her and prayed the Our Father before giving them both Holy Communion. They knew the routine quite well and prayed along with her.

When visitors were present, Jacob would sit at his wife's side in order to repeat loudly into her ear whatever was said. As Del tucked away the empty pyx and settled back into the chair for a little visit, she expected things to get interesting. They always did.

"Well," she began, speaking as distinctly as possible. "I'm happy to see you."

Jacob leaned closer to his wife and shouted into her ear, "She says she's had the flu."

Una, concern on her face, quickly returned with, "Well, ask her how she's feeling now."

Del shook her head.

"Oh, no, I'm really quite fine."

Jacob looked surprised, but dutifully repeated to his wife, "She says she'd like some wine."

Una frowned, looking troubled. "I'm sorry. I don't think we have any in the house."

"Oh, bless your heart, but I'm not thirsty."

Jacob gave her a funny look. "'It's not Thursday'? Is that the only day you drink wine?"

Del bit her lip to keep from smiling. She decided to try another topic.

"It sure is cold today."

Once again the husband leaned toward his wife and relayed, "She's got a cold today."

Una looked sympathetically at their guest and declared, "She's had the flu and now a cold? Jacob, maybe we should be bringing *her* Communion!"

They laughed companionably together while Del stood up.

"I have to be going."

Jacob said to Una, "She says it's snowing."

"Oh, do be careful while driving, dear!" exclaimed Una to Del, as Jacob got to his feet to usher their visitor out. Del went to the side of the bed to kiss the precious lady on her cheek. They thanked her and she left the house. Jacob, standing in the doorway, waved goodbye as she got into her car. After the elderly man closed the door she chuckled out loud, but the amusement soon gave way to reflection.

Driving away, she thought about the love which had flowed, totally unnoticed by the world, in this humble home for over fifty years. It was love based on sacrifice made for the sake of the beloved, and it brought a real beauty to this one small part of the earth. Words from something she had read in the past kept tumbling through her mind and they finally coalesced into sharper focus:

Sacrifice is always tedious and irksome.
Love can make it bearable – perfect love makes it a joy.

18

Do You Hear What I Hear?

At her kitchen table Del finished her morning prayers, closing her Bible and pushing it to the side. She spent a little while sitting there, staring dreamily out the window at her garden. There wasn't much to be seen at this time of year. A few hardy flowers still bloomed, but overall the effect was *brown*. Wilted leaves, bare branches, sodden wood-chipped paths and untidy clumps of dry ornamental grasses would be enough to depress any gardener's heart. Yet Del accepted each and every change through the seasons. She liked to think of Windmill Gardens as simply resting, storing energy for another outstanding season come spring.

Just as God planned it, she said to herself.

Unwilling to launch into the chores which needed doing around the house, she stayed there in her chair by the window for a longer time than was usual.

It's all the fault of that law of physics, she thought. *'A body at rest tends to stay at rest.' No wonder I can't get going this morning. This body tends to stay at rest longer all the time!*

Her thoughts meandered everywhere until the ring of the telephone startled her.

"Eva, it's you!" she exclaimed into the phone. "I've been wondering what's been happening! Do you know anything about the fire yet?"

The voice on the line sounded discouraged.

"A little. The fire inspectors sifted through the mess. They found an incendiary device."

"Oh, no!" exclaimed Del. "Do they know who did it?"

"Not yet. The police have been asking around town to see if anyone saw anything out of the ordinary." Eva seemed tired as she continued, "It was thrown through a back window. There are bushes back there and not much else. It would be easy for someone to hide in them and no one would notice.

"The fire was caught pretty early, but everything inside the building was waterlogged. Most of the baby equipment had to be thrown out. A few of the baby clothes are salvageable. They just need to be washed. But all the office equipment, including our computer, was damaged." Eva stopped, taking a deep breath before going on.

"Amazingly, we saved most of our clients' paper records, although they were pretty wet. The police lent us a big conference room downstairs in their building to spread out the papers to dry. However, someone went through the records while they were drying and took down names and the like."

Del broke in, "Isn't that invasion of privacy or something? Is that legal?"

"We have our lawyer looking into it. I'm not sure what happened, but I think it was some inexperienced hotshot on the force who was looking for any lead in order to solve the case. Meanwhile, Del, we're trying to get letters out to our supporters to let them know what happened. Please pass the word around at your church. We'll need donations of baby items and office equipment in order to keep helping the women who come to us. Of course, cash is always welcome!"

"But what are you going to do about the building?"

"Well, that's one piece of good news in all this. A business just down the street has donated some office space for us to use while our place is being cleaned and repaired. It's a little cramped but we're grateful to have somewhere to go."

As their conversation ended, Del promised to let her parish know about the desperate needs of the crisis pregnancy center. For starters, she promised to bring it up at choir practice that week.

Wednesday was All Saints' Day, a holy day of obligation.

Obligation, my eye! fretted Del as she arrived for the evening Mass. *Nobody seems to feel obliged to come to Mass any more on holy days.* She looked around at the half-empty church.

Why don't we start calling it a holy day of 'invitation?' Jesus invites us to come and receive him in the Eucharist. If we really thought about it, would we turn down his invitation? That's like someone offering us a million dollars and we say, 'No, thanks, I'm too busy to come and pick it up.

67

She went to the choir loft where she picked up her music and the thread of her thought again. A long time ago she had heard a homilist say that Jesus loves us so much that he has prepared a special place for us in heaven, united with him forever. *But Jesus couldn't wait for that union to happen – he wants union with us even now! And so he gave us his very Body and Blood in the Holy Eucharist to be united with us even while we're still on earth. Incredible!*

Del was still pondering that thought as they stood to sing the opening hymn. *Not only are we in union with Jesus, but at Mass we experience the unity of the whole body of believers. All the faithful who have died – and all of us here. How blessed I am to have so many brothers and sisters in the faith who are praying with me!*

After Mass that evening the choir stayed for rehearsal. Del mentioned the distressing news of the fire and several members made immediate plans to drop off donations in the next few days. Then a committee was formed to work on the piano fundraiser. Del hoped that there would be enough volunteers so that she wouldn't be needed, but it was clear that the printing and assembly of the cookbook would take every available hand.

"We need to get this finished by mid-December," declared Harriet. "People will be happy to buy them as Christmas gifts."

Laurie looked nonplussed. "You've got to be kidding! Do you realize how much work you'll have to do in the next six weeks?"

Harriet waved a hand in dismissal. "Don't worry! We've already started to sort and categorize the recipes. Franklin is typing them on his computer, Mae Beth is proofreading them and Ernestine is calling people who haven't contributed a recipe yet. It would be nice if someone would volunteer to draw a few illustrations for the cookbook." Over the top of her glasses she looked pointedly at Del.

Del quickly found reason to examine her fingernails. Luckily for her, Joe Nagley spoke up, stating that his wife was pretty good at drawing and that he'd ask her. When the cookbook business was finished the group dispersed, but the choir director asked Del to remain a minute longer.

"Del," she said hesitantly, "do you remember when you asked us if we knew anyone who could sing like an angel? Was it here at our church where you heard that person singing?"

Del nodded. She had thought often of the mystery singer. The beautiful, haunting voice came to her mind all the time, but she was no closer to figuring out who it might be.

"I tell you," Laurie went on, "it was the strangest thing. I came in on Monday afternoon this week. I had a day off from work and was catching up on things I hadn't had time for. I was in the office printing our music schedule and then started to walk back through the church to go home. Then I heard someone singing. I looked up at the choir loft and could see a head, but the window behind her was too bright to see who it was."

Del nodded again. She knew exactly what Laurie was talking about.

"The voice was just absolutely incredible. I don't think I've ever heard anything quite like it. I stopped, because I felt if I moved, I'd break the spell."

Del smiled, saying, "I know what you mean."

Laurie was not even looking at her, but staring off into space, remembering. She continued, "The hymn was in Latin. It was the *Ave Maria*, but the melody was different from any I've ever heard." She looked at Del quizzically.

"Did you hear the *Ave Maria?*"

Del shook her head. "The words were different. They were vaguely familiar but I couldn't place them. Anyway, did you see who it was?"

"No," Laurie replied. "When the hymn was over I went to the back of the church, but whoever it was must have left in a hurry. I even walked around the church outside, hoping to see her, but there was no one in sight."

The conversation ended, the enigma leaving them both mystified as they locked the church. Del decided to pray about it.

After all, she figured, *maybe we could add this tremendous voice to our choir. What an improvement that would be!*

19

Market Day

Del was in the family-size cab of Richard's pickup, chatting amiably with her neighbor. Today was the first Saturday of November and they were making their monthly trip to the farmers' market in the city. Del missed the days when Richard's wife and children would come along. However, since the baby's birth, Ann was finding it easier to stay home. Even Sean wasn't with his dad today.

"I've been tellin' him all along," said Richard grimly, speaking of his son, "that if he doesn't stop neglectin' his chores, he wasn't goin' to the farmers' market. I guess he thought I'd give in when the day rolled around. When he found out this mornin' that I really meant it, he got pretty upset."

Del was surprised. Sean was usually good about doing what he was told. Now, if it had been Abby, the problems would have been understandable.

"Well, he's getting close to that magic time – teenagerhood! Just wait!" she warned with a grin.

Richard shook his head. "I tell you, Del, it's been one thing after another lately. Sometimes life seems to be spiralin' out of control. My father's been back and forth to the doctor, tryin' to get his heart medication adjusted correctly. My brothers have always been there to help him with the farm, but now with Russ gettin' married it seems he's always off doin' something. Paul still lives at home but he's been callin' me more and more to lend a hand over there. And, of course, I've got all my work to do at my own place. Ann's doin' the best she can, takin' care of the kids and the house and the egg business. Is it too much to ask for my son to pitch in without havin' to be told all the time?"

Del had to smile to herself. Sometimes farmers had the reputation of being the "strong, silent" type. Over six feet tall and well-muscled, Richard was certainly strong. But silent he wasn't. He was never hesitant to share his opinions and feelings with anyone who would listen. The reason he and Del got on so well together was that she, too, was the sort to give those around her a piece of her mind. Maybe that's why she had no hesitation now to tell him what she thought.

"I'm not surprised you're feeling overwhelmed," she said. "But Richard, that's just how it is at this point of your life. Just as seasons come and go on the farm, the seasons of our life pass too. Try to enjoy the good things that each day brings and remember that the hard times will pass."

"Sure," the man replied, sounding unconvinced. "But there's so much pressure every day to get everything done that I find myself grouchin' at Ann and the kids. I spend more time apologizin' to my wife than eatin'!"

This time Del laughed out loud. "At least you're apologizing! That's the best way to keep your marriage on track!" She shifted in her seat in order to look at him.

"You know, Richard," she said in a more serious tone, "marriage is a sacrament. You and Ann have grace coming to you by virtue of that sacrament. I don't think married couples realize how much grace is given to them by God, for the strength and courage they need to live out their everyday lives together."

"Well, I don't see that grace workin' in *my* life!" broke in Richard.

"I'm not sure any of us do at the time. Usually it's only when looking back that we can see how much God has had his hand on us all along." Del reflected that that was certainly how it had been in her marriage. All through the hectic years of raising her children, the heartache of losing her teenage daughter and then caring for her husband through his final illness – no, she didn't always see the workings of grace at the time, either.

"But," she continued, "we can believe in God's promise that he will give us *all* we need. I think the problem is we fail to activate the graces given in to us in the sacrament of marriage."

Richard glanced at her. "Uh, Del – 'activate' graces?" he asked skeptically. "I went to catechism classes all my years growin' up and I never heard anything about that. I think you're makin' that up!"

Del chuckled. "Okay, so I'm using my own words! But think about it this way – when you get a new credit card, don't you have to do a little more, like call a certain number to activate your card? If you don't, the card is virtually useless. Well, when you and Ann were joined in matrimony, you were given grace through that sacrament. But to really activate it you need to do a little more."

"Like what?" asked Richard, staring down the highway.

"Well, several things. First of all, you need prayer."

"Now, Del, don't start on that again. I told you before that I pray. But I'm just so busy."

"I know you are," cut in Del sympathetically. "But it's worth it to keep trying. And don't forget that your everyday work can be prayer, too."

"Hmm, make a morning offering, right? I remember hearin' that from someone along the way."

Del smiled. She was probably the *someone* he had heard it from. "Right. Anyway, there's no substitute for personal prayer. But, Richard, there are other ways to activate that grace that we don't think about much. Like the Holy Eucharist."

"I've been goin' to Mass every Sunday," Richard quickly objected, although Del already knew that.

She explained further, "But we often forget that when we receive the Body and Blood of Jesus in the Eucharist, little by little, week after week, he changes us to be more like him. Think of it this way. When we eat regular bread, it goes into our bodies and becomes part of us. When we eat the Bread of Life, which is Jesus, we actually become part of him."

"I don't think it's happenin' in my case, Del," her neighbor said, shaking his head.

"Believe me, it is, even if you're not paying attention. *I've* noticed," Del teased. "Besides," she went on, "how often have you actually *asked* God for the help you need in your marriage and family?"

Richard took one hand off the steering wheel and rubbed his chin thoughtfully. "I guess I really haven't, at least not very often."

"Try it," urged Del. "Especially at Communion time, when you're united most closely with him. Also, don't forget about the other way to activate grace. Do you know what it is?"

Richard pondered a moment before replying, "Okay, I give up. What is it?"

"Going to confession."

The man groaned. "I was hopin' that wasn't it."

Del laughed. "For heaven's sake, how can a big, strong man who isn't afraid of anything, be so afraid of the Sacrament of Reconciliation?"

"I do go – once a year. Isn't that enough?"

"But you're missing out on *all* the graces God wants to give you! You know, Richard, when Joey and I got married, we had a lot of growing up to do. We had to learn a lot about forgiveness, and things sure got better after we started going to confession frequently. I had more patience with my family because I had more peace in my heart." Del didn't go around telling this private stuff to just anyone, but felt that she and Richard, long-time friends, had a special rapport.

Since they had reached the city, Richard began to look for a parking spot near the market and the conversation ended.

At least for now, figured Del. *I'm sure Richard will have more to say later.*

They hastened to get their booth set up with the items they brought. Ann had somehow managed, even as busy as she was, to complete half a dozen wreaths. Decorated with dried flowers and set off with a fabric bow, they would certainly attract attention from customers. Bundles of rushes, tied with raffia, were propped in the rear of the booth and Del lined up jars of jam and jelly on the table, along with bags of dried herbs. In coolers on the ground were cartons of eggs and jars of cream from the Spencer farm, and under the table were tools.

Richard tended the booth by himself for awhile so Del could search the market for bargains. She came back with dozens of canning jars.

"Only ten cents each!" she said smugly.

She then sent her neighbor off to look around. It was while he was gone that Del had a surprise visitor.

20

Del Explains All

Del was counting out change into a customer's hand when she heard a familiar voice. She quickly looked up.

"Mara!" she cried, delighted. "What are you doing here?"

The customer left and Del came around the table to give the girl a hug.

"Hi, Del!" the teenager exclaimed, a big smile on her face. "I figured since today is the first Saturday, I'd find you here. Hey, I want you to meet someone!"

The girl turned, took the arm of a man standing near her and drew him forward.

"This is my dad."

Del was nonplussed. It wasn't often that the woman was speechless, but she didn't know quite what to say as the man stretched out his hand to shake hers.

"Nice to meet you," he said. "I'm Scott Ramsey." Del finally found her voice and returned the greeting.

Mara's father was slender and tall, nearly as tall as Richard. He had sandy hair and his eyes seemed friendly enough behind a pair of wire-rimmed glasses. He was dressed in a tan pullover sweater, blue jeans and worn tennis shoes.

"My daughter has told me how you gave her a place to stay this past summer. I'm grateful to you," he said. He sounded a little uncomfortable.

Del noticed Richard returning. She introduced the men to each other and then asked her neighbor if he would watch the booth for a while. He shooed them off with a wave, and Del led the way through the busy market to an area set up for eating. Brushing a few dried-up curly fries from the chairs, they seated themselves at one of the round wooden tables. It was still noisy here but there would be fewer interruptions. She asked if she could get them something to eat.

"No, thanks. We had a hamburger and fries at that place you used to take me to," replied Mara, followed by her dad asking, "Can we get you anything?"

Del declined, saying she had eaten also. There was silence for a moment. No one seemed to know how to begin a conversation. Finally Del asked, "So, what brings the two of you to the city today?"

Scott started to answer but Mara jumped in.

"Oh, we went shopping! Dad said he'd buy me some clothes so we went to a big mall on the other side of the city. At first it didn't even occur to me that this was the first Saturday in November. But then it suddenly hit me. When I realized that you and Richard were probably here today, I asked my dad if we could drive over. We only got a little lost, didn't we?" She turned to her father.

Del wasn't accustomed to the teenage girl talking so much. Generally Mara was pretty quiet, but now she seemed animated. Her eyes sparkled and she smiled more than usual. She was clearly thrilled to be spending the day with her dad.

Her father picked up the conversation.

"Luckily for my wallet she didn't want much." He smiled at his daughter and then addressed Del.

"I hear that you've got the most beautiful garden in the whole world."

At that, Del threw back her head and laughed heartily.

"Well, I don't know about that! But I guess it does have a bit of a reputation hereabouts. Mara was a big help to me, taking care of it this summer. There's a lot of work involved."

They spent some time chatting about gardens before Scott asked his daughter, "Hey, isn't this the place you told me you got some really good hot pretzels? I could go for one right now."

Mara eagerly arose and Scott handed her a ten-dollar bill.

"Why don't you get one for each of us?"

They watched as the girl wended her way past vendors and shoppers, then the man looked at Del.

"I really did mean what I said. I'm truly grateful that you took her in when she ran away. I get chills when I think about where she could've ended up."

Del responded, "She's a wonderful girl. But it's God you need to thank for directing her to my place."

Scott nodded. He rested his arms on the table, leaned in closer and said more intensely, "I'm glad you're a Christian. I am too. But as you can probably guess – I'm having an awfully hard time accepting that my daughter is pregnant because she was raped."

His eyes glinted and narrowed and his jaw tightened. Del said nothing so he continued.

"As a Christian, I believe that abortion is wrong. But, still, I can't help thinking that Mara would be better off if she had gotten one. Now, please don't misunderstand me," he said, putting up his hands to ward off objections, "I'm glad that you helped her, and I know you thought you were giving her good advice. But I just don't know..." He shook his head, dropped his hands to drum his fingers on the table and his voice trailed off. He sat back and looked away from her.

Del appreciated his frankness and decided to be just as direct with him.

"I can understand that you're worried about your daughter, and it's good that you are. But an abortion would further complicate an already complicated situation. Mara is still much like a child, and to take the life of her own child would be something that would affect her the rest of her life."

Now it was her turn to lean in more closely.

"Did Mara tell you about Eva, her counselor?"

The man's eyes were on her. His face inscrutable, he nodded silently.

"Well, Eva has counseled hundreds of pregnant girls. Some even as young as eleven or twelve. She's told me these girls, even though they were raped, seldom want abortions. It's usually a mother or someone else who's pushing it. The girls themselves, being so young, seem to instinctively want to protect the helpless child they're carrying. And do you have any idea what the aftereffects of abortion are?"

The man stared back at her, not saying anything, so she went on.

"Did you know that there's a higher incidence of suicide after abortion? Of drug abuse? That girls who get abortions often develop eating disorders? Sometimes it's easy to think that an abortion will allow a girl to get on with her life, but the opposite is often true."

Del said all this in a calm voice. She understood that the man only wanted what was best for his daughter. She started to say something else when he interrupted.

"But Mara informs me that she intends to keep the baby! That's crazy!"

"I know," Del agreed quietly. "But there's still time for her to change her mind. Eva is helping her to sort out all the options. We have to keep praying and trusting God."

Scott's face was grim, his lips set in a hard line. He glanced up and saw Mara making her way back to the table, so he fell silent. In spite of her inborn cautious nature that whispered, "Be careful, don't trust him too much," Del felt sorry for the man. He was hurting, too, and seemed at least to be trying to make amends for what had happened in the past. She thanked Mara as the girl placed a soft pretzel, steaming in a paper napkin, in front of her.

As they ate, Mara told them about the animals for sale which she had passed. Before leaving, Scott asked Del if he could see this garden of hers sometime. She claimed that there was not much to see right now, but that next Saturday was free. Why didn't the two of them come over for lunch?

Scott quickly agreed and thanked Del again as he and Mara left. Del tarried for a few more minutes, unsure what to think about the encounter.

Okay, Lord, I talk a lot about trusting you. Now help me to put those words into action myself.

21

The Golden Keys

Del bundled up well for her outdoor trek, as the sun shone brightly but didn't provide much warmth on this November afternoon. She wasn't on a quest for anything in particular, but just enjoyed being outside in the brisk weather.

The maples had already shed their foliage. The oak trees still clung to theirs, the leather-brown leaves rustling incessantly in that characteristic sound of the autumn woods. The beeches with their smooth, silvery bark stood here and there like sentinels, and Del smiled to see squirrels scampering off with the triangular beechnuts they loved.

She came to a small brook meandering through a field with large willows clinging to its edge. Their leaves were long gone but their trailing yellow branches swept the surface of the water. Spying a mound of mud covered with dried cattails in the distance, she briefly considered wandering in that direction to try to spot the muskrats who built it. However, she decided that she had more interest in the flora than the fauna and headed back into the woods.

Del missed nothing as she walked, noticing everything from the high-hanging orioles' nests to the red berries clinging to the hawthorns, but her mind was otherwise engaged. She was mulling over the conversation she had had with Richard on the way home from the farmers' market a few days earlier. Her neighbor had been in rare form.

"Just what are you goin' to do with all those pumpkins you bought today – start a pie factory?"

Del, tired after the long day, didn't even try to come up with a clever response.

"No, I think I'll make some pumpkin jam – I've never tried that before. You have to admit, they were quite a bargain!"

The pumpkin-seller at the market had been happy to unload his leftover wares and sold a dozen to Del for just five dollars. She planned to cook up the flesh of the pumpkins and dry the seeds for squirrel food. She didn't consider it such a strange thing to do, but Richard obviously did.

"And those chocolate chips? Don't tell me you're goin' to eat five pounds of chocolate chips all by yourself!"

Del sighed. She had to admit it was a pretty hefty bag she had bought. But it was only a dollar eighty-one! They had stopped at a warehouse store before leaving the city so Del could stock up on sugar and other canning supplies. How could she pass up a close-out sale on chocolate chips?

"I'll make cookies for your kids. And maybe take some to choir on Wednesday. If I hadn't bought them, they might've been thrown out! I just can't see good chocolate chips going to waste."

Richard grinned. He had a feeling that that the chocolate might be going to *waist*. But he switched to a different topic.

"So that's Mara's dad, huh? What does he have to say about leavin' his wife and kid?"

In her fatigue, Del wanted nothing more than to close her eyes and lean her head back against the headrest. Somehow, though, she knew she'd never get any peace unless she answered.

"We really didn't have much time to talk. He mostly told me he was grateful that I gave Mara a place to stay when she ran away. The two of them are coming for lunch next Saturday."

"Uh, oh," responded Richard. "Is that a good idea?"

Del responded wearily, "I don't know. I guess I'll find out."

Richard was quiet for awhile. Then he started again, returning to the subject they had discussed on their way in.

"Now – about this matter of marriage. I hear what you're sayin' about the graces of the sacrament and activatin' them and all that. But Ann's not Catholic so she doesn't receive Communion or go to confession. Yet she's better than me!"

Del had to chuckle at that.

"Richard, even the fact you're admitting it shows that grace has made inroads in your life! As for Ann, I know that she prays. God will give her what she needs in her vocation as wife and mother. But the sacraments of Eucharist and reconciliation are special keys that God has given *you* to unlock what he's called *you* to be. Why not take full advantage of them?"

There was no answer, so Del closed her eyes and before long began to doze off. Thinking back on it, she wasn't sure, but she *thought* she might have heard Richard muttering to himself, "I dunno. I suppose it all makes sense. But – I'd hate to admit she could be right!"

Out in the woods, Del's thoughts came back to the present. She looked at the afternoon sun dipping lower in the sky and turned her steps toward home. She had mixed up some chocolate chip dough earlier and still needed to bake the cookies for tonight's choir practice.

She arrived at church only a little late. But no one noticed her anyway until she set down her plate of cookies and removed the foil covering. Then they all descended like crows on carrion. With a cookie stuffed in her mouth, Harriet demanded to know if Del had brought her recipes yet for the cookbook. Hesitantly, Del handed over the papers she had written out earlier.

Harriet took one look and almost choked on her cookie.

"What are these, Del?" she said, shuffling the papers to look at each one. "Are you serious? 'Daylily Salad?' 'Cattail Flower Pickles' and 'Dandelion Greens With Bacon?'"

George guffawed but Del just smiled serenely. She figured that that would be the reaction she'd get. She had thought long and hard before choosing these particular recipes, knowing ridicule might be the price she would pay for her decision.

"Well, look at it this way," she tried to explain. "What's wrong with having a little variety in our cookbook? I mean, do we really need half a dozen recipes for meatloaf?"

One look at Mae Beth's face told Del that she had picked the wrong example.

"Mae Beth," she quickly amended, "I'm sure that your meatloaf recipe is delicious. However, nobody would want *my* meatloaf recipe. And another thing, maybe people should get to know how tasty and nutritious wild foods are!"

George was following the conversation with interest. He started to bite into another cookie before suddenly pulling it away from his mouth and examining it carefully.

"All right, Del," he exclaimed. "Did you put something funny in *these* cookies?"

"Why?" she asked evasively. "Do they taste different?"

80

The entire choir nibbled carefully, trying to determine if there was anything strange about the chocolate chip cookies. After a moment Franklin declared, "Well, I don't care what's in them. They're darn good!"

A small secretive smile touched Del's lips.

After choir rehearsal, Ernestine and Del chatted as they made their way down the stairs.

"Thanksgiving is just around the corner! Can you believe it?" asked Ernestine. "Are your boys coming home for Thanksgiving?"

"No," replied Del. "Robert called to say they're going to Emily's parents for Thanksgiving, but they'll see us at Christmas. And John said that he won't make it for Thanksgiving, either, but he's going to come the Sunday before." Del stopped with one hand on the outer door and looked at Ernestine.

"Says he's bringing a girl he wants me to meet."

"Oh!" exclaimed the older woman with a broad smile. "Is it serious?"

Del shrugged. "Don't know. He hasn't told me much about her. I think he's been seeing her for several years off and on. I hope it's not getting too serious. He's still pretty young."

"You and I were about the same age when we got married."

Del shook her head. "It's different now. These days it seems so much tougher to stay married. Young people today want so many things. I think that when you give in to every whim – have to have this and have to do that – you don't learn the meaning of sacrifice. And sacrifice is just what's needed for a good marriage."

"Well, you never know, Del. Maybe this young woman will surprise you," Ernestine said as they left the church together.

A couple weeks later, Del realized that Ernestine's words turned out to be truer than she could ever imagine.

22

Suspicions

The next day after lunch, Eva left Del an urgent message. Del didn't answer the phone when it rang as she was up to her elbows in pumpkin. What a mess! She had decided to tackle only half the pumpkins and store the others in the cold garage for use in the winter. However, even six good-size pumpkins were proving to be a challenge. She cut them into halves and scraped out the slimy strings and seeds before sectioning them and slicing off the rind. By the time she had put the chunks of flesh into a large pot to cook, discarded the stringy mess and washed the slippery seeds thoroughly, much of the afternoon was gone. After scrubbing her hands and arms at the kitchen sink, she grabbed a towel and was drying off as she went to the bedroom to see who had called.

When she heard Eva's voice on the recording machine, she returned her call immediately.

"What's going on?" asked Del without preamble.

"Oh, it's you," Eva said, sounding relieved. "I was in a meeting all morning with the center's lawyer and just got off the phone with him again. I just can't believe everything that's happening."

"Like what?"

"Omigosh, Del, the police have been questioning Mara's father!"

"What?! Whatever for?"

"You remember I told you that the inspector found a device which started the fire? And that someone had written down names from all our clients' files? The lawyer is still working on that one. Anyway, the police started checking at businesses in town. You know, our town isn't very big. People notice when strangers are around. Well, the cops started asking questions and one of the names that popped up was Scott Ramsey's."

Del wasn't following her line of thought and said as much.

Eva explained, "The day before the fire, Scott apparently stopped for gas here on the way to visit Alyssa. Someone at the gas station remembered him and a search through credit card records turned up Scott's name, which was also listed on Mara's file at the center. The police have already called him to come in for questioning."

"Do they have any kind of proof?"

"No. I think they're just looking for any kind of connection. Of course, it doesn't help that he has a jail record."

Del was uneasy. Mara and her dad were coming over for lunch in two days. This new information wasn't something she had bargained for.

Eva was still talking. "I saw Mara yesterday when she came in for her session. She was telling me about her dad and that he had met you last Saturday. So I was just wondering what you thought of him."

"Well, I don't know, really. He seemed nice enough. He told Alyssa that he had a religious conversion in prison. I don't know if he was sincere or just using it as a tactic to see Mara. It's hard to know, just meeting him once." Del didn't mention that she would see him again soon, figuring that Eva would just worry.

"But, anyway, why would he want to destroy the center? I would think he'd be happy that Mara's getting the help she needs."

Eva replied, "I don't know. It doesn't make much sense to me, either."

Del asked to be kept abreast of any new information and went back to finish her pumpkin tasks with a heavy heart.

Just when things seem to take a turn for the better for Mara, they get worse. Lord, how much more? What good could possibly come out of all this? Would Scott really do something as horrible as arson? Del tried to think what his motivation could possibly be.

The fire was the day after he and Alyssa had a big blowout. Was he so angry that he just took it out any way he could think of? Wouldn't he know that this would just hurt Mara more? It really doesn't make sense! Oh, my Jesus, I need help! Please help me give him the benefit of the doubt. Help me not to judge him without even knowing if he's guilty.

That night and all the following day she brought the problem to prayer often. By the time Saturday arrived, she found that she was at least willing to give Scott a chance.

Mara and her dad arrived promptly at noon. Del greeted them at the door and took their jackets, then led them into the living room. His daughter scooped up Coco to show her dad, talking animatedly all the while. Scott didn't say much and Del didn't have to.

After they spent some time playing with the kitten, Del invited them to the table for lunch. She had prepared a simple casserole and served it with homemade rolls and fruit. And freshly-baked chocolate chip cookies.

The garden could be seen through the large picture window in the kitchen and it became the main topic of their conversation. Mara asked if she could give her dad a tour of the garden after lunch.

The teenager led the way through the back room and they stepped outside. She showed him one garden after another, explaining about the plants. Her dad nodded his head, asking questions, and Del followed along quietly. She was still amazed at how much information the girl had absorbed in her few short months here.

"Look here," the girl continued. "See these small plants all over? They're forget-me-nots. You should see them when they're blooming. They're such a pretty blue! They spread everywhere like crazy if you don't watch'em!"

Then she showed Scott the vegetable gardens close to the garage. Even though the windmill was hard to miss, towering as it did over the backyard, neither Scott nor Mara alluded to it in any way. Del suspected that the girl may have told her dad about the lightning which had hit the windmill back in August and how it had instantly killed Tom. Even now, Del shuddered when she thought of it.

May God have mercy on his soul, she thought, *but I can't say as I'm unhappy he's out of their lives.*

Mara tugged on her dad's arm and drew him over to where Del grew fruit trees.

"You should see how many peaches Del gets from this little tree!" the girl exclaimed. "We must have picked thousands!"

Del laughed. "Well, it only seems that way when you have to peel them."

Mara announced at that moment that she needed to use the bathroom, and left Del and Scott standing there uncomfortably with each other. However, Del wasn't one to beat around the bush for long. She used the opportunity to look the man straight in the eye and say, "I understand the police are questioning you."

Scott's eyes widened in momentary surprise and then he frowned.

"Who told you that?"

"Well, I have my ways. Does Mara know about it?"

He shook his head. "No, and I'd really prefer that she didn't. She has enough problems of her own." His voice sounded strained and he looked away.

Okay, Lord, what do I say now? Should I come right out and ask him?

Del pondered the question only a split second before blurting out, "So, *did* you start the fire?"

Startled, Scott looked sharply at Del, his blue eyes unreadable.

"No," he said tersely. "I didn't. Is there anything else you want to know?"

Del searched his face for a moment before shaking her head. Mara was coming back from the house anyway and Scott was saying that they had to go.

Well, I don't know any more than before, she decided. *I'd like to believe him. But can he be trusted?*

23

The Sunday Before Thanksgiving

Del was flitting about nervously. An elaborate dinner was in the oven and the kitchen table set with her best dishes. John and his girlfriend were due to arrive any minute now. Since this was the first time Del was to meet her, she found herself fussing more than usual to have everything right. She had made sure the house was straightened and dusted, all the dozens of books put back on their shelves, her garden paraphernalia properly stowed, the living room rug vacuumed and the kitchen floor washed.

Okay, she admitted, looking around at the unusually clean house, *I'm trying to impress her. But I don't want to embarrass my son!* She gave the kitchen counters one last swipe with the dishcloth and heard footsteps coming up the front walk.

Perhaps John's tall and slender frame didn't fill the entire doorway when Del swung open the door, but even so, he was all she saw – wavy brown collar-length hair, warm dark eyes and an angular face so like his father's. He grinned at her and she grabbed him in a bear hug. Delighted to see him, she looked up at him with tears in her eyes.

"Now, Ma, don't cry!" he warned, but he was laughing as he tried to extricate himself from her embrace. "I want you to meet someone special."

Turning slightly and beckoning a young woman forward, he said, "Ma, this is Natalie."

Tearing her eyes from her son's face, Del turned to greet Natalie and her smile froze instantly on her face. In an instant she forced her lips into an even wider smile and cordially shook the hand that was being offered to her. Del invited them in while scolding herself.

Now, Del, appearances can be deceiving. At least give her a chance.

Normally, Del wasn't one to judge people on how they looked. It's just that this time she was a bit taken aback. Not long ago, John had shown her a snapshot of the two of them together. At the time, the girl had long brunette hair framing an attractive elfin face. Now her hair was cut short and spiked all over. That may not have been so bad, but it was also a bleached shade of blond – with red streaks.

Didn't I read somewhere that they color their hair with Kool-Aid? Well, maybe it's better to put it on the hair than to drink the stuff! she rationalized.

She settled herself in the easy chair across from where they were on the couch and tried not to stare at Natalie.

But those earrings! Oh my goodness!

Technically, "earrings" would not be the correct term, for Del was looking at a stud piercing the left eyebrow and a ring through a nostril. There were also actual earrings, and she surreptitiously began to count all the silver loops decorating the outer edges of the girl's ears. Then Del swallowed hard and turned her attention to John who was speaking to her.

"It took a little longer to get here than I expected. There was an accident on the freeway…"

Del nodded her head dutifully and glanced over at Natalie. The girl sat quietly looking at John as he talked.

Del finally found her voice.

"So, Natalie, what do *you* do?" she asked, and was a bit relieved to find that the young woman held a job in fashion design.

Well – maybe she needs to look a bit different in her field of work. Thank goodness she's not in show business or something.

Seeming a bit reticent, Natalie warmed up as Del asked her more questions. By the time dinner was ready, the two of them were chatting away. While they ate, John hardly had a chance to get a word in. He grinned at them, looking happy that his mother and girlfriend were finding something to talk about.

Natalie thanked Del for inviting them to dinner, saying how much she enjoyed the chocolate chip muffins. Del complimented the blue lace shawl that Natalie was wearing and the girl seemed pleased, explaining that she had made it. John cut in to ask his mother how the old computer was working and went off to take a look at it.

After he left, the conversation began to run out of steam. Del tried talking about the garden, pointing out different features through the window. Natalie smiled politely and nodded, but it soon became obvious that she knew nothing, and cared even less, about gardening.

Well, I guess that's okay, decided Del, trying to be understanding. *Not everybody has to like flowers.*

And yet it was well nigh unthinkable to her that there was actually someone walking the face of the planet who didn't like flowers. She turned the conversation back to the girl's interests – which she soon discovered were sewing, hiking and horses – and found they had enough topics to keep them going until John announced that it was time for them to go.

"We've got a long drive ahead of us, Ma, but we'll see you at Christmas."

Del hated for them to leave. Even though she had plenty to keep her busy, she greatly missed her youngest son. Del made John promise that he would call and let her know he'd arrived safely. She waved to them from the doorway until they were too far down the road to see her any more.

She cleaned the kitchen and closed everything down for the night before collapsing on the couch. She brought her Bible into the living room and had some quiet devotional time while waiting for John's call. Was she praying or was she thinking? It was hard to tell as it all tended to blend together.

Lord, please set your angels around them to keep them safe on the roads tonight. I wonder if he's almost home. His car looked kind of old. I hope it doesn't break down. Dear Jesus, guide them in this relationship. If it is not in your will, then please help them to see that. Boy, she sure looks strange. Wouldn't it hurt to get pierced like that? I wonder why she feels a need to look so different. Father, help her to know how much you love her, that it's okay to just be herself. Okay, I suppose I wasn't exactly being myself today either. I admit – I was trying to impress her.

How could it be that she doesn't like flowers? Lord, I don't know about this girl. I guess you're going to have to help me to see her through your eyes. I can tell that John's crazy about her, and I don't know if I can love her on my own.

Was that a little cross I saw on a chain around her neck? I wonder if she's a Christian? I'll have to ask John about it when he calls... But by that time, Del had long since drifted off into dreamland and forgot what she wanted to ask him.

"Ma, we're home," he said over the phone. *Home,* Del knew, meant his apartment in Chicago. Even through her just-awakened fog, she thought she heard something in her son's "we're home" that she didn't like.

"John," she asked, a little more sharply than she intended, "are you and Natalie living together?"

"Oh, Ma!" he replied, sounding exasperated.

"Don't 'Oh, Ma' me!" Del took a deep breath and tried to speak calmly. "John, you know how I feel about that!"

"Yeah, Ma. You've told me often enough."

He paused for a second, then said, "Natalie and I are planning to get married."

Del sucked her breath in sharply. She wasn't expecting that. *But I guess I should have known.*

"Ma?" came the query over the telephone line. "Are you still there?"

Del answered in what she hoped sounded like a composed voice.

"Yes, I'm here. Congratulations, John. I really am happy for you. Natalie seems like a nice girl." *Even if she looks strange. And doesn't like flowers.*

She heard John chuckle. "She *is* a nice girl. I know it must have been a surprise for you to see her, considering what she's done to her hair." He didn't say anything about her earrings.

If Del hadn't been so tired she might not have jumped in right away with advice, but would have waited until she could sit down with her son and talk to him face-to-face. As it was, she rushed on.

"Oh, her hair isn't that important. But John, marriage *is.* Building a marriage which will last is like building a house. You've got to start with a good foundation. If the foundation is cracked, the house is going to have problems, and so will a marriage. If a couple lives together before they get married, they're laying an awfully poor foundation for their life together."

John broke in before she could go any further.

"Yeah, yeah, Ma, I know."

Del wondered if he'd be upset with her, but instead there was a hint of merriment in his voice. He must be in a better mood than she'd expected. Sounding a little as if he were the parent, patting a troublesome child on the head to appease her, he continued, "Listen, everything will be fine. Thanks for dinner and everything. I'll call you closer to Christmas and let you know when we're coming. Love ya."

"I love you, too," answered Del. It was only after hanging up and crawling wearily into bed that she realized her son had never answered her question.

24

Expect the Unexpected

"Do you think we can have dinner together tonight? I want to ask you something."

Del felt her heart jump. With surprise? Foreboding? Maybe anticipation? She and George were talking on the phone. It was not even lunchtime on the Monday morning before Thanksgiving and her mind was still busy with the previous day's conversations. She wasn't ready yet to take on any more emotional issues.

I can just guess what he wants to ask me! I've been avoiding the topic of marriage for so long that he's finally taking the direct approach. Del decided that maybe it was better to get the issue on the table and settle it once and for all, so she agreed to meet him for dinner at the Hampstead Inn.

Hope I'm not expected to dress up for this, she grimaced that evening as she changed into nice slacks and a sweater. *I suppose I could put on a dress, but would that look like I'm expecting something important? Don't want to get his hopes up.* Sometimes Del had a tendency to fret over trivial things. She smoothed her hair, grabbed her purse and coat and was out the door.

The way to the restaurant led down the highway in the direction of the city, right through the middle of town. As she passed St. Bernard's church, she made the sign of the cross in greeting to her Lord who was present there. That was a long-time habit of hers, taught by her mother, as a way to acknowledge the Real Presence of Jesus in the church's tabernacle. It also served as a reminder that she could speak to her Lord anytime and any place, and she used the solitude of the rest of the drive to ask for his guidance in this matter of George and his intentions.

George was already at the restaurant and stood when she was brought to the table by the hostess. Del found herself with a fluttery stomach, which wouldn't go away no matter how much she chided herself for being silly. It was even difficult for her to find anything that sounded appetizing on the menu, unusual for a person who had quite a fondness for food.

They made small talk while waiting for their selections to be brought. Over dinner, George entertained her with stories about his grandchildren, and it was only as they finished eating that he finally got around to the topic on his mind.

"Uh, Del," he said, clearing his throat. "I wanted to ask you something."

Oh, oh, here it comes! Take a deep breath. Lord, give me the words to let him down gently.

George seemed nervous. He fidgeted with the silverware and started again.

"Uh, Del, it's like this. Do you remember my sister Edna?"

Del nodded, wondering what his sister had to do with a marriage proposal.

"I was telling Edna about the choir's plans for doing a cookbook and then I just happened to mention your recipes. You know, the ones with wild plants in them?"

Del, puzzled over the turn in the conversation, nodded again.

He usually says 'weeds,' thought Del. *And what does this have to do with anything?*

George looked as if he'd rather be anywhere else at the moment, but he stalwartly plunged on.

"Well, uh...Edna wants to know if you have any more recipes like the ones you submitted for the cookbook." He looked a bit sheepish asking her this, after all the teasing he had done.

"She's been reading some books on wild foods and has become really interested in teaching her own grandchildren how to cook and use those plants."

Del stared at him, uncomprehending for the moment. Expecting him to ask her one thing and having him change horses in the middle of the stream...for heaven's sake, her mind wasn't quite taking in what he was saying.

"You want...more of my recipes?" Del knew she was probably sounding quite stupid, but she still wasn't catching on.

George nodded. "I know, I know," he said, embarrassed to look her directly in the eye. "You have a right to laugh at me if you want. Go ahead, rub it in. But I have to tell you…my sister was excited to actually hear about someone who knows about this kind of stuff."

After a prolonged moment of silence, Del found herself saying that, of course, she would be happy to pass along more recipes and anything else that Edna would like to know. George looked relieved and thanked her heartily. She remembered him saying one time that he had a soft spot in his heart for his younger sister and that he would do anything in his power to help her in any way. It must have taken some swallowing of pride for him to admit that his own sister didn't think it strange to be eating "weeds."

With great self-control, Del smiled and thanked him nicely for the dinner and said she would see him Wednesday at choir rehearsal. As she left the inn and got into her car, she was starting to build up a full head of steam.

Of all the nerve! He was supposed to ask me to marry him! I was practicing the words to let him down nicely. He didn't even give me the chance!

Now Del was really fuming.

To get me all nervous and then…nothing! She was on a roll now and saw nothing illogical in her feelings.

"Recipes, huh?" she said loudly to no one in particular. "I'd like to give that man some recipes!"

25

Thanksgiving on the Farm

"Oh, these look delicious!"

Ann gratefully accepted the three pies that Del was trying to balance in her arms. The younger woman handed them to her husband and son with the admonition, "Don't you dare try to sneak a taste!" They grinned nearly identical grins, carried the pies into the dining room and set the pies on the sideboard.

Ann took her coat and hung it up before leading her guest into the living room. Del greeted Richard's parents and brother Paul. Then she followed Ann to the kitchen where the mouth-watering aroma of roasting turkey wafted through the air, promising a great meal to come.

"Ann," she said, "I passed along your dinner invitation to Alyssa. Actually, I left it on her answering machine. Did she ever call you?"

Ann nodded. "Yes, she did. But she said that Mara's counselor had already invited them to have dinner with her family today. She said thanks anyway."

Del smiled, knowing that Stephie was going to enjoy a ride in the pony cart. Yet she was a little disappointed as she had been looking forward to seeing them.

"And," Ann continued, "I also invited George." She looked at Del with an impish grin on her face. "But he said he was going to his son's."

Del tried not to wince when George's name was mentioned. She turned away from Ann's questioning smile. She was still feeling a bit put out over what happened at dinner on Monday and did not intend to share her chagrin with anyone.

"Oh, that's too bad," she answered noncommittally. She turned her attention to the pies she had brought.

"I'm glad you asked me to bring the dessert. I have an awful lot of pumpkin these days. Who would have guessed that just six pumpkins would give me so much? I'm getting a little tired of pumpkin bread and pumpkin waffles! I even made pumpkin jam to sell at the market. So that's why I brought two pumpkin pies today. I figured Richard will make short work of any leftovers!

"And this apple pie," she indicated with her hand, "was a last-minute substitution. I had intended to make a new recipe I found – a custard pie in a crust lined with chocolate chips. But when I pulled out my chocolate chip bag, there were hardly any left."

It was Del's misfortune that Richard just happened to be passing the kitchen at that precise moment and overheard her remark. He poked his head through the doorway.

"Hardly any chocolate chips left! Now tell me, Del, where did five pounds of chocolate chips go in just a few short weeks?" He smiled broadly at his neighbor's discomfiture.

"Ah...Well," Del started to explain, "I did make cookies for the choir."

Richard said nothing but kept grinning at her.

"And there were the cookies and muffins I made for guests," Del continued a bit defensively.

"And?" he prodded.

Del decided that he was not going to let her off the hook easily. "Oh, all right," she finally answered, figuring that maybe honesty would be the best policy. "I admit I ate a few here and there."

"A few chips or a few pounds?" Richard guffawed.

Del picked up a kitchen towel and threw it at him. He caught it deftly in mid-air and tossed it back at her, whereupon she launched a potholder at him. Ann put an end to the volley by asking her husband to start carving the bird. However, Del didn't seem to mind Richard's teasing too much.

"Don't you think," she asked Ann with a twinkle in her eye, "that cocoa beans should be considered a vegetable?"

Ann chuckled and asked Del to get the dishes from the china cabinet. With help from Richard's mother, the large, old-fashioned dining room table was soon set. The three women concentrated on putting out the side dishes – roasted potatoes, sweet potato whip and homemade rolls with farm-fresh butter – while Richard sliced the meat from the gigantic turkey and finally brought the heaped-high platter to the table.

No one had to be called twice to dinner. They all took their places eagerly and Richard led them in a prayer of thanks for God's bounteous blessings over the past year. As they passed around bowls of food, laughter and animated conversation rippled through the old farmhouse.

Richard's father began a discussion about the difficulties of making ends meet in the dairy farming business. His son Paul jumped in with his own thoughts, leading to a spirited exchange which some might call the beginning of an argument.

"Dad," interjected Richard. "Have you ever thought about making a corn maze?"

"A what?"

"A corn maze. I've been readin' all about 'em. Farmers go and cut mazes in the middle of their cornfield, and people pay good money to go through 'em."

"Are you nuts?" Paul asked his brother, none too charitably.

"Okay, then don't believe me!" Richard declared amiably. He pushed back his chair and went to the living room where they could hear him shuffling through papers.

"Here it is!" he called from the other room and returned with a newspaper article in his hand.

"Look! Here's a picture of one."

He handed his father a folded newspaper. Bill Spencer opened it, and his wife and other son peered over his shoulders at the black-and-white aerial shot of a cornfield. There, right in the center, was an intricate maze carved through the full-grown stalks of corn.

"Well, lookee here!" Bill exclaimed.

He read to them parts of the accompanying article which explained how farmers cut mazes, advertise them and charge people an entrance fee.

"Imagine that! This story says that they are a darned good money-maker!"

Paul looked skeptical but Richard grinned.

"See, Dad? Your troubles could be over!"

His mother harrumphed, "Seems like they'd just be starting! Can you imagine – all those people traipsing through our yard? Where would they all park? And they're not coming into *my* house to use the bathroom! And who's to say they'd stay in the maze and not go wandering off and get lost somewhere? And what about insurance? How much insurance would you need to cover all the possibilities of people getting hurt? And how would you...?"

Her husband held up a hand. "Whoa! For heaven's sake, Frieda, I never said I would even consider this!"

Richard laughed. "You're right, Mom, there'd be a lot of things to work out. But you have to admit, it's certainly an interesting idea!"

While Ann dished up the pies for dessert and passed them around with some of the farm's rich whipped cream on top, the discussion on mazes and farming continued. Baby Jacob, sitting in his rocking baby seat on the floor by the table, must have felt left out of the conversation and began to fuss. Del, turning to smile at him, picked up one of his toys, a plastic clown with a large suction cup on the bottom. Since she couldn't find a smooth surface on which to stick it, she smacked it solidly onto her forehead. As she bobbed her head at the child, the clown rattled away merrily.

At first the baby looked a bit startled, staring at her with his eyes wide as saucers. As she continued to talk to him, one corner of his mouth turned up. Then he grinned widely and finally a chuckle burst from him. Del laughed, too, and played with him until it was time to clear the table. She pulled the toy off her forehead, surprised that it was still stuck so tightly.

As she gathered the dirty dishes and stacked them carefully, Del decided to throw a little levity into the conversation.

"Hey, you guys," she said loudly. "Do you know what the Golden Rule for dairy farmers is?" When she had their attention, she answered the riddle herself. "Do unto udders what you'd have udders do unto you..."

There was dead silence.

It wasn't THAT bad of a joke, was it? Del wondered.

Paul stared at her and a slow smile spread across his face. He elbowed his dad. Bill also grinned, nudging his wife. Abby giggled, covering her mouth with her hands, and Sean laughed out loud. No one said a word until Richard, trying to keep a straight face, looked up at his neighbor as she stood perplexed next to him and said, "Hey, Del, that's a lovely decoration you have there!"

She plunked the dishes down and scurried into the bathroom. Leaning closely into the mirror, she was appalled to see a large, startlingly red circle smack dab in the middle of her forehead. She rubbed at it and was dismayed to see that it only got brighter. She found a washcloth in the cabinet, doused it in cold water and held it to her head for a few minutes. It didn't make one bit of difference. She concluded that the suction cup must have pulled blood to the surface of her skin, and it looked like there was nothing to be done but wait until it would fade on its own.

Sheepishly she returned to the gathering. Frieda was helping Ann clean up and the men had resumed their conversation. Abby tugged at Del's arm. The little girl inquired worriedly if the "ouchy" was hurting Del. Reassured that her friend was fine, she ran off to play. It wasn't long before Bill, with one last sideways look at Del's forehead, announced that it was milking time. After they left for home and Richard and Sean headed outside for their own chores, Del joined Ann in the kitchen.

Once Ann was convinced that there was nothing she could do about Del's "problem," their conversation drifted to Mara.

"This Sunday is Mara's birthday," said Del. "They've invited me to have dinner with them at the restaurant where Alyssa works." She shook her head with apprehension.

"That ought to be interesting," Ann responded.

Del sighed. "You don't know the half of it. Mara insisted that her dad be invited to the celebration."

"Oh, dear! I'll be praying for you, that you won't be caught in the crossfire! And...Del?"

With a wide smile she peered once again at her neighbor's forehead.

"Maybe I'd better pray, too, that that thing goes away by then. Or you'll need to change your hairstyle. I suggest bangs!"

26

Birthday Party

It was Sunday morning and Del was comfortably ensconced in the front pew at church. It was way too early for anyone else to be there for the noon Mass, but that was how she liked it. She needed some time this morning to spend with Jesus in quiet. Tonight was Mara's party and she was feeling a need to fortify herself with prayer.

Opening her Bible, she prayed along with the Psalm for the day. She read a line and then added her own words of praise or petition to it before going on to the next line. This was one of her favorite ways to pray. It helped her to feel a connection with all God's people down through the ages who have prayed the ancient Psalms. With great intimacy she spoke to her Lord, knowing he was right there with her, present in the Eucharist.

She closed her eyes to meditate on that thought.

He had no earthly possessions to leave us, she reflected, *but he did far more. He left us himself. What a gift!*

In return, Del held nothing back from him. He was her Lord, her Savior, her greatest love. Not a day went by when she didn't express her gratitude to him. For she was a sinner, once lost and now found, a wandering sheep who had come back to the fold. Remembering her own failures helped her humbly intercede for others, as she was doing now for Mara and her family.

As other people arrived to get ready for Mass, Del finished her prayers and went up to the choir loft. This day as she sang with the choir, she continued to lift up her concerns to God.

Let your mercy be on us, O Lord, as we place our trust in you...

When Mass was over, Harriet made an announcement.

"All the recipes are typed and ready to go!" She picked up a sheaf of papers from a chair and waved it around. "Joe finished them this week and Mae Beth and I have been checking them. And Nicki drew some wonderful illustrations!"

Joe Nagley grinned, saying that his wife had been most happy to help out.

"So…" Harriet paused dramatically. "We are ready to print!"

The entire choir broke into applause.

Laurie asked, "Are you sure you've done everything? How about the cover? The table of contents…"

Harriet waved her hand imperiously.

"All taken care of."

She gave the stack of papers to the music director and asked that it be passed around so everyone could take a look at it.

"But be careful," she warned fussily. "These are our originals and we don't want them wrinkled or torn."

Laurie riffled gingerly through the pages and handed them to the next person, saying, "Looks great! So what's next?"

Mae Beth answered, "Well, we'd like you to place an article in the bulletin about the cookbooks. We could start selling them the second week of December. And do you think you could get Father Mike to make an announcement?"

Laurie nodded. "Sounds like my job's easy. Who's going to do the copying?"

"We all are!" chimed in Ernestine. "Listen, everyone! Whoever's available needs to be here tomorrow morning at ten. Bring a lunch with you so we don't waste any time. Then if it's necessary, we'll continue later in the week."

Del groaned inwardly, but she could think of no plausible excuse why she couldn't come the next morning. She glanced over at George, thankful that a little makeup had covered up fairly well the pinkish circle still remaining on her forehead. He would surely have had something to say about it.

"You're retired, George," she said pointedly. "You're planning to come and lend a hand, aren't you?"

George made a mock bow and smiled broadly at her.

"Your wish is my command, m' lady!"

Del rolled her eyes in mock dismay. She had finally forgiven him for last Monday evening, having come to realize how silly her feelings of rejection were. Instead, she should have been relieved that he *hadn't* popped the question.

It's nicer this way, she thought. *Let's just be friends.* She smiled warmly at him and waved as she headed down the stairs.

That evening she arrived at the restaurant where Mara's party was being held and immediately spied the group in a corner booth. Mara was in the place of honor, Stephie was in a high chair and Alyssa was speaking to one of the waitresses as Del walked over.

"Hi, Del," Alyssa greeted her. "Thanks for coming. I'd like you to meet my friend Rochelle, who was kind enough to work my shift tonight."

Del shook Rochelle's hand before seating herself in the booth. They decided to delay ordering until Mara's dad came.

There was an air of unease about them as they waited and talked for quite some time. Alyssa kept glancing at her watch. She was just about to suggest that they go ahead and order when Scott came through the restaurant door. He went right away to his daughter, leaning down and kissing her on top her head. He wished her a happy birthday before greeting the others. As he slid into the booth next to Del, he winked at the child in the highchair, saying, "And this must be Stephie."

Predictably, Stephie hid her face shyly, and Del chuckled.

After Rochelle had taken their orders, the conversation became a little awkward. Del tried valiantly to find things to talk about until their dinner came. As they began eating there was talk for a few minutes, but before long an uncomfortable silence descended.

Del looked over at Mara with compassion. *She looks pretty nervous about this whole thing.*

When Rochelle brought out a birthday cake, the other restaurant employees came over to sing "Happy Birthday" to Alyssa's daughter. It was only after the cake was taken back to the kitchen to be cut up that Scott apologized for being so late.

"Uh, huh," muttered Alyssa quietly, but loud enough for them all to hear, "so what's new?"

Scott glanced sharply at her. He frowned and replied, "I said I was sorry. I tried coming by what I hoped would be a shorter way and got turned around."

Mara looked pleadingly at her mother, then her dad, and finally stared down at the table. Stephie banged her plastic cup on the highchair and her mom yanked the cup away. The child began to wail.

Alyssa hurriedly tore open a cellophane package of saltines for Stephie and the crackers flew onto the floor. She turned around to the empty table behind her and grabbed another pack. Teeth clenched, she threw in Scott's direction, "Always an excuse."

Mara looked up, her eyes pleading.

"Mom – please!"

Alyssa shot an angry glance at her daughter.

"Of course! It was always me who was the bad guy! But don't forget, I was the one who was always there when your dad wasn't home." She glared at Scott. "Which was most of the time."

Del could see tight lines forming around Scott's mouth. She hurriedly tried to intervene.

"Oh, look!" she declared brightly. "Here's our cake and ice cream!"

No one, except Stephie, of course, said anything else until dessert was finished. When Mara opened her gifts, it triggered another cutting remark from Alyssa.

"It's nice that you can buy your daughter a pricey gift, isn't it?" she addressed Scott icily. "While *my* money has to go to pay the bills."

Scott reddened as if she had slapped him across the face. He started to say something, but a glance at Mara's agonized face stopped him. He clenched his lips together, rested his elbows on the table and stared fixedly out the window.

Alyssa busied herself with cleaning up Stephie, instructing Mara to get ready to leave. Scott said in a tight voice, "I'll pay for dinner tonight. Don't worry about it." He looked over at his daughter and noticed her eyes brimming with tears. He got up to give her a hug.

"It's all right, babe. Go with your mom. And give me a call when you have a chance, okay?"

The teenager nodded. She gathered up her presents and trailed out slowly after her mother and sister. After they left Scott noticed Del still sitting there and slid into the seat opposite her.

"I'm sorry," he apologized. "You didn't need to witness that ugly scene." A grim smile crossed his face. "Me, now, I'm used to it. But I'd give anything to go back and start the evening over so Mara wouldn't have to go through that."

He closed his eyes and rubbed the back of his neck, then sighed. Looking again at Del he asked, "Did Alyssa tell you anything about our break-up?"

"Not much. Except that you walked out on them."

He nodded. "Well, that part is true. I wish now that I had had the smarts to insist on counseling. At the time it just seemed easier to leave."

Scott, grief shadowing his eyes, looked over at Del. She had the distinct impression that he was the kind of man who didn't find sharing his thoughts very easy to do.

Mara must have inherited her reserve from her father. Her mother never hesitates to tell a person anything!

He continued, "I admit, I was very caught up in my job. Alyssa is right about that. At the time I convinced myself I was working hard for my family. I wasn't home much, as the business I was in started to take off. And when I did have some free time, I'd spend it with friends."

He looked down at his hands clenched together on the table.

"But on the other hand, she wasn't easy to live with either. Nothing I did was ever good enough for her."

He stopped abruptly, just as Del was thinking, *I can believe that.*

Then he shook his head.

"Sorry. I shouldn't have said that. Marshall has been trying to get me to focus on my own shortcomings, not hers. Marshall," he went on to explain, "is a friend of mine. I'm renting a room in his basement until I get back on my feet. Right now I'm trying to save up to get a car. He lends me his car every weekend so I can come see Mara."

Scott leaned back in his seat and Del noticed how haggard his face was. He was probably only in his mid-thirties but his weary-looking eyes made him seem older.

He continued, "The job I have right now doesn't pay much but I'm looking for a better one. My goal is to pitch in and help Alyssa with expenses. I know I can't make up for the past," he said, running his fingers through his thinning hair, "but at least I can do something. Marshall says that restitution is a biblical concept."

Del asked, "Do you read the Bible much?"

"Every day. I pray, too. I even ask God to bless Alyssa…"

Del smiled, realizing that that prayer was probably the most difficult.

He stood up and tossed some bills on the table for the tip. He thanked her for coming to celebrate Mara's birthday before going

103

over to the cashier. Del lingered a few minutes longer as he drove away.

I don't know, she reflected. *He seems sincere. But poor Mara is the one caught in the middle. And there's still the matter of the fire. Eva says the police still don't have any evidence against him, but I can't help but wonder. Underneath, he might still be a very angry man.*

27

Missing!

The workroom at the church was warm and stuffy. There were too many people in the small space and they were constantly bumping into each other. George and another man found a long table which they set up in the hallway as a place to put the reams of copier paper. Mae Beth was given the task of unwrapping the paper, while Harriet directed the others in using the machine and stacking the finished copies into boxes.

After an hour in that stifling room, Del stepped out into the hall and mopped her brow.

"Isn't it awful in there?" sympathized Mae Beth.

Del nodded. "It's hard to believe that it's so warm in there when it's so cold outside. Wasn't it a surprise this morning to find snow on the ground? Anyway, it's just lucky that more people didn't show up as there's not much we can do. Put the paper in the machine, make copies, stack them…"

Just then a collective groan issued from the direction of the workroom.

"Darn machine!" That sounded like Ernestine's voice.

Del poked her head back in and saw George down on his knees attempting to retrieve a jammed piece of paper from the copier's rollers. By turning a dial or two and pressing a lever, he was able to pull it out piece by little piece. Then the machine worked fine, at least for another five minutes when the same thing happened again.

George placed his hand on the glass top.

"Gosh, this is awfully hot!" he declared. "You know, we're asking a great deal from this old machine. We're making a lot of copies. I really think we'd better let it cool down every so often."

From there on, the pace of the work slowed to a crawl. Then the crew dwindled a bit. Mae Beth got a call from the school saying her daughter was ill, and several others left after complaining that all they were doing was standing around. Del stayed on, as did George, and they were the ones that Harriet had to send out to track down a toner cartridge when the ink ran out.

By four thirty they decided to stop for the day. They were only half done so they made plans to return, with yet another toner cartridge, later in the week. As Del drove home, she couldn't believe how exhausted she felt.

I can make jelly all day and not be this tired! A cup of hot ginger tea sounds awfully good about now. And I think I have some turkey soup left over from the weekend. That'll be an easy supper. Maybe I'll curl up this evening with a good book.

However, that was not to be. The light was flashing imperiously on her answering machine.

"Del!" she heard when she pressed the button. It was Alyssa's voice. "Is Mara with you? Call me back!"

Del frowned. *What's this about?*

The next message was playing. "Del, it's Alyssa again. Mara's still not home from school and I don't know where she is! Please call and tell me she's with you!"

Del sat down heavily on her bed, a feeling of dread coming over her, while the final message played.

"Mara should have been home over an hour ago!" The voice sounded panicky. "If I don't hear from you by five, I'm calling the police!"

It was nearly five now. Del grabbed the phone to call.

"Alyssa! I just got home. What's going on?"

"I don't know where she is!" Alyssa's voice was strained and her words were rushed. "I just can't believe this! I'm afraid she's run away again!"

Del's heart began to pound loudly but she tried to stay calm.

"Okay, okay," she said. "Slow down and tell me what happened."

"I told Mara to come right home after school today to babysit! I was supposed to be at work at three thirty."

Alyssa took a deep breath and continued, "When she didn't come home I called the school. They checked their records and said that she was there for all her classes today. So I waited longer, but when she still didn't show up, I put Stephie in the car and drove around looking for her. Then I came back home to see if she left me a message."

"Maybe she went to a friend's house or something." Del wasn't sure if Mara had made any friends at school, but it was worth asking.

"She hasn't mentioned anything about any friends. I wouldn't know who to call. And she knows I need her to babysit today!" Alyssa sounded a bit hysterical.

"Hold on, let me think for a minute," Del said. She stared out the bedroom window. The thought of Mara running away again was too awful to contemplate.

Lord, she thought desperately, *where could that girl be?*

Finally she spoke into the phone again. "Why don't you call Eva and see if somehow Mara managed to go over there? I know she likes Eva's family."

"How could she do that? Eva lives in the next town!"

"I don't know, but anything's worth a try. The only other people that I can think of are the Spencers. You call Eva and I'll give Ann a call."

Del's hand was shaking a little as she dialed. When Ann answered, Del blurted out, "Ann, is Mara there?"

Ann sounded a bit surprised. "Here? Why would she be here?"

Del explained the situation, then asked if maybe Richard had seen the girl.

"Well, I don't know how he could have. He had to run into town earlier to pick up some medicine for one of our cows which is sick. Then he came home and went right out to the barn. Do you want me to go ask him?"

"Yes! Would you please?"

She stood tapping her shoe against the wood floor, impatiently waiting for Ann's return. If Alyssa were to call now, she couldn't get through.

Ann's voice came back on the line.

"Richard said he gave Mara a ride to your house!"

"What? When?"

"He said he saw her in town and she asked for a ride. That must have been around three. He didn't think anything of it. Figured that you two had made plans to do something together. He dropped her off at your house and came home."

"Where did she go after he dropped her off?"

"Don't know. He was in a hurry and didn't wait around. Does she have a key to your house?"

"No," replied Del. She exhaled sharply. "Well, that gives us something to go on, anyway. Thanks, Ann."

She hung up after promising to let Ann know when she had any news. She ran quickly to the front door, opened it and poked her head out. The afternoon sun had melted the snow on the driveway, sidewalk and front porch, but enough remained on the lawn that she could see faint footprints leading around the side of the house. She hurried into the kitchen to peer out the window.

Sure enough, instead of a smooth expanse of untouched white, a dark woodchip was turned over here and there. As her eyes went to the old workshop at the very back of the yard, the phone rang.

28

Heart to Heart

Del pulled on a warm coat and stepped out the back door. She headed toward the workshop, thinking about the conversation she'd just had with Alyssa.

Told her I'd call back after I talked to Mara. She was relieved to find out she's here, but I'll bet that won't last long. She's going to be awfully angry at Mara for pulling this stunt! Dear Lord, I'm going to need some guidance here. What am I going to say to this child?

As she drew closer, she could see a faint red glow through the row of front windows on the small structure. Yanking open the door, Del was greeted by radiant warmth from an old space heater on the floor.

Mara was on the padded bench which was built along the back wall. She had her legs tucked underneath her, her coat pulled loosely around her and her head leaning back against the wall. She opened her eyes a crack when Del came in and closed them again. The woman seated herself at the other end of the bench in silence.

"Well, hello," she said finally, but wasn't surprised when the girl didn't answer.

"Your mom's been worried about you," she tried again.

When there was still silence, Del reached over and touched the girl's leg.

"Child," she said, then realized how silly it sounded to address the girl in such a way when she was shortly to have a baby herself.

"Mara," she began a second time. "Why did you run away again?"

The girl's eyes flew open.

"I did *not* run away!" she snapped.

Del's eyebrows shot up but she said nothing.

"I just needed some time to think, that's all!"

Del nodded. She did understand. She sat there for a while without saying anything before asking softly, "Honey, what's going on?"

At Del's kind question, a tear rolled down the girl's face. As she shook her head slowly, a sob escaped and she whispered, "I can't take any more. I just can't take any more!"

Mara began to weep harder. She threw her legs over the side of the bench so that her feet touched the floor. With her elbows resting on her thighs and her head buried in her hands, she continued to cry. Del moved closer and put a hand on the girl's shoulder but didn't say anything. Wiping the back of her hand across her eyes, Mara cried with deep heart-wrenching sobs. Del handed her a tissue, then gently brushed the teenager's hair back from her face. She waited patiently for the sobbing to stop.

Finally the girl began to suck in deep, slow breaths. By that time Del had tears in her own eyes. *The poor child! Carrying such burdens on her young shoulders.*

The girl was starting to regain some control, so Del decided to try asking some less emotion-provoking questions.

"How did you come to be here in the workshop?"

Mara sniffed before answering.

"I tried calling you from school to talk to you, but you weren't there." The look she threw at Del was almost accusatory, as if the woman was supposed to be glued to the phone in case she was needed.

"I walked around town for awhile, but then it just happened I saw Richard. He was coming out of a store and I decided to ask him for a ride here. But you still weren't home."

"But, child...I mean, Mara! Your mother was so worried when you didn't show up!"

The girl shrugged but didn't say anything.

After a moment, Del decided to try another line.

"It seems," she said, feeling her way along, "the party yesterday didn't go so well, did it?"

The girl looked devastated. Another tear escaped.

"I felt so bad for you," Del continued. "But I do know that both your parents love you. They didn't mean to hurt you."

"Well," Mara sniffled, with bitterness in her voice, "couldn't they've tried harder – just this once – to get along?"

That was Del's opinion too. Personally, she felt that Scott had made more of an effort than Alyssa, but she kept that thought to herself.

"I called my dad later last night," the girl said tearfully, staring out the windows. "I asked if I could come live with him."

"And?"

Mara took a deep breath, broken by a sob which caught in her throat, and answered, "He said he doesn't have room for me."

"Well, that's true," confirmed Del. "He told me he's just renting a room from someone."

Mara had her head down and was continuing to weep softly. Del patted her on the arm.

"Try to get hold of yourself, okay?"

The girl wiped her eyes and blew her nose.

Del said, "Things do look pretty bleak right at this moment, I grant you. I know you have a lot going on in your life. But sometimes you simply have to hold on through the bad times. Your parents both love you, but they have a lot of things to work out."

"No kidding. Especially my mother. She can be so mean sometimes." Large tears again ran down the girl's face.

"Is she still trying to talk you into having an abortion?"

Mara shook her head. "No, but she yells at me all the time. Or, a lot of the time, anyway."

Del said thoughtfully, "I imagine she might be pretty worried about the prospect of you trying to raise this baby yourself. Being a mother is an awfully hard job even in the best of circumstances..."

The teenager straightened, glaring through her tears.

"I can hardly do as bad as *she* did, can I?"

"Mara, please listen to me. I know things between you and your mom aren't so good right now. But she's carrying a heavy burden, too."

With compassion, Del continued, "You have to understand that every time she looks at you, she's confronted with the evidence that she failed you. Mothers are supposed to protect their children – and she realizes every day that she didn't do that. She's torn between her love for you and her feelings of guilt. Can you try to understand that?"

"I don't know. I get so mad at her sometimes and I don't know what to do. It's me who has to face other people every day. I know the things they're saying about me at school."

"Tell me about it."

Mara shook her head. "It doesn't matter. There's nothing you can do about it. Oh! I just want to drop out of school! I can't concentrate anyway. I sit there in class and I can feel the baby kicking inside me."

She cried softly, "I wonder what difference it all makes, when no one seems to care anyway!" before breaking down again.

Del answered quickly and more sharply than she meant to.

"That's not true! Your parents love you and they *do* care! Your mother was panic-stricken when you were missing today. And *I* love you and care about what happens to you."

Del made a valiant attempt to control her emotions and continued in a quieter voice. "And Eva cares, and her family too. Then there's Ann and Richard. They like you and care what happens to you. And, of course, there's your friend Peter. You told me you e-mail him all the time. Even through everything that's happened, he's supported you, hasn't he?" She smiled at Mara. "See? Right there is a lot of people who care about you!

"Tell you what." Del had a sudden thought. "Let's brainstorm together and see if there are solutions to at least some of your difficulties."

"What do you mean?"

"Let's think about school first. I can understand how there would be problems there. Maybe there are other solutions than dropping out of school entirely."

Mara frowned through her tears.

"Like what?"

"Well – what about home-schooling?"

"You mean my mother would have to teach me?" The girl's voice began to rise.

"Oh, dear, no. I guess that wouldn't work out very well. But isn't there a way to do your schooling online? Maybe you could do some research on the internet and see if there's anything like that available."

The girl looked skeptical. "I don't know about that. Anyway, to stay in my apartment all day, I'd go crazy! And my mother...well, she'd have me babysitting all the time if I was there."

"Hmm. You're probably right. So let's try another angle. Let's say you remain in school. What would make it easier for you?"

Mara sat teary-eyed for a few moments, thinking.

"I don't know," she said finally with a big sigh. "Maybe it would be easier if I just had someone to hang around with. Like all the other kids do."

"Isn't there anyone there that you think of as a friend?"

Her blond hair falling over her face, the girl lowered her eyes and shook her head. But Del didn't give up easily.

"Okay, then, you claim that all the other kids avoid you or talk about you. But isn't there even one person who has talked to you, maybe smiled at you in the hallway?"

Mara didn't say anything for some time before finally replying, "There's Amy."

"Amy?"

Mara glanced at Del, saying, "Amy's younger than me. I think she's a junior. She has a twin sister, Mandy. Actually, both of them have talked to me, and once they even sat with me in the lunchroom. I think their father is a pastor at one of the churches in town."

"Well, there you go! Have you tried calling them or anything?"

Mara shook her head, so Del continued.

"It sounds like they might have tried to be friendly. But you can't expect them to keep trying if you don't respond. Do you think, when you go back to school tomorrow, you could make an extra effort to talk to them?"

The girl shrugged.

"Tell you what," Del said. "Ask them if they'd be available this Friday evening to go to a movie. I'll be glad to pick you girls up and drop you off at that theater that's near the counseling center. And if you have to babysit, I'll watch Stephie for you. Okay?"

A few tears still ran down Mara's cheeks, but after a moment she said, "Well, maybe."

"Honey, sometimes it's hard to see the answers to problems when you're right on top of them. It helps to take just one small step in a positive direction. You never know what kind of good things it can lead to.

"How 'bout if you look at it this way? What if it was Stephie who was in the same circumstances that you are? Pretend that she's a teenager and these awful things have happened to her, just like they happened to you. You're her big sister and you love her. What advice would you give her?"

Mara bit her lip, then wailed, "Oh, I hope nothing like this ever happens to her!"

"But what advice would you give her?" Del persisted.

The girl sat wiping her eyes and thinking.

Finally she replied, "I guess I'd tell her not to give up. To keep trying. And that I would help her through anything."

"Good advice." Del smiled. She reached over and gave the girl a hug.

"And Mara? Keep trusting in God. He can bring good out of the most awful circumstances."

"I don't see how anything good can come out of this!" The girl started weeping again. "And I can't seem to pray. All I do is think about my problems."

Del chuckled lightly. "That usually happens to me, too, when I try to pray. But remember – even when it doesn't seem like it, God is close to you. He's loving you and guiding you. When you feel like you can't pray, try to picture God reaching out to you. Just put all your troubles in his hands, and keep doing that every time a worry creeps in. You'll find it really helps!"

She fished around in her pocket and handed something to the girl.

"This is a prayer card I've been meaning to give you. On the front is a picture of St. Gianna Molla. There's a prayer on the back."

The girl looked at the photograph of a dark-haired, smiling woman holding a small child.

"Who is this?"

"Gianna was a young mother who was diagnosed with a tumor while she was pregnant with her fourth child. She had to make the hard decision whether to have an operation which would save her life but would mean the death of her unborn baby, or try less drastic measures. She was a doctor herself, so she knew the second option might cause her own death. But she insisted that her child's life be preserved at all costs. And it did turn out that she died not long after her baby was born.

114

"Mara, Gianna gave her life so that her child could live. And you, too, in a manner of speaking, have given up your life, the life you once had, so your baby can live."

A tear fell on the card as the girl gazed down at it. She turned it over to read the prayer.

Del explained, "I've been praying that St. Gianna will help you in everything. Why don't you ask her to pray for you, too?"

Del stood up.

"Come on, let's go back to the house. It's getting cold out here! We still have to call your mother. If it's all right with her, you can stay overnight and I'll drop you off in the morning at school.

"And Mara? Remember what I said about taking one small step?"

The girl nodded.

"Right now you probably should take a small step with your mom. How 'bout if you tell her you're sorry for making her worry today?"

29

The Singer Returns

It was Sunday after Mass and this was the day the choir was planning to assemble cookbooks. Del declined joining them for lunch at McDonald's as she was picking up Mara, who had offered to help. She still had a few minutes before needing to leave, so she sat in one of the back pews at church and closed her eyes. There was plenty to think and pray about. So much had happened that week!

The morning after finding Mara in the workshop, she had dropped the girl at school and then stopped by Alyssa's apartment. Del wasn't really too surprised when the other woman acted a bit cool toward her. Oh, she was grateful, certainly, that Del had found her daughter and had had a talk with her. Yet Del could see that there was resentment settling into Alyssa's heart.

I'm sure it seems to her that I'm coming between the two of them. Mara always comes to me when there's a problem. But hasn't it always been so – mothers and daughters, loving each other but unable to connect? And this situation is especially difficult. I guess only prayer – and time – is going to bring healing. She sighed.

Then there was the cookbook project. They had finally finished the printing, which took most of Wednesday. *And* part of Thursday. By late Thursday afternoon, she was really beginning to appreciate George's willingness to lend a hand where needed. No matter what difficulties they ran into, he pitched in with a smile, always there when called upon and patient when things went wrong.

You could do worse than marrying a man like George, whispered a small voice in her head. She pushed the thought away. There were other things to think about.

Friday had been cold, with several inches of snow which fell overnight. But that didn't deter Del from gathering what she wanted to take to the farmer's market the next day. She enjoyed being out in the woods in spite of the snow.

Other people might look at the woods in winter and not see anything other than leafless trees and dead plants. But you, my God, are the Lord of all seasons. How much there is to see if we just open our eyes!

Del's eyes saw dried stems of Queen Anne's lace topped by puffs of snow on their seedpods, like fluffed-up cotton balls. Black haw berries and scarlet winterberries still clung to their branches, providing food for wildlife through the lean months to come. Red stems of dogwood and yellow willow, a colorful and welcome sight, stood out in contrast against the snow.

Even though enjoying the woods, she was happy she didn't have to go *too* far on this cold day. She headed directly to where she'd find hemlock, arborvitae and holly for cutting. Other interesting specimens, like prickly barberry with its red pendant berries, were added to the pile of branches which she bundled carefully in an old sheet. Back in her garage, she placed them all in buckets of water. Her customers at the market always looked forward to purchasing her fresh greenery for their Christmas arrangements.

By Friday evening she was pretty well tuckered out, but held to her promise to drive Mara and her new friends to a movie. Since her babysitting services were not needed, she dropped in at Eva's while the girls were at the theater.

It was a nice chance to visit. Thank you, Lord, for the good news she gave me. Eva told her that there had been an outpouring of help from the community, enabling the counseling center to get re-established.

"A lot of baby items have been donated and money has been coming in so we can clean up the building. We should be able to move back in soon." Eva seemed tired. "It's been a lot of work and more money is still needed."

"What about the person who started the fire? Have there been any leads?"

Eva shook her head. "Nothing yet. But the investigation is continuing. The police are still checking out tips."

"What about Scott Ramsey?"

"He's still not off the hook. There's really nothing to link him to the fire except the fact that he was in town the day before. Unfortunately, there's no witness to his whereabouts at the time it happened, because the fellow he lives with was away for the weekend." Eva shrugged in bewilderment. "Who knows?"

Well, I know that you know, Lord. Please let the truth be known in this matter. If Scott is innocent, help them find the person who did this hateful thing.

After picking up the young people from the theater, Del declared that her tired old bones needed an infusion of hot cocoa to warm them up. The four of them crowded into a booth at a fast-food joint. She was delighted to see Mara laughing and forgetting herself as the girls discussed the movie they'd seen. However, Del was one tired woman by the time she got home that night, and she still had to be up early the next day for the long ride to the city.

Del was pleased when she sold nearly everything she had brought to the farmers' market. Even the pumpkin jam was a hit.

Thank you, Lord, as now I'll have a little extra money for Christmas.

Since the market was close to the cathedral, she went to Mass and lit a votive candle for Mara. *Just a little sign of faith that you, Lord, are never forgetful of our petitions.*

Then, before they left the city, Richard made an additional stop to buy a few Christmas presents that Ann wanted for the kids. It had turned into another late night for Del.

No wonder I'm so tired today! What a week!

Del checked her watch and realized she'd have to hurry to pick up Mara. On the ride back to the church, the teenager was talkative for a change.

"My dad came yesterday and we did some stuff together. Oh, and he has a new car!"

"Really?"

"Well, it's not *new* new. Actually, it's kinda old and stuff. But he says it's all his. And you know, Del," she thought a moment before continuing, "that's kinda weird."

"What do you mean?"

"'Cuz he always liked nice cars. I mean, before – like, he'd *never* have a car like this one. 'An old junker,' he woulda called it."

"Where'd he get it?"

"He said some people from this church he's been going to with Marshall gave it to him. At first he was gonna sell it and use the cash as a down payment for a new car. But he changed his mind."

Mara continued thoughtfully, "When he dropped me back at the apartment, he gave me an envelope to give to Mom and said it was to help pay the bills. It had a check in it for quite a bit of money! He told me he's going to start sending child support money every month from now on."

Del glanced over at the girl.

"What did your mom say?"

"She was pretty surprised. She didn't say anything."

Mara was silent until they pulled up at the church.

"Del?" she finally asked. "Do you think people can change?"

The woman turned off the ignition and looked at her.

"I suppose so. I mean, I'm sure they can. Your dad is going to church again and this Marshall fellow really seems to be helping him. But Mara, he still needs lots of prayer. And your mom too. I've been praying for them. Are you?"

Mara stared out the window.

"I used to pray for them, that they'd stop fighting and stay together. But it didn't help. They still got divorced."

Del nodded. "That happens a lot. It seems like God doesn't hear us and bad things still happen. When I don't get answers to prayer, I find it helps to ask God what kind of prayer he wants me to pray. Maybe, in this case, he just wants you to pray that your mom and dad will be open to whatever his will is for their lives. How does that sound?"

Mara shrugged without a word.

"Why don't we go in?" suggested Del.

They proceeded into the church and up to the choir loft. The area was being prepared for a cookbook assembly line.

"All right!" crowed Harriet. "Everyone's here! We're on a roll now! Joe, how about if you and George man that tool which punches the holes. And you two," she beckoned to the other men in the choir, "once the holes are punched, you can be in charge of inserting the spines. Have Joe show you how to use that gadget.

Ernestine, maybe you can help them by sitting here in this chair and handing them the spines from the box."

Harriet tended to be a bit bossy at times, but there was no doubt about it – when she was around, things got done.

"And everyone else," she beckoned to Del, Mara, Mae Beth and the other women from the choir, including Laurie, "we're going to collate the pages assembly-line fashion!"

All the piles of pages had been laid out along the wide railing which was the edge of the choir loft. Harriet instructed the ladies to line up and pick up the top paper from each pile as they walked along. At the end they would hand their stack to the men, go back to the beginning and start again.

It started out quite orderly, the line moving smoothly along. With much laughter and joking, the camaraderie between the workers was obvious as they all pitched in with good will. However, after a few times through, there were some who moved too slowly and soon others began cutting around them. Harriet fussed at them, warning them not to miss any of the piles, "or we'll all be here 'til Christmas checking through every cookbook!"

The initial high spirits, after an hour or so of this routine, started to dampen. When a few snide remarks were overheard, Del tried to throw a bit of levity into the situation.

"Hey, you know," she called out, "this reminds me a little of a conga line!" She started knocking out a rhythm, "Duh-duh, duh-duh, duh – *huh!* Duh-duh, duh-duh, duh – *huh!*"

With the "duh's" she swung her shoulders back and forth, and on each "huh!" she kicked a leg out to the side. Mae Beth behind her picked it up and soon all the ladies were dancing to the beat, picking up pages as they made their way along. All except Mara, of course. No teenager, pregnant or not, would be caught snaking along a conga line with a bunch of old people to assemble a *cookbook*, of all things.

Eventually, even this attempt to make a deadly dull task more interesting had its limits. It wasn't long before total silence set in and the mind-numbing task was simply suffered with resignation. No more bantering, nor even talking – they just went about putting one foot in front of the other as the endless stacks of pages began to diminish.

At one point, several of the choir members prevailed upon Mara to sit down and get off her feet for a while. Del, too, was becoming so tired that she was about to beg Harriet for a break, when suddenly her shoe caught on the carpet and she pitched forward against the choir loft rail.

"Oh!" she cried, as a pile of pages sailed off the edge and beyond her grasp. In dismay she looked down to see papers fluttering onto the pews below, the same instant she saw the startled, upturned face of a young woman in the nave of the church. The stranger – wearing a dark coat with a scarf wrapped around her head – stood there rooted in the shadows for a split second while cookbook pages settled around her like snowflakes. Then she spun on her heel and rushed toward the back of the church.

"Wait!" Del shouted, and flew down the steps as fast as her tired legs could take her. Before she could reach the bottom, the heavy wooden door banged shut. She yanked it open and ran outside. Wrapping her arms around herself in the biting cold, she looked first in one direction and then the other.

Where'd she go? wondered Del. *I don't get it. Is this the same woman from before – the one with the beautiful voice? If so, why does she keep showing up and then running away when anyone tries to talk with her?*

30

Invitation

It was Friday, the eighth of December, the Feast of the Immaculate Conception. At the evening Mass, the singing had sounded exceptionally lovely, or so Laurie told the choir afterward.

Del, however, felt their director was being kind. *I guess it's as lovely as it can get,* she thought. *But I don't think we can blame all of those screechy notes on the piano.* She glanced furtively at Ernestine before remembering that she herself did not contribute a great deal to the music, either.

Oh, well, she sighed, *thank goodness Our Lord listens to the heart, not the voice!* Del was just grateful that Mass was offered at St. Bernard's this evening. At first, Father Mike had planned to have only a morning Mass. After all, he was trying to keep up with the needs of two parishes and the other, being larger, was to have the evening service. Eventually he was able to locate another priest to help him out.

Not that Mass started out so well, grimaced Del at the memory. *Poor Mae Beth!*

The young woman, as the assigned cantor, had stood in front of the congregation and announced what she thought was the opening hymn. When the music didn't start as expected she glanced up at the choir loft. She saw Laurie gesticulating wildly and pointing to the board where the hymn numbers were posted. As Mae Beth stepped forward to check the hymn board, her foot slipped off the step and she toppled in a heap onto the floor.

Unhurt but mortified, she got up with the help of several people and smoothed down her skirt. With a flushed face, she announced what she thought was the correct hymn number.

Unfortunately, in her haste and confusion, she transposed two of the digits. Laurie began the music anyway, but Mae Beth wasn't able to lead as she was flipping back and forth in her hymnal trying to find the right hymn. Flustered, she finally gave up, put on a brave smile and did her best from memory.

After Mass, Laurie brushed away the embarrassed apologies. "Don't worry about it, Mae Beth. Believe me, any of us could have done the same thing. Liturgical accidents do happen!"

Del smiled as she put away her music. She was just grateful that *she* had never been asked to cantor. Hearing a male voice, she turned around.

"Del?" George smiled at her, looking especially handsome this evening. "I was wondering if we could go out to dinner next Friday."

"Friday?" Del frowned. "Well, George, I'd love to, but I've offered to watch both the girls for Alyssa next weekend. Could we do it a different night?"

They were interrupted by Harriet. She had her arms full of cookbooks and was handing out a dozen to everyone in the choir.

"These are yours to sell!" she instructed firmly. "Buy them yourselves for Christmas gifts or get other people to buy them from you. And don't forget that this Sunday we're selling them before and after Mass."

She paused for a breath. "Did everyone see the article about the cookbook in the paper?" Heads dutifully nodded. Harriet had somehow managed to get her own photo on the front page of their local newspaper. No one minded *too* much as the church phone was already ringing with requests for the cookbook.

Choir members leafed through the nicely-illustrated pages, admiring how well it had turned out. Del grinned when she saw her recipes in print and nudged George.

"Okay, okay! I won't say anything else!" he laughed. "So when are you going to give me those recipes that Edna wants?"

They returned to their original topic, trying to come up with another night for their dinner which was mutually agreeable. However, between them they had every evening tied up.

George looked crestfallen. He explained that in eight days he was leaving for his daughter's house in California for Christmas, and he would be gone a month. Del was always amazed at how much this man traveled. *Not that I'm envious,* she said to herself.

Of course not! But it would be nice sometimes to have enough money to go here and there.

In the past George had invited her on several of his trips, but she didn't feel right traveling with him. Besides, he would insist on paying her way, and she really didn't want him spending that kind of money on her when the two of them were just good friends.

She thought for a moment.

"Tell you what. If we have dinner at five, I can still get to Alyssa's apartment at a reasonable time Friday night. Why don't we try for that?"

George quickly agreed. As they left the choir loft, he inquired why Del was watching the girls for an entire weekend.

"Alyssa's been invited to the wedding of one of her college roommates. Mara told me her mother wasn't originally planning to go. She didn't want to leave a teenager in charge of a two-year-old for a whole weekend. But I told Mara to tell her mom that I'd be happy to come over and stay with them.

"You know," Del said at the bottom of the stairs, "Alyssa hasn't been too friendly towards me lately, but I think this was just too good a deal for her to pass up!"

She chuckled before continuing, "Maybe she'll thaw a little towards me now. At any rate, I'll enjoy it. I'm sure that Mara can watch Stephie until I get there Friday night, then on Saturday I'll take the child to my house while Mara goes with her dad for the day. I'll take Stephie back to the apartment on Saturday evening so she can sleep in her own bed. And on Sunday after church, my friend Eva has invited us all over for dinner. Alyssa's coming back Sunday evening."

George laughed as he pushed open the door and held it for Del.

"I am so glad," he said, "that we're going out to eat *before* you babysit. Running after a toddler all weekend! By Sunday night you're going to be one frazzled woman!"

As things turned out, Del *was* pretty frazzled, but not for the reason George thought.

31

The Presence

The Saturday morning after her conversation with George, Del received a phone call from a disappointed Mara. Her dad was down with the flu and was unable to come that day.

"Oh, honey, I'm so sorry to hear that. Too bad he doesn't live closer. I'd run over to him some elderberry syrup. You know, it's so good for the immune system!"

She could almost see Mara smiling at the other end as she answered, "That's okay, Del. He promised he'll be better by next Saturday and we'll go Christmas shopping together. But also, tonight after my dad left I was going to meet Amy and Mandy in town and go to McDonald's with them. When my mom found out I was staying home today, she cancelled our neighbor for babysitting and told me to watch Stephie."

Del was thrilled to hear that Mara had made plans with her friends. Since the girl had connected with the twins, she seemed to be a little happier. Del wanted to encourage this budding relationship.

"Well, I'm not doing anything! Check with your mom and if it's okay with her, I'll watch Stephie for an hour or so tonight, so you and your friends can go out."

That evening it was an exhausted Del who crawled into bed. *How will I ever be able to keep up with that child all next weekend?* she wondered. *And why did I ever introduce her to hide-and-seek?*

Even in her weariness she smiled, asking God for a quick return to health for Scott and for safe travel next weekend for Alyssa. She prayed for Mara and the baby and then for her own family. As the prayer intentions continued, her eyelids grew heavier. Before she knew it, Sunday morning had arrived.

She went a little early to church in order to help set up a table in the vestibule. Even as she and Ernestine laid out the cookbooks, people arriving for Mass were lining up to buy them.

"Phew!" breathed Ernestine finally, their customer base trickling out as Mass time approached. "Who would have thought these would be so popular?"

Del grinned. "Maybe folks are impatient to try out my 'wild' recipes!"

Ernestine laughed. "Sure, why not? But the cookbook *is* well-done. And just possibly the entire congregation can't wait to replace that old piano!"

After Mass, the cookbook sale wound to a close without Del's help. While the other choir members manned the table, she turned her talents toward renewing the flower arrangements in the sanctuary. In keeping with the season of Advent, there were a few purple chrysanthemums among the greenery, but Del realized that they would not last until the following Sunday. She carried the large vases to the maintenance room. Dumping out the wilting flowers and rank water, she saved as many of the evergreen branches as possible. After adding fresh water, she placed the vases back on the floor in front of the altar. Then she located a carpet sweeper in the closet and made short work of the old, curled up leaves and debris on the carpeting.

As she was finishing, Harriet poked her head through the vestibule doors.

"Del?" she called. "The rest of us are leaving now. I don't have a key to lock the church doors."

"I've got one," answered Del. "Go on. I'll lock up when I'm done."

"Okay. See you tomorrow night at practice."

For a moment Del was confused, thinking Harriet must have meant *Wednesday* night. She then remembered that they now had two rehearsals a week until Christmas. She waved to the other woman and the head disappeared.

Del returned the sweeper to its place, turned out all the lights and pulled a chair over in front of the tabernacle. There, with closed eyes, she sat before her Lord. She began, as she always tried to do in her prayers, with thanksgiving and praise. After that she mentioned all the petitions which were uppermost in her mind.

On days like today when she had no place to rush off to, she would finish up her quiet time with the Lord by simply waiting with an open heart for his leading. Once in a great while she could feel his promptings in her heart. More often than not, there was only silence on his part and distractions crowding in from all sides on hers. Yet she would remain there anyway, like a child just enjoying being with a loving parent.

This day she never made it to the last part of her prayer, as she suddenly heard soft footsteps behind her. Startled, she turned quickly and saw a figure shrouded in darkness standing in the center aisle.

Del was a bit alarmed. She squinted her eyes in the dim interior of the church. The winter sun streamed yellow and orange through the stained glass, pooling in patterns on the carpeted floor. It was difficult to see beyond its brightness. After a moment a woman's soft voice was heard.

"I'm sorry. I didn't mean to interrupt your prayers."

Del rose to her feet and walked through the sanctuary to where the stranger stood. As she got closer, the woman took a small step backward.

Del stretched out a hand toward her.

"It's okay. Please don't go."

The woman stopped. She had on a long black coat and winter boots. A blue scarf was wrapped loosely around her head, shadowing her features and making it difficult to see her face.

Is this our mystery singer? Lord, please give me the words to say. I don't want to scare her away again.

Del smiled and asked gently, "Why don't we sit down?"

The woman hesitated before moving into a pew. Del followed her in silence.

After a long moment, the woman spoke. Her melodious voice sounded uncertain.

"Are you a...a member of this church?"

Del nodded. "My name is Del. And you are...?"

"Trish. Trish Allbright." The woman pulled off the scarf that partially hid her face and, using her fingers like a comb, attempted to tidy her long dark hair.

Del saw an attractive young woman in her twenties, but one with a countenance marred by tragedy. A large area of shiny skin on her left cheek reached all the way up the side of her face to her

127

brow. Her left eyelid was pulled slightly out of position by the raised scar which bordered the patch of mismatched skin.

Trish saw Del's expression and lowered her eyes.

"I was burned," she said in reply to Del's unspoken question.

"I'm so sorry," Del said compassionately.

The woman shook her head. "It's all right. It looks a lot better than it did before I had a skin graft. I'll eventually have plastic surgery which should improve the looks of the scar."

"Are you the person with the beautiful voice I've heard singing here in the church?"

Trish looked embarrassed, but nodded.

"Why do you run away when anyone hears you?" Del persisted.

Trish's eyes began to glisten with tears but Del quickly assured her that it was all right.

"Well," the younger woman said slowly, "I'm just not very comfortable around people anymore."

Del understood. She remembered how self-conscious she had felt about the red circle on her own forehead. She asked, "Would makeup help hide the scarring?"

"It does a little. But it takes so long to apply correctly that most of the time I don't bother. I work in the office of Stowe-Barnes."

Del recognized the name of the small shipping company which had a building next to the church.

"And no one there minds how I look. So I only use the makeup when my husband and I go somewhere, like to church."

"Here?" Del asked, surprised.

Trish shook her head. "No, we go to the Hill Street Bible Church, outside of town. Actually, Adrian, my husband, isn't much of a churchgoer, so we don't go there a lot."

She continued her explanation. "Sometimes I take a walk when I have a break at work, and one day I decided on a whim to stop here in this church. When I tried the doors they were unlocked and no one was around."

Del knew that was entirely likely. Father Mike resided in the rectory at the neighboring parish. Therefore, quite a few St. Bernard parishioners had keys to open up for meetings and rehearsals and the like. But human nature being what it was, forgetfulness set in and the doors often remained unlocked.

"But this is the second time I've seen you here on a Sunday," Del wondered. "Do you work on Sundays too?"

Trish said no. "My husband and I live close, so sometimes I tell him I'm going for a walk and I come by hoping the doors will be open."

Del was watching the young woman's dark expressive eyes and said, "You know, there's something familiar about you. I can't quite put my finger on it. Would I have seen you somewhere else?"

Trish shrugged, saying, "I grew up in the area." She went on, "Anyway, the first time I walked into the church here, it seemed different somehow."

She stopped, glancing around the church before continuing. "It wasn't so much how it looked. It just seemed that there was a *presence* in this place, like God was really here."

Del looked at Trish and smiled.

"God really *is* here."

She waved her hand through the air and explained further.

"Actually, I guess you *could* say that God is everywhere, that he's in you and me and in the very air we breathe. But more than anything, right here," she gestured to the tabernacle near the altar, "is his Real Presence in the Holy Eucharist. Jesus did say, 'This is my Body' when he held up the bread at the Last Supper. He also said, 'I will be with you always, even to the end of the world.' And this is the way he remains with his followers – through this Holy Sacrament, the real Body and Blood of Our Lord."

Trish was staring at the altar. She seemed to accept Del's explanation and simply nodded.

"I absolutely love," she whispered, "to come and sing for him."

Del brightened, thinking of the woman's marvelous voice.

"Why don't you join our choir?"

Surprised, Trish exclaimed, "But I'm not Catholic!"

Del thought about Mara, and also Ann Spencer who often came to Mass with her husband.

"Well, others come who aren't Catholic either! Since they're not in union with the Church, they don't receive Communion. But *everyone* is welcome in God's house," Del emphasized.

She paused a moment in thought.

"I wonder," she asked, "why you don't employ your beautiful voice at your own church."

Trish smiled then, a rather lopsided but engaging smile. "Somehow, I don't think I'd be invited to sing the 'Magnificat' there. It's not exactly their style of worship music."

"So *that's* what I heard you singing! I thought the Latin words were sort of familiar, but I've never heard that version before."

Trish dropped her gaze.

"That's because I wrote the music for it."

Del was astonished.

"*You* composed that? It was incredible! I've never heard anything like it!"

The other woman shyly replied, "Thanks."

With enthusiasm swelling in her voice, Del asked, "Why don't you come by tomorrow night when we have choir practice? I'll introduce you to Laurie, our choir director. Believe me," she said, her eyes crinkling in delight, "a voice like yours would help raise the caliber of music in our entire church!"

Trish's eyes sparkled. "Maybe I will! I don't think my husband would mind. He's been encouraging me to start singing publicly again, which I haven't done for ages. I don't like to be in front of audiences."

She turned in the pew to look up at the choir loft.

"But here," she gestured and laughed softly, "I'd be in the back!"

32

With Heart and Soul and Voice

"Come on, guys, settle down! There's only two weeks to go until Christmas! We have to get this music learned."

Laurie sounded a little exasperated. It was Monday night's special rehearsal and it was late getting started. The cookbook sale had gone so well on the weekend that the ladies were abuzz with plans to sell even more of the books. Adding to the commotion, everyone was in a festive mood and sharing holiday plans with each other.

Del had drawn Laurie aside earlier and mentioned the mystery singer who might join them. Unfortunately, Trish hadn't shown up and Del was terribly disappointed. While the others were busily conversing and laughing, she kept glancing back toward the stairwell in the corner.

I was so positive she'd come. Darn! I wish I'd gotten her phone number.

At last, Laurie was able to get the rehearsal underway. They worked on the music for Midnight Mass, trying to make some headway on the complex pieces. Frustration was setting in as Laurie had them go over and over the more troublesome sections. They were more than an hour into practice when light footsteps were heard on the stairs and Trish's head came into view.

Del smiled delightedly at her, beckoning her to a seat nearby. Trish removed her heavy coat but left her scarf wrapped loosely around her face. She took the seat indicated and someone behind her handed her a pack of music.

"Hey, everyone!" Del called out. "This is Trish! Trish, this is our music director, Laurie."

131

Laurie walked over to the newcomer and shook her hand in welcome. Trish smiled shyly. Then everyone else introduced themselves in a clamor until Laurie tapped on her podium and sternly requested they get on with rehearsal. Del pointed out to Trish the page they were on in the octavo.

The young woman's professional training was evident as she quickly joined in. Yet she didn't make any attempt to stand out above the others, modifying her volume to blend in. Del was grateful for that.

Don't need any comments from the others about this new person trying to be the star of the show. But this choir is already sounding better!

At the end of practice that night, Trish received many compliments on her lovely voice. If anyone had noticed the scarring on her face they were too polite to comment on it – at least in front of her. Since it was late the other choir members left quickly. Trish and Laurie were talking quietly together so Del just waved to them before heading down the stairs.

On Wednesday evening when they gathered again for practice, Laurie announced that Trish would be singing *O Holy Night* as a prelude to Midnight Mass this year. Out of the corner of her eye, Del saw Harriet shift in her seat and frown.

Oh, oh. I'll bet she was hoping to snag that solo, thought Del.

As practice was drawing to a close that evening, there came the unexpected sound of a *lot* of footsteps tromping up the stairs. Mara and her two friends, their cheeks ruddy from the cold, blew into the choir loft with the enthusiasm of young people. Del was surprised to see them. She motioned to Laurie to continue with practice and she slipped back to where the teenagers stood brushing snow off their coats.

"What are you guys doing here?" Del whispered to them, puzzled.

The twins giggled and Mara answered in a low voice, "Oh, we were just walking around looking at Christmas lights."

Teenagers walking around looking at Christmas lights? That's small-town entertainment for you! Del grinned.

Mara continued, "We were going by the church and I noticed your car in the parking lot. So we decided to stop in and surprise you."

"Well, I certainly am surprised! And it's so good to see you girls."

Del gave each of them a quick hug, adding, "Practice is almost over. Why don't you have a seat and warm up a bit? I can talk to you more when we're done."

The girls commandeered chairs in the back and Del picked up her music again. Rehearsal was soon over. While Harriet and Ernestine straightened up the choir loft, Mae Beth walked over.

"Say, you girls look sort of familiar," she said to the twins. "Aren't you the daughters of Reverend Symon from the Presbyterian church in town?"

Amy and Mandy nodded, smiling, and Del was quickly drawn into a conversation with them and Mae Beth. She didn't immediately notice when Mara wandered over to where Trish was organizing her music. When Del next looked around, she saw the two of them talking with their heads bent close together.

Almost as if they know each other, Del mused, perplexed. She nodded to the others and excused herself, intending to ask Mara how she was acquainted with the other woman, when the choir director called Trish over to the piano.

Laurie ran through the intro to *O Holy Night* and Trish started in softly and sweetly. As she gained confidence, her clear soprano voice soared upwards into the high places.

"…the weary world rejoices! And yonder breaks a new and glorious morn…"

The talking that had been going on in the corners of the loft ceased. Not a stirring was heard as the magnificent sound echoed through the still church.

"Fall on your knees. O, hear the angel voices…"

Those were precisely the voices that the listeners must have thought they were hearing, as even the sounds of their breathing seemed to cease. If anyone had been looking, a tear might have been seen in an eye here and there. They were all mesmerized by the beautiful music unreeling through the air like a ribbon of purest gold.

"…O-o-o-o-o night divine!"

Trish brought the beloved hymn to a heart-rending finale and the last inspirational notes faded away. There was only awed silence in the choir loft. Del had closed her eyes in order to listen more intently and realized suddenly that she had been holding her breath. Her eyes still shut, she murmured, "Oh! How beautiful…"

With that, the spell was broken and the others crowded around Trish, congratulating her on the spectacular rendition. A bit embarrassed, the young woman smiled. Del noticed that Harriet was the first to march over to Trish.

Even Harriet knows when she's been outdone! chuckled Del to herself. *It's rather doubtful that she'll ask for ANY solo now. Trish is a pretty hard act to follow.*

There was excitement in the air as they all left that night. Not to mention a thrill of hope that maybe, after all, the choir might be able to do justice to the Midnight Mass music.

As Del wrapped her scarf around her head, buttoned her coat up tight and headed out into the cold, snowy night with the girls, Mara asked, "Did you get the message Mom left for you?"

Del shook her head.

"I haven't been home since lunchtime. What's it about?"

"She was wondering if you could stop over tomorrow. She wants to give you some instructions about watching Stephie this weekend."

"I guess I can. Tell your mom I'll call her in the morning to see what time would be good. Okay?"

Mara nodded and she and her friends headed toward the apartment complex. It was only as Del was on the way home that she realized she had forgotten to ask Mara about Trish.

Oh, well, I'll do it next time, she figured. However, with all the events which would happen that weekend, "next time" turned out to be a long way down the road.

33

A Novel Idea

It was nearly one o'clock when Del rang the doorbell to Alyssa's apartment. She had meant to get there earlier but she'd been delayed by a phone call after lunch.

"Hi, Mom!"

She had heard the bubbly voice of her daughter-in-law over the phone. "How are you?"

Del smiled with delight at the greeting. Emily was as dear to her as a daughter and a blessing to the entire family. She was the sweetest thing, her honey-colored hair always caught back in a large barrette on one side, her hazel eyes dancing as if enjoying some inside joke and her enthusiastic personality drawing people toward her like moths to a flame.

Or like bumble bees to bee balm! And how wonderful she loves flowers, too!

Del had immediately liked this young woman when her son Robert had first brought her home, and continued to enjoy her company whenever her son's family was able to come in from Colorado. Of course, that wasn't often enough for Del, especially now that there were grandchildren.

"I just wanted to let you know our Christmas plans," F was saying. "We've got a ten o'clock flight from International on the morning of the twenty-third. We' Metro in Detroit at two-forty. We'll rent a car ar ' you can expect us for dinner that Saturday even¹

"Wonderful!" cried Del. "And the Christmas Eve to spend together! Mayb' choir sing at Midnight Mass."

"Well, of course!" laughed Emily. "We'll just bring along some blankets and let the girls sleep in the pews."

Del couldn't wait to see her granddaughters who were two and four now. They must have grown so much since their last visit.

"How long will you be here?" she asked.

"Until the twenty-seventh. Unfortunately, Robert has several meetings on Thursday or we'd stay longer."

"That's all right," Del said quickly. "I'm just glad to have you here for however long you can stay."

She was still smiling as the buzzer sounded to let her in to the apartment building. She climbed the wide stairway and was about to knock on the door when Alyssa suddenly opened it.

"Come on in!" the other woman exclaimed. She closed the door and invited Del to be seated while she poured a soft drink for herself.

"Can I get you anything to drink?" she called from the small kitchen.

Del declined and Alyssa returned, settling in a corner of the sofa. Pepper immediately jumped onto her lap and was unceremoniously pushed off.

"Thinks he owns the place," scowled Alyssa.

There were toys scattered on the floor but Stephie was nowhere to be seen. *Must be naptime*, Del decided, just as Alyssa began talking.

"Thanks so much for coming. I suppose that Mara could have told you most everything, but I feel better knowing that nothing important was forgotten."

Alyssa explained Stephie's schedule, where everything was located, the emergency phone numbers posted by the phone and the like.

"What time are you leaving?" asked Del when Alyssa stopped for a breath.

"I want to get out of here by one. It's a four hour drive to Cleveland where the wedding will be, and I'd like to be there for dinner with some of my old college friends tomorrow night. My neighbor will keep Stephie at her place 'til Mara gets home, and said you'd be here around seven to stay the night. Oh, yeah, change my bed before I go so you can sleep in it. The sofa isn't comfy!"

Del was grateful. Years ago she may not have minded camping out in such a fashion, but these days her old hinges needed a little more support.

As Alyssa went on with instructions, Del reflected that the woman seemed to have warmed up toward her.

Amazing what an offer of free babysitting for a whole weekend will do to change a heart!

Alyssa continued talking animatedly about her friends.

I can just imagine how excited she is to be going, getting together with old friends and all. She said it's been years since she's seen some of them.

"Oh, it's just so romantic!" Alyssa was saying breathlessly. "Del, you wouldn't believe it. My friend Marcy, the one who's getting married, gets flowers from her fiancé every month on the anniversary of their first date! He's never missed in three years! And his proposal! He hired a carriage pulled by two white horses, then he…"

The woman became ever livelier as she talked. She described every detail she could remember of the courtship and every plan she knew about the wedding. Yes, it all sounded very romantic indeed.

Del had been nodding and smiling when Alyssa began talking, but as the one-sided conversation continued her smile began to fade. *Is this a real-life relationship she's talking about – or a fairy tale?* Del began to wonder. *Sure, there's a place for romance. But I haven't heard a word about the marriage. Hopefully it's going to be built on a more solid basis than what I'm hearing.*

Alyssa, her cheeks flushed and her eyes sparkling, wound down her tale. "Now *that's* the kind of guy I'd like to find!" she finished dramatically, throwing an arm across a sofa pillow.

Del said nothing for a moment, then looked over at the younger woman and asked gently, "Alyssa, if you were writing a 'recipe' for a good marriage, what do you think would ' most important ingredient?"

The other woman sat up straight and s⁺ suspiciously.

"For heaven's sakes, Del! A recipe ᶠ obviously, *love* would be the main ingredie

"What about sacrifice?" Del asked.

Alyssa looked sharply at Del.

137

"What are you talking about?"

"Well, of course," Del said, "love is important. But we have to understand whether we're talking about *feelings* of love or about *real* love."

"That's goofy. Love is love."

"But real love isn't a feeling. It's more like a...well...like a...like an act of the will," she finished lamely.

Alyssa looked puzzled. "Huh?"

Del breathed a silent prayer. *Help, Lord! This isn't coming out right!*

She tried again. "Real love," she explained, "the kind that lasts for a lifetime, is about *sacrifice*."

Seeing the blank look on Alyssa's face, she sighed and leaned forward to look into the other woman's eyes.

"Alyssa," she said a quieter voice, "feelings can come and go. Romantic love is notoriously short-lived and isn't the best thing to base a marriage on. But when love causes you to want to sacrifice for the other person, *that's* the kind of love which will carry you through anything."

"Sacrifice? Like giving up your life for each other? And how often does *that* happen?"

Del laughed. "Why...every day!"

"Every day!?"

"Yep. It's a sacrifice every time you *don't* squeeze the toothpaste tube in the middle because you know it drives your spouse crazy. Or you get up a little earlier to start the coffee pot so your husband can wake up to his favorite cup. Or you sew the buttons back on his shirt – for the umpteenth time – even though you hate sewing!"

"Huh! Those are little things. They're not exactly giving up your life for one another. Now *that* would be something!"

Del wished she was better at explaining all this.

"But Alyssa," she said, "a person will never make a big sacrifice if they're not willing to make little, everyday sacrifices – like putting the other's needs before their own."

Del thought of the couples she knew, like the Sigorski's, ho made a lifelong habit of putting the other person first – one at a time. Her eyes wandered to the overstuffed bookshelves to the television. In a seeming change of subject, she asked, e you read all those paperbacks?"

Yeah. I *love* reading!"

"Me, too," responded Del, smiling. "But the books you have are all romance novels."

"So what? They're just stories. I've been reading them for years." Alyssa flipped her hair back from her face. "And they're certainly more exciting than *my* life right now!"

And more exciting than living with a real-life husband. No wonder Scott could never make her happy.

"Alyssa," Del said firmly, turning once again to look at the woman, "those kinds of books are like pornography for women."

"What?" Alyssa snapped at Del. "I'm a Christian! I don't read stuff like that!"

"I hope not," Del responded calmly. "But still... it seems to me that pornography gives men unrealistic expectations of women. Don't you think that these romance novels tend to give women unrealistic expectations of men?"

"So? It's just romance! What's wrong with that?" Alyssa was frowning at her again.

Del shook her head sadly. This conversation didn't go well and here they were, come full circle, back to where they had started. It was fortunate that Stephie had awakened and was calling out, because Del didn't know what else to say.

She smiled appeasingly at Alyssa, wishing her a safe trip.

"Enjoy yourself and don't worry about the kids. We'll get along fine and we'll see you on Sunday night."

She hurriedly put on her coat and made her exit before Stephie saw her.

There'll be enough time for hide-and-seek this weekend, she thought. *I'd better save my strength!*

34

A Later Love

It's our annual Christmas dinner, Del reminded herself on Friday afternoon as she pulled one thing after another from her closet, looking for something festive to wear. She finally decided on a long black skirt and a red blouse. Her mind was preoccupied with many things as she absentmindedly changed her clothes, packed an overnight bag for staying at Alyssa's and drove to meet George at the Hampstead Inn.

He smiled at Del when she approached the table and complimented her on how nice she looked. The red top *did* set off her lovely olive skin and sparkling dark eyes. If George remembered that she had worn the same outfit the year before – *and* the year before that – he was too well-mannered to mention it. He pulled out the chair for her before seating himself again and handing her a menu.

While waiting for their meal to arrive, she gave him a large manila envelope.

"Here it is. The information that Edna wanted."

"Oh!" George responded. "Thanks. I'll see her next week and give it to her. On the other hand, maybe I'll mail it to her after Christmas. I don't want her trying out the recipes on me!"

Del chuckled amiably. As they ate dinner, she was surprised at how much she was enjoying the evening with George. Ever since they had worked on the cookbook project together, George seemed to be more and more on her mind. For some reason, she was mightily impressed with how he had handled himself in that stressful situation.

Patient, gentle and kind, Del mused, charitably dismissing the teasing he had dished out over her love of wild plants.

140

Nobody's perfect – certainly not me! And he puts up with my foibles. There's something to be said for that.

Later she would come to wonder if it had been the fine wine they had for dinner, or perhaps the soft, low lighting and the candlelight sparkling in the crystal wineglasses. But whatever the reason, the good-looking, silvery-haired gentleman seated across from her seemed more appealing than ever as the night wore on. She realized with a start – and a smile that wouldn't stop – that yes, she did feel she loved this good man.

She knew that she was talking all too much – and laughing even more – but she couldn't seem to help herself. As they finished their dinner and ordered dessert, Del felt as giddy as a schoolgirl. She leaned closer to him while they talked companionably together of many things.

After the dishes were cleared, George suddenly said, "Hold on." He reached under the table and drew out a gift-wrapped package.

"I've got something for you," he said, a hint of a nervous grin on his face.

"Why, George, you know we agreed not to exchange Christmas presents!"

"I know. But this is special. Go ahead, open it!"

Del hefted the package in her hand. She looked quizzically at George over the top of her little round glasses and pulled the wrappings off the gift.

"Well, George, this is lovely!" she exclaimed, turning the hardcover book over. "*Planting Seeds of Love: A Book of Poetry.* Just look at this gorgeous garden on the cover!"

She held it up so George could see it but he nodded, saying, "I know – I bought it!"

Del laughed and began to read the first page, before George insisted she turn to the poem he had bookmarked.

"It's called 'Evening Garden,'" she said and looked up at her companion.

He urged, "Go ahead – read the whole thing. It reminded me of you. Of *us,*" he amended quickly.

Del began, "When evening settles gently and the blossoms hide in shadow…" Her voice softened as she continued to read in a whisper to the very end. When she looked up at George her eyes glistened in the flickering candlelight.

"It's about a beautiful garden in the later hours of the day, comparing it to a love which is found in the later years of life. I guess you already knew that, huh?" A small smile touched her lips.

George reached his hand over and covered one of hers.

"That poem says exactly how I feel about us. Del, I love you. Would you ever consider marrying an old guy like me?"

Del was speechless. All her pre-rehearsed lines went right out the window as she looked helplessly at George's expectant face. Another long moment of silence passed, until she finally blurted out, "Why, I don't know what to say!" Then she laughed lightly. "And that's something when *I* don't know what to say!"

George leaned back in his seat and chuckled, too. The tension seemed to ease somewhat and he said, "That's all right. I didn't really expect an instant answer. I figured you'd tell me you needed some time to pray about it."

Del nodded gratefully. "That's right. You know I never make big decisions without prayer."

George put an elbow on the table and rested his chin thoughtfully on his hand. "You know, Del, that's one of the things I love about you. I know that you'll help me grow closer to God. There's so much I still need to learn about him."

"I do, too," Del responded quickly.

"Anyway, I'm leaving tomorrow and I'll be gone for a month. Do you think you can give me your answer when I get back?"

"I'll try to, George."

"Will you try really hard? You know, we're not getting any younger!"

"Of course."

Del stood up to put on her coat.

"And George," she looked at him with a twinkle in her eye, "I give you my solemn promise..."

George leaned forward expectantly.

"...that I won't marry any other man while you're gone!"

35

Christmas Eva

Saturday morning started far too early for Del. She hadn't slept well, with George's proposal churning through her mind. However, when she awoke rather bleary-eyed, it was the previous night's conversation with Mara that she thought of first.

Del had no sooner come in the door Friday evening and taken off her coat, than Mara was putting on hers.

"Why, Mara! Wherever are you going?" asked Del in astonishment.

"Out."

Del just stood staring at the girl. She didn't think that the impertinent reply really answered the question and waited, a trifle annoyed, for more information.

Mara zipped up her roomy coat over her large stomach and glanced at Del. She frowned, saying in a defensive voice, "I'm just going Christmas shopping."

"I thought you were doing that tomorrow with your dad."

Mara look irritated. "I can't exactly buy a present for my dad when he's with me, can I? Mrs. Symon's taking me and Mandy and Amy to that new mall outside of town."

She tossed a brightly-colored scarf around her neck and quickly left the apartment.

"Be careful," called Del in motherly fashion. "Don't be too late."

She closed the apartment door, stopping Stephie from following her sister. The little girl started to cry.

Teenagers! thought Del in frustration.

She invited Stephie to cuddle next to her on the sofa so they could read together. To herself she admitted that she felt acutely

143

disappointed, as she had hoped to spend time with Mara this evening. *Well, anyway, maybe we can talk when she gets home later.* But by the time Mara arrived home, Del had fallen soundly asleep on the sofa.

The next morning she was up before either of the girls. She wanted to make a good breakfast for Mara before her dad picked her up.

"Do you know what time you'll be getting back tonight?" Del asked while they ate.

"My dad said he'd drop me off by six." Mara got up to peer through the front blinds. "Oh, he's here! Gotta go!"

She rushed out. Del and Stephie finished their breakfast and headed to Del's house. The two of them baked Christmas cookies, made ornaments out of beads and colored pipe cleaners, decorated pictures of Santa with cotton balls and glitter, and together had a messy, grand time. In the afternoon, Del managed to coax Stephie into resting on the bed for awhile and it wasn't long before Del was lying there next to her.

I'll just pray my Rosary until she's asleep.

It was nearly five o'clock when Del awoke with a start. She got Stephie up quickly and hurried back to the apartment to start dinner. But Mara didn't arrive home at her predicted time, and it was after seven when the phone finally rang.

"Del?" came Mara's voice through static. "We're having some car trouble."

"What's the matter?"

"I dunno. My dad says there's more things wrong with his car than right."

"What are you going to do?"

"Well, there's some guy here trying to help us." A big sigh was heard before the girl continued, "It might be a couple more hours. Oh, my gosh, I'm so tired!"

"Where are you?"

The crackly voice answered, "We're still in the city."

Del replied, "Well, I guess there's nothing I can do, then. Try to get off your feet for a while, okay?"

"Okay. We're gonna get something to eat in a few minutes. So I guess I'll be home whenever I get there."

Del prayed for a quick resolution to the car problem. As she got Stephie ready for bed that night, the child became clingy.

Missing her mama, Del figured, and she was glad when the little one drifted off to sleep. Around nine-thirty Mara finally arrived home, too tired to say much except that the car was fixed before she headed off to bed.

Over breakfast the next morning, Del reminded Mara that they had been invited to Eva's after church that day.

"That's right!" Mara exclaimed. She still looked tired but she smiled. "I almost forgot. Oh, Stephie!" she said to her sister. "Maybe you can have a ride on their pony!"

Stephie clapped her hands and shouted, "Hurray!" Del asked Mara if she'd like to go to church with her, but Mara declined, saying that she'd just stay home and Del could pick up the two of them later. Looking compassionately at the girl's drawn face, Del agreed that that might be the best thing.

"Try to get some rest," she ordered as she left.

When she returned to the apartment after Mass and let herself in with Alyssa's key, she found Mara fast asleep on the sofa, one arm trailing down to the floor. Stephie was also slumbering soundly, curled up on the living room floor, her favorite stuffed rabbit clutched closely to her. Pepper was the only one moving as he prowled around looking for someone to play with. He bounded happily over to Del when she came in, rubbing against her leg and looking up at her with a hopeful expression in his golden eyes.

"I guess it's just you and me, Peppy," whispered Del, reaching down to scratch him behind the ears. She looked around.

Yikes! This place is a mess!

Quietly Del picked up toys and straightened up around the sleeping bodies, then headed to the kitchen. She washed the dishes and fixed a snack for the girls before waking them.

"Time to get up, sleepyheads!"

Mara groaned, slowly sitting up. Stephie rubbed her eyes sleepily then jumped to her feet.

"Going ride on pony!" she shouted, delight written all over her face.

As they drove to Eva's, a few snowflakes were starting to fall. The little girl watched everything out the window and became excited every time they passed a Santa or snowman in someone's yard.

"It's beginning to look a lot like Christmas," Del sang out, then quickly switched to "Jingle Bells" so Stephie could sing along. Mara just shifted restlessly in her seat and was silent.

"You okay?" Del stopped singing for a moment to ask.

"My back is hurting."

"You've been on your feet a lot this weekend. Maybe you can lie down when we get there."

The outside of Eva's house was festooned with garlands of cedar and tiny, twinkling lights. Two large fiberglass reindeer, looking quite real, stood on the front lawn. Long, red ribbons connected them to a weather-beaten, full-size wooden sleigh.

"Look at that, Steph," said Mara, pointing to the display. "Looks like Santa's here."

Del glared at Mara as she helped the little girl out of her car seat. "Don't go telling her that," she whispered to the teenager. "Now she'll want to see him!"

As they rounded the corner from the driveway to go to the back door, they suddenly stopped. Santa *was* there, right in Eva's back yard. Twelve feet tall, big and bulbous and blowing in the brisk winter wind, Santa quivered and shook against his tethers as an electric motor kept him inflated. Stephie, wide-eyed, grabbed Del and buried her face in her coat.

"Isn't that thing hideous?" came Eva's cheerful voice from the back doorway. She urged them to hurry into the warm house and explained that her husband had won the Santa in a contest at work.

"I told him it was awful and that he should give it away. But for some strange reason, he likes it! To keep the peace, I said he could keep it – but only if it stayed in the back yard." She laughed. "I don't know about Kirk sometimes!"

They followed the welcoming scent of cinnamon and cloves into the cheery kitchen.

"Warm apple cider," said Eva. "Let me get you some."

From a pan on the stove, she ladled the spicy drink into mugs for Del and Mara and a sippy cup for Stephie. As they sat down at the kitchen table, Del inquired about the rest of the family.

"I'm afraid they won't be back 'til close to suppertime. Kirk's dad had a stroke this past summer, so he asked them to come over today to help with the Christmas tree. Kirk and the kids will cut it, then I imagine they'll set it up and put the lights on. I told them you were coming, so Kirk said he'd try to get back as soon as possible. Sorry, Mara. You probably wanted to see the girls."

Mara shrugged, saying nothing. Del explained to Eva, "Her back is hurting. I thought maybe she could lie down for a while here."

"Sure! Go make yourself comfortable on the family room couch, sweetheart." Concerned, she looked more closely into the girl's face. "Are you feeling okay?"

Mara nodded and Del spoke for her. "Christmas shopping like she did this weekend would tire *anyone* out!"

Mara drained her mug and headed to the family room to rest. When Stephie was finished with the cider, Eva took the two of them around to each room to see the decorations. How beautifully she had done the house for Christmas! She had brought out her collection of crèches and had set up at least one in every room. Homemade ornaments made by the five children over the years mingled with antique angels, and red candles were everywhere. There were several Christmas trees – real ones, of course. One was decorated with favorite mementos of the family and the other with heirloom ornaments. Stephie was dancing with delight and had to be reminded more than once to "look with your eyes, but don't touch with your hands."

It was obvious that Eva enjoyed making her house lovely for the holiday season. *And I haven't even hauled my decorations out of the attic yet!* thought Del. *I've been so busy! Well, there's still eight days to go,* she reminded herself. *Anyway, my mother never decorated until the last minute. 'Advent should be observed first,' she'd say. 'Time enough to celebrate when Christmas comes.'*

Interrupting Del's thoughts, Eva asked, "Would Stephie like to see the pony?" Silly question! It was difficult to put a coat and hat on the wiggling, excited toddler. Mara wasn't interested in going, so the others trudged out into the cold, blustery weather. This time Stephie was too keyed up about seeing the pony to mind the gigantic Santa and she broke away from Del to run ahead. By the time they caught up, she was trying to open the heavy barn door.

From the brightness outside, they stumbled into the dark warmth of the barn, its pungent manure smell immediately assaulting their nostrils. Del steered the child to Old Paint. Stephie fearlessly climbed the open wooden boards on the side of the stall, hanging over the top to pat the pony's back.

"Hi, pony!" The little girl greeted him like an old friend.

"Would you like a ride?" asked Eva.

The child's blonde ringlets bounced up and down like springs as she nodded gleefully.

Eva entered the gate to the stall and took hold of the pony's halter. "Come on, Stephie, let me lift you onto his back."

The toddler held out her arms. Eva plucked her over the rails and deposited her on top of Old Paint. He looked totally disinterested as to who might be the featherweight on his back, but Stephie squealed with delight as Eva led the pony in circles around the roomy stall.

It was difficult to talk the little girl into leaving. She first had to pet Woolly the sheep and say hello to the chickens. Then she peeked into the rabbits' cage and Eva told her all the bunnies' names. But it was Old Paint she was most interested in.

"Bye, pony. Bye, pony," she kept saying as they finally left the barn and headed back through the snow which was falling steadily. Del went right to the family room to ask Mara if she'd like more cider. The couch was empty. She looked around, seeing only the family's large dogs dozing in front of the fireplace.

"Mara?" she called. Eva came in and pointed to the light showing under the bathroom door.

"She's in there."

They returned to the kitchen and talked for a time before Del noticed that Mara was still in the bathroom. She knocked on the door.

"Mara?" she asked, concerned. "Is everything okay?"

She heard the toilet flush and then the doorknob slowly turned. Mara walked out, her face white as a sheet. She was rubbing the side of her stomach.

"I'm having pain," she said, a panicky look in her eyes. "And I think my water broke."

36

Dashing Though the Snow

Del blanched. She insisted that Mara sit down, as Eva came in quickly and asked the girl a few questions. Then she and Del returned to the kitchen for a hurried conference.

"I don't think her water's broken – but it's definitely leaking," said Eva in a low voice.

"Dear Lord!" murmured Del, her heart racing in trepidation. "She's only, what, about seven months along?"

"She needs to get to the hospital immediately. I'll call an ambulance."

Del reached out and stopped the woman with a hand on her arm.

"You live too far away. It'll take a half-hour to get here! It'll only take me that long to drive to the hospital."

"But Del! It's snowing!"

Del glanced out the window. "Yes, but it's not sticking to the roads. They're still pretty clear."

"Then I'll go with you."

Del protested in a hushed voice, "No! I'm going to have to leave Stephie with you." She glanced over at the child who was busily making crayon marks in a coloring book Eva had given her.

"Take her to another room while Mara and I slip out or she'll start crying."

Del pulled a paper out of her purse.

"Here's the phone numbers for Mara's mom and dad. I don't know if you'll be able to reach Alyssa. She may have started home already, or maybe that's her cell phone. I don't know."

She hurriedly scribbled another number. "And could you call Ann Spencer? That's my neighbor. She's a nurse and knows Mara, and I'd like to have her come if she can."

Eva turned quickly and went over to Stephie.

"Hey, Steph," she said in an upbeat tone of voice. "Want to see our guinea pigs?"

The little girl jumped off her chair and latched onto Eva's hand. As the two of them disappeared down the hallway, Eva called back over her shoulder, "I'll phone Dr. Walkerman, and I'll be there as soon as I can. Del, please drive prayerfully."

Del and Mara threw on their coats and hurried outside into the snow. As Del backed the car down the driveway, she was praying with all her heart. She prayed as she turned off the dirt road onto the highway toward the city, and she prayed every time she glanced over at Mara, huddled in her seat, sniffling.

"Are you doing all right?" she'd ask occasionally. Each time Mara would nod but Del could tell she was in pain. *Labor pains? I hope not! Dearest Lord, please don't let her go into labor! It's too soon!*

"Take deep, slow breaths," she instructed the girl. "Don't fight the pain. Try to relax your muscles. Here, let's breathe together. Take a deep breath, relax, now breathe out. Breathe in, relax as you breathe out. You're doing great. Don't worry. Everything will be fine," she reassured Mara, trying to believe it herself.

On a winter day such as this, there was nothing more enjoyable than being out in the country for a leisurely drive along snow-bordered roads, the white stuff sticking to every limb of every tree, making a pretty picture-postcard out of everyday scenes. But today's drive wasn't leisurely and it certainly wasn't enjoyable. Del, driving faster than was her wont, became impatient at every red stoplight and every slow-moving vehicle.

"Hurry it up there, mister!" she muttered at an old, rusted-out pickup, obviously being driven by someone's great-great-grandfather.

"You there, who taught you how to drive?" she exclaimed through clenched teeth at someone who turned onto the highway, far too slowly, directly in front of her. Coming upon yet another slowpoke, she pounded the steering wheel with her hand. She was just about to shout in frustration when she glanced over at Mara's agonized face.

Calm down, Del, she grimly told herself, *take a deep breath. Breathe in, relax, breathe out. Breathe in, breathe out. That's better. It isn't going to help Mara to be getting so upset. Lord, please calm me down. We're almost there. And help this poor child and her baby. Please, Lord, it's much too soon!*

"Are we almost there?" the girl wailed.

Del pointed at the hospital building looming up a short distance in front of them and in just few minutes she pulled into the parking lot.

37

The Waiting Continues

Several of the other people in the waiting room had left, but Del remained in the same place as when Ann had talked to her earlier. The small crèche on the endtable was still flanked by the ugly sledders. Since Del had never carried through with her threat to loosen them, no one had walked away with them. Right now, though, her eyes were closed, an elbow was propped on the arm of the chair and her head was resting on her hand. Thoughts and memories had been reeling around inside her mind for quite a while and Del had lost all track of time.

All of a sudden Del was abruptly brought back to the present when Eva rushed in. Her dark hair sparkled with melting snowflakes.

"Is anything happening?" she asked breathlessly.

Del shook her head, trying to shake off her sluggishness before saying, "Ann Spencer's here. She's been hanging around in the hallway and bringing me reports."

Del looked up at the clock on the wall. She and Mara had arrived around four-thirty in the afternoon and now it was six-fifteen. She tried to remember how long ago Ann had last talked to her.

"Ann said the doctors are trying to stop the contractions by giving Mara something – I can't remember what it was. Anyway, they're also giving her injections of steroids to help the baby's lungs develop."

She looked at Eva. "Did you call everyone?"

"I phoned her parents right away but had to leave messages. Then after I got hold of the doctor I called Ann and she must have left right away. Within a half-hour Scott Ramsey got back to me.

He was pretty upset, as you might imagine. Anyway, I told him to call the hospital immediately in case they needed his permission to treat Mara. She's still underage."

"Is he coming?"

"He said he'd be here about six-thirty, but I don't know about that. The snow's coming down heavier now. It might take him longer."

"What did you do with Stephie?"

"Kirk arrived home," Eva glanced at her watch, "a little less than an hour ago. I gave him the neighbor's number, the one who watches Stephie, and asked him to call and see if he could drop the child off there. I figured Stephie would be better off with someone she knew."

Eva chuckled. "You know, when I left the house, that little lass had three new playmates – my kids – playing hide-and-seek with her!"

A moment later, Ann reappeared to report that the medication seemed to be working. The contractions had stopped and an ultrasound had shown that Mara hadn't lost a lot of amniotic fluid.

Thank you, Jesus! Del breathed a sigh of relief. "Do you think we'll be able to see her?" she asked.

"Maybe in a little while. They're going to get her settled into a room. Then it'll probably be okay if you keep it short. I need to be heading home. Please keep me informed what's happening."

Del thanked her warmly and the younger woman left. Sitting closely together, Del and Eva bowed their heads in prayer, and that's how Scott first saw them when he arrived.

When Del heard a male voice, she looked up to see Scott brushing snow off his coat. He asked, "How's she doing?"

Del introduced him to Eva, whom he hadn't yet met. Eva returned his greeting with a polite smile and a measured look. However, Scott didn't notice, turning immediately back to Del. She brought him up to date on what had occurred.

Scott asked, "Have you heard from Alyssa?"

Eva said that she had left her cell phone number and asked Alyssa to call as soon as she got the message. Then an uneasy silence descended. Del stared at the nativity scene next to her, Eva seemed lost in her own thoughts and Scott shifted restlessly in his seat, occasionally getting up to pace the room. It was close to eight o'clock when they were finally told they could see Mara.

At the door to her room, the women stayed in the hallway so Scott could visit his daughter first. They could hear his hearty greeting, "Hey, baby, how're you doing?" After that, there were only muffled sounds of talking. Finally Scott reappeared with a grim face and running his fingers nervously through his hair.

"I'm going to see if I can find the doctor," he said over his shoulder as he headed down the hall. "I want to get more information."

Del and Eva stepped into the room and went to Mara's bed. The teenager's face against the white sterile pillow looked pale and frightened. An IV was attached to her arm, and there were monitors nearby to check both the heartbeat of the baby and any contractions Mara might have. Del reached over to grasp her hand.

"We hear that you're doing better now and the contractions stopped," she said. The girl nodded, her eyes brimming.

"How are you feeling?" asked Del gently.

Tears escaped and ran down onto the pillow.

"I'm scared," said Mara with a sniffle. "I thought I had more time."

She looked up at Del. There were deep shadows beneath her watery eyes.

"I don't know what to do."

Eva spoke up. "You're doing exactly what you're supposed to be doing right now," she said in a positive voice and with a smile. "You need to rest and let the medication do its job of stopping the contractions. Every day that passes gives the baby a little more time to grow and develop." She paused.

"In our sessions together," she went on, "we really didn't go into what happens during labor and delivery. I was thinking that we had 'til February."

Del addressed Mara. "Maybe we should make sure someone explains everything to you."

"I can do that," Eva stated. "But I think that tonight, since you're not in active labor, you just need to rest. I'll come back tomorrow and answer any questions you might have. Okay?"

The girl seemed relieved and nodded. At that moment Eva's cell phone rang and she stepped out of the room.

Mara looked up at Del who was still standing beside her.

"But, Del," she said, tears pooling in her eyes once more, "what's the point of all this?"

"What do you mean, child?" Without realizing it, Del slipped back into using her earlier affectionate term for Mara.

"Well, why did I have to go through all this if the baby is just going to die anyway?"

Del's eyebrows shot up.

"Why, child! No one said the baby's going to die! I mean, even if it's born right now, there's a really good chance that he or she would make it. There are a lot of premature babies born all the time and many of them do just fine."

Mara compressed her lips, looking uncertain.

"Child – I mean, Mara," Del smiled at her and spoke gently. "You have to trust in God. He's created this baby for a purpose, just as he has a purpose for you and for me. There's nothing to do but leave this little one in God's hands. The baby will most likely be just fine. But in any case, you'll be able to have peace in your heart, knowing that you did everything you could. You've given up an awful lot to have this child."

Del squeezed Mara's hand more tightly and continued talking to her quietly.

"You know, we all have a natural, human desire to create something which is beautiful. Something beautiful which will last. Nothing is more beautiful or lasts longer than a human soul – which lives forever! And you've cooperated with God in bringing another soul into the world, even though it wasn't initially your choice. If you only knew how much God loves you! Whatever happens, he will be watching over you *and* the baby."

"But I'm so scared!" Mara was crying openly now.

"I know. But I'll be with you through all this and so will your mom and dad, and Eva too. Why don't we ask the Lord right now for his help?"

Del, still holding the girl's hand, closed her eyes and prayed that God would send his angels to guard Mara and the baby, and that he would put his hand on her to heal whatever was in need of healing. She finished quickly when she realized that Eva had returned and was holding out her cell phone to Mara.

"It's your mom," the other woman said with a smile. "I told her what's been happening up to now. But she wants to talk to you."

Del and Eva stepped out of the room and saw Scott returning down the hall. When the three of them returned to the room, Mara handed the phone back to Eva.

"She was calling from a rest stop on the freeway," she explained tearfully. "She's worried about me but I told her I'm okay. Dad said he's going to stay the night here," she glanced at Scott and he nodded, "so I told her not to come tonight. Stephie will be needing her, anyway."

"That'll work out fine, then!" Eva exclaimed cheerfully. "You just stay in bed and get a good night's sleep. I'll see you tomorrow!"

Del leaned over and kissed the girl on her forehead.

"I'll be back as soon as I can, too."

As she and Eva left, Scott was dragging over a chair closer to Mara's bed.

38

Let Nothing You Dismay

At choir rehearsal the next evening, Del requested prayers for Mara. Del explained that she had been planning to visit the girl that afternoon, but Eva had called from the hospital saying it was possible that Mara would be released sometime during the day.

When she returned home after rehearsal that evening, there was a message on her machine from Alyssa.

"I'm calling from the hospital to let you know the doctor decided to keep Mara here for another night. Everything seems okay. I guess it's just a precautionary measure. Scott's here and he has a cell if you want to call. Here's the number."

Del called right away, telling Mara that she'd come the following morning. Upon arriving, she found that Scott was still there.

"Have you been here all this time?" she asked, astonished. He nodded, and she knew it was true with one look at his haggard and unshaven face. Del turned to Mara who assured her she was doing better.

"At least the doctor's letting me up to go to the bathroom!" the girl said with a wry grimace. "But poor Dad. He's the one who had to sleep in that awful chair for two nights!"

Del asked whether she'd be going home that day.

"I don't know. Later on, they're going to have me walk around to see how I do. They might release me before dinner."

"Great to hear!" exclaimed Del. "Has your mom been in today?"

Scott answered, "She was here most of the day yesterday, but she's nervous about losing her job. She said that Rochelle covered for her this past weekend, and she can't expect her to do that every day. I told her I'd be here, that she needn't come today. It's okay."

Del was watching him as he talked and she realized that it really *was* okay. Here was a man who, in many ways over the past few years, had been through some tough times, and yet they may have changed him for the better.

Perhaps, as he told her, it had been a selfish attitude which had driven him when he was younger. However, this new Scott was consistently putting others' needs before his own. Del realized that she harbored no more lingering suspicions about his guilt in the matter of the arson. She prayed that he would soon be cleared of that dark cloud hanging over his head.

"And what about you?" she asked him solicitously. "What about your own job?"

Rubbing his tired eyes, he answered, "I'm very fortunate. My friend Marshall has been helping me out." He stifled a yawn before continuing. "Marshall not only rented me a room in his house, he also found me a job at the place he used to work. When I told him that my daughter was in the hospital, he just said, 'Go. I'll step in for you.' And he has. When I called him last night, he said to stay as long as I was needed."

His voice broke as he stared at his shoes, studying them intently. To give him time to get his emotions under control, Del talked to Mara.

"I called the Symons' house and talked to Amy. I told her what's been happening and that you'd probably enjoy a phone call. She put her mom on and I asked if their church could pray for you. And *my* choir sends you their love and prayers."

Del told Scott she would stay for awhile and sent him out to find a place to shower and take a nap. When he returned several hours later with fast food for Mara, Del headed home. Scott called that evening just as she was finishing her bedtime prayers.

"Mara insisted I call you. Sorry it's so late. We're still here – at the hospital. When Mara walked around earlier the contractions returned. So she went back on bed rest and they've stopped."

Del said she'd be there the next day.

That promise turned out to be more easily made than kept. When she went out to her car the next morning, a tire was completely, maddeningly flat.

"This old car!" she complained out loud, kicking the tire.

Next she discovered there had been a slight but steady leak in the trunk lid gasket and her jack had rusted. She hated to bother Richard, but finally decided that she had no choice. Her neighbor arrived within the hour with another jack.

"Del, you just gotta get rid of this old heap o' junk!" he proclaimed. "Get a newer car. You need somethin' more reliable."

"With what money?" she retorted.

Her neighbor shrugged and made short work of changing the flat.

"It's fixed," he said, "for now. But I don't recommend you go too far on that spare. It's seen better days. You'd better stop in town and get the other tire fixed before drivin' all the way to the hospital."

Del was annoyed but figured she'd better take the well-meaning advice. She left the car in capable hands at the repair shop and trotted over to the church for a short visit. In front of her Lord in the tabernacle, she prayed fervently for the girl and her child. There was also safety on the roads to be petitioned for, especially with her own family members coming in for Christmas. And then there was George.

Good heavens! With everything else that's been going on, I nearly forgot about George.

She chased that problem around for some time in her mind. She felt she really did love him.

Then why do I feel such hesitation? Is it fear? Fear of loving again, after losing Joey? Or fear of the changes in my life that marriage would bring?

Del sighed. She just didn't know, and decided she needed to trust in God to work it all out. After getting her car back, she arrived at the hospital by mid-afternoon.

Mara was still on bed rest. Scott had gotten a motel room nearby, so he went off to get a little rest while Del sat with Mara.

"Eva and Mom came by this morning," the girl announced. "Mom brought Stephie, but you're really not supposed to bring children under twelve."

"How'd she work that out?"

"She and Eva took turns staying with Stephie in the families' room down the hall while the other would visit me. But eventually Mom managed to smuggle her in. Stephie climbed into bed with me and kept talking a mile a minute and playing with the bed controls. It was fun while it lasted. Nurse Terminator saw her and demanded that my mother take her out of here."

"Nurse Terminator?"

"Yeah. That's the one who's forgotten how to smile."

They both laughed. Mara had a wry sense of humor, in between all the complaining. How often Del was hearing her say, "I'm bored." "My back hurts." "I'm sick and tired of this." "Why can't I go home?" Patiently Del talked to her, read to her, told her jokes and funny stories. When Scott returned that evening, Del wearily decided to skip choir rehearsal and go home to sleep instead.

Thank you, Lord, that one more day has passed, one more day for the baby to grow.

The next morning Del called Mara to tell her that she wouldn't be coming that day.

"I need to get things done for Christmas. My sons are coming and I have nothing ready. But I'll be there tomorrow."

Although the girl was disappointed, she told her that Amy and Mandy were off school now and their mother was bringing them to visit her in the afternoon.

Del escaped out to the woods that afternoon. It was wonderful to breath in the clean, crisp air instead of the antiseptic smell of the hospital. The sun hid behind a thick cloud cover. It was pretty cold but Del didn't intend to go far. In the circular meadow just beyond the garden she tramped around the young fir trees, eyeing each carefully. She had planted these as seedlings and every year one became her Christmas tree.

No small one this year! The grandkids are coming. Have to have one that'll reach to the ceiling.

With a bright yellow ribbon she marked the perfect tree for Robert to cut when he came. Carrying an armload of greenery, Del returned to the warmth of her house with a big smile on her face. Getting out for a walk in the fresh air had been just what she needed. In large vases she arranged the holly and the pine boughs. Arborvitae was twist-tied together to form long roping around her doorways. Finally, from the attic she brought down boxes of ornaments.

All ready for when the kids come!

She was tired. Planting herself in a kitchen chair, Del said her evening prayers in front of the large kitchen window where she had an unobstructed view of the backyard. A light snow which had fallen during the previous night clung to every tree limb. Mounds of perennials, awaiting the return of warmer days, hid with tranquility beneath the blanket of white. A slight haziness hung in the air as evening approached. The sky, still overcast and ashen, was beginning to take on a pinkish hue with the setting sun. As the rosy pastel washed across the garden, the scene took on the serene appearance of having been painted in the softest of watercolors.

With grateful heart, Del basked in the peacefulness of the moment as twilight faded into night. She knew that peace might be hard to come by in what were sure to be hectic and stressful days ahead.

39

The Purple Coat

When the phone rang the next morning it startled Del. She grabbed the receiver, her heart pounding, afraid that the call was bad news from Mara's parents.

"Did I get you up?" Eva's voice rippled cheerfully through the phone line. Not waiting for an answer, she continued, "Hey, Del, I have some news. Actually, I have good news and bad news. Which do you want first?"

Del sighed to herself. It was too early in the day for this.

"I suppose," she said with resignation, "I'd like the good news first."

"Well, here it is. Scott's off the hook!"

"What? What happened?"

"It seems that the police picked up some kid – a teenager – for drunk driving. One thing led to another and before long he admitted to starting the fire at the center."

"Why would he do something like that?" interrupted Del.

"Do you remember, years ago, when some of the center volunteers were involved in a court battle? When they were trying to keep an abortion clinic out town? It turns out that this kid knew some of the people involved on the other side and all this time the idea of retribution somehow stuck in his mind. According to him, it wasn't preplanned or anything. He was drinking one night and decided on the spur of the moment to do this stupid thing."

"Dear me," muttered Del. "That *was* stupid. So what does this mean for Scott?"

"The police have already contacted him that he's no longer under suspicion."

"Alleluia! Of course, I believed he was innocent anyway," declared Del.

"Me, too," said Eva.

Sure, Del grinned, keeping the thought to herself. "Okay, now what's the bad news – or would I rather not hear?"

"Well, it's the matter of money. You know how the center had promised to help Mara with some of her medical expenses? The problem is, if the baby arrives prematurely, the hospital bills are going to be staggering."

Del furrowed her brow. She hadn't thought of that.

Eva was continuing, "We were fortunate to have received a lot of donations after the fire but I just don't know how far we can stretch them. We have other clients, too, in need of help."

"What about insurance? Is Mara covered?"

"Luckily, Alyssa has insurance and it'll probably cover most of Mara's hospital costs. But I don't know if it'll include the baby. She's going to look into it."

"What about Scott?" Del asked.

"He doesn't have insurance at his present job. But he said he'll do what he can, even if he has to pay it off a little at a time. I'm really impressed, Del, with his attitude in this whole matter."

"Well," she said, "I'm not sure what *I* can do. I don't have a whole lot either."

"Oh!" Eva sounded surprised. "I wasn't asking you to contribute financially. I'm just throwing out the problem for any thoughts you might have."

Del added the new request to her ever-lengthening prayer list. She then phoned Alyssa for a status report and was told that every time Mara was up she would get contractions. There was also a risk of infection with her water leaking, so now it was definite that she would be in the hospital until the birth of the baby.

"Alyssa, how are *you* doing?" Del asked sympathetically.

"I'm okay." A big sigh. "It's just hard for me to juggle everything, what with work and running to see Mara. I feel like I'm on a never-ending roller coaster ride."

"I can understand that. If I can do anything, like watching Stephie, let me know."

"Thanks. But my neighbor has been really great. Stephie loves it there and I watch her little boy for her whenever I can."

Del said she was going to the hospital later and asked Alyssa if she would like a ride.

"I have to work. Scott said he'd call if anything happens. Tell Mara I'll be there tomorrow."

Since Del had a little time before leaving for the hospital, she decided to drive into town for Christmas shopping. Just this morning she had had the inspiration to buy something for Mara. She already had one present for her, a book about flower gardening, but she wanted to get the girl something a little more personal. What she had in mind was a pretty sweater. Whether the baby arrived now or in February, Del figured that Mara would be thrilled to have something new to wear.

She also wanted to get a gift for the baby.

Holding a cute little sleeper might give Mara hope that the baby will be all right.

Del headed to town, marveling that the sun was out, the temperature far above freezing and most of the snow already melted. *Only in Michigan,* she thought. *Tomorrow the weather will change completely.*

When she walked through the doors at Bean's Discount Store, her attention was immediately caught by a rack of winter coats. Exactly why she stopped to look at them she was never quite sure.

This is ridiculous, she said to herself. *I don't need a coat.*

She glanced down at the coat she was wearing. Navy blue wool, countless years old and hardly the height of fashion, yet it had served her well. Del knew it would give her many more years of dependable wear.

However, her eyes went immediately to a purple one. She pulled it off its hanger and held it up to look at it.

The coat wasn't a garish shade of purple, but a deep, rich, *royal* purple. It was three-quarters length and lined with velvety black pile. She ran her hand over the coat in loving admiration. Del was sure that she had never seen a coat so beautiful. Already she could picture herself in it.

She held the purple coat up again, and right then decided that she wanted it more than anything else in the world. She kept caressing its silky softness.

But I don't need a coat. Probably doesn't fit anyway.

Del shrugged off her old, worn coat, dumping it unceremoniously on the floor. She quickly donned the new one. It fit perfectly.

She looked at the price tag. It was on sale for only forty-five dollars! She spied a nearby floor-length mirror and sashayed over to admire herself, turning this way and that, in the purple coat. Then she walked slowly back to the rack, thinking hard.

Forty-five dollars. Hmm. I brought forty with me for the gifts – and I know I have a few extra dollars tucked in my purse somewhere. She frowned as another voice in her head argued, *But that money is for the gifts for Mara!*

She took the coat off and cradled it in her arms, uncertain what to do. A niggling thought crept in, reminding her that she really didn't spend much money on herself and that she did a lot of nice things for other people. Didn't she deserve something special like this, just this once?

And anyway – I didn't tell Mara that I was planning to get her something, so she wouldn't realize I didn't. And I still have the book for her.

As Del shifted from one foot to the other, her thoughts ran first in one direction and then in another. She put the coat back on its hanger and a few seconds later took it off again, holding it up once more to look at it. Such a beautiful shade of purple! How nice she would look at Mass on Sundays!

But on the other hand, I was really looking forward to seeing Mara open the gifts I was going to get her.

Del sighed in vexation. *Lord, have mercy – I'm not usually this indecisive!*

Slowly she picked up the hanger once more. Sliding the coat onto it, she stuffed it back into the overcrowded rack. In the deepest recesses of her heart, she knew beyond a shadow of a doubt that the new coat would not bring her that much satisfaction.

Every time I'd wear it, it would remind me of the gifts I could have bought.

Later that afternoon Mara, lying in her cheerless hospital room, opened a gaily-wrapped package and found a soft turquoise pullover sweater.

"I don't think this will fit!" she said, ruefully.

Del laughed.

"It will! Sooner or later you'll be wearing it."

Then the girl held up the yellow terrycloth stretch sleeper with teddy bears on the collar.

"It's so tiny!" she said, tears in her eyes but smiling. "Thanks!"

"You're welcome. I know it looks pretty small, but the baby will probably swim in it!"

Del left the hospital that night with the desire for that purple coat still firmly entrenched in her mind. Yet on her face was a bright, joyful smile. When the guard at the door nodded to her, saying, "Happy holidays!" she responded, "And happy *holy days* to you!"

By noon the next day Del had too much going on to dwell on the coat. She was in a real tizzy trying to clean the house, bake cookies and pumpkin bread and put fresh linens on the guest beds.

My grandbabies are coming tonight! her heart sang each time she had a moment to think. She couldn't wait to have them help decorate the tree on Christmas Eve.

Children in the house again – just like the old days.

Del still had much to do and was grateful that Scott had told her to stay home this day. *How thoughtful of him!* Of course, it never occurred to her that he could be concerned about the likelihood of Mara being happier to see Del than her own mother.

In the midst of all the Christmas preparations, the phone rang. The tidings it brought were not of comfort and joy.

40

O Tannenbaum

"Mom?" came Robert's voice over the phone line. "What's the weather like there?"

"Here?" asked Del, looking out the window with apprehension. A few snowflakes drifted lazily down from leaden skies.

"Not bad. Why?"

"Haven't you been listening to the radio? We're being socked by a snowstorm."

Del's heart sank. She'd been too busy to listen to the radio.

Robert continued, "All flights coming and going are being cancelled. We heard about the storm coming and kept hoping it would pass us by. But during the night we got six inches on the ground and now they're predicting more than a foot total. It's near-blizzard conditions."

Del felt like crying. How she'd been looking forward to Christmas with her family here!

"Isn't there any chance it might stop in time to get another flight?" she asked hopefully.

She could hear Robert's breathing in the receiver. *He's thinking. He's always had a way of pondering things before speaking. Just like his dad.*

"I don't think it's going to be possible," her son finally said. "It's supposed to continue through tomorrow, and everybody's going to be trying to re-book their flights for Christmas. I just don't know what we can do."

"Well, if it's dangerous to be traveling, I certainly don't want you to try it. But it won't be the same here without you."

Emily came on the line next.

"Oh, Mom, I'm so sorry. You don't know how much we wanted to be there with you on Christmas. It's been more than a year since we last saw you!"

Del struggled hard to look at the situation philosophically. "Well, there's nothing anyone can do about the weather. I'll miss you too. Maybe you can call on Christmas and say 'Hi.' Can I talk right now to my favorite little girls?"

After Del hung up, she sat down heavily in her easy chair. The sharp disappointment she felt was almost too much to bear.

What if John can't make it either? she worried. *Robert said the storm is moving east. It will probably hit Chicago just when John's planning to leave!*

Bringing all her willpower to bear, she tried bravely to put things into perspective. *I'd rather have them safe. Lord, please watch over them and protect them. We can always get together at another time.*

However, there was a lingering sadness deep inside her. She reached over to the end table and picked up her rosary. As she prayed on the beads, she laid the burdens in her heart squarely in the heart of Jesus. With the repetition of the Rosary prayers, she put her hand in the hand of her Mother Mary, sharing the sorrows of universal motherhood. *And my problems are nothing compared to what she went through.*

When Del finished the Rosary the disappointment was still there, but it was time to turn her attention to some practical matters.

"Like that turkey!" she exclaimed out loud. "Whatever am I going to do with Mr. Turkey if no one shows up?" The eighteen-pound bird was even now defrosting in the refrigerator. Del knew she didn't want to be eating turkey stew for the next six months.

"I know!" she answered herself. "I'll cook it anyway! Surely the turkey I can't use will help Alyssa's budget a bit. She probably won't have time to do much cooking with everything else going on."

That problem settled, she decided to ask Richard to help with the Christmas tree. It was already dark by the time he finally showed up that evening, saw in hand and Sean and Abby in tow. Del was delighted to see the children. She gave her neighbor precise directions on where to find the tree she had selected. Sean went along to hold a flashlight. While they were gone, Del opened a carton that was sitting on the living room floor. She took out a rustic wooden stable, setting it on the floor, and then began to hand Abby the nativity pieces. The figures were made from heavy plywood with painted clothing and features.

"My husband cut these out many years ago and my daughter painted them," she explained to the little girl. Del held the figures for a moment, studying them with a tender smile, before showing Abby how they stood up by themselves. Abby got down on her knees, arranging shepherds, kings and sheep around the stable.

"I know," said Del. "Let's read the Christmas story!"

Taking her Bible, she turned to the book of Luke and began, "In those days a decree went out from Caesar Augustus..."

As she read how Joseph took Mary to Bethlehem to be enrolled, she saw Abby pushing the figure of Mary, balanced on the wooden donkey, toward the stable. When the child had them safely ensconced in their proper places, she quickly trotted in Joseph. She'd obviously heard the story before.

When the angel of the Lord made its appearance, Abby flew all the angels up to the end table where they could peer down from the heavens onto the waiting world. The shepherds were next to be moved. All swooped together in a group, they were deposited in Bethlehem to visit the Child wrapped in swaddling cloths, lying in a manger.

Del glanced up from her reading and saw Abby trying to pile Joseph and Mary on top of baby Jesus.

"Why, child, whatever are you doing?" she asked, perplexed.

Abby looked up, her innocent face framed by dark curls. Her usually mischievous eyes were solemn as she insisted that the Holy Family were *all* in the manger together. Del looked down again at the words she had read – "And they went with haste, and found Mary and Joseph and the babe lying in a manger." Sure enough, the Bible story *had* said that. With a smile, Del started to explain what the words really meant when Sean burst through the back door in a cloud of cold air.

Richard followed, struggling to pull the large tree through the small doorway. Between the three of them they managed to set it in its stand. While Richard held it upright, Del and Sean crawled underneath to tighten the thumb screws.

"Hurry it up!" Richard said. "This thing is heavy!"

"We're trying," muttered Del. "Which way do these things go, anyway?"

"Good grief!" complained her neighbor. "It's rightsy-tightsy, leftsy-loosey."

Once it was steady, Del asked if they could help put the light strands on the tree before leaving. Then she talked them into hanging the ornaments while she made hot cocoa for everyone. She could see that Richard was getting impatient to leave, but there was still one last thing to be done. She handed her tall neighbor the heirloom angel to be placed on top, then threw on the light switch.

"Ooooh! Aaaah!"

Even Richard was caught up in the magical moment. He grinned, leaned down and planted a kiss on Del's cheek.

"Merry Christmas, Del."

"Merry Christmas to us all," Del returned, her eyes shining. "And to all a good night!"

41

Hopes and Fears

Del had a good night's sleep and woke up refreshed. *It's Christmas Eve!* she remembered first thing upon opening her eyes. It was also Sunday, and Del reflected to herself on the way to church that she was happy the choir did not have to sing.

"I'm giving you the noon Mass off," Laurie had decreed. "I want your voices to be rested for Midnight Mass."

After Mass, many of the choir members asked how Mara was doing. Del caught them up to date, expressing her intention to visit the girl in the afternoon. She also voiced her concern about the financial problems that could develop and asked them to keep that also in their prayers.

"Please give her our love," Ernestine said sincerely. "Let her know we care about her."

It was after four o'clock when Del finished her final preparations at home. She hadn't yet given up hope that John, at least, would be able to make it the next day. She had called him earlier to see if he and Natalie were still planning to come but had had to leave a message. On the radio news she heard that the worst of the snowstorm was heading a little north.

Maybe it will miss Chicago, she thought as she left to visit Mara.

It was Eva she saw first when she stepped off the elevator. The other woman looked troubled.

"The contractions have started again. They've been trying different things and nothing seems to be helping much."

"Can I see her?"

Eva shook her head.

"Both her parents are here and they're talking to the doctors now. There's too many people in the room. We have to wait out here."

Before long Scott and Alyssa joined them in the hallway. Scott's face was grim and Alyssa's was filled with worry.

"They kicked us out," she stated with irritation, while Scott said, "They're doing everything they can. We were just in the way."

Before long a grandmotherly woman in a lab coat strode purposely toward them.

"Mr. and Mrs. Ramsey? I want to make sure that all your questions are answered before I go."

Eva introduced Dr. Elena Walkerman to Del. Then Alyssa asked, "What's going to happen if the medication doesn't work? If the labor pains don't stop?"

The doctor answered, "If that happens, we'll be moving your daughter down to the delivery room." She smiled kindly. "If the baby is determined to arrive early, there's really nothing else we can do."

Del asked how big the baby would be at this point.

"Well, Mara's about thirty-two weeks along, so the baby's probably around three pounds right now. Of course, every day that she can hang on is one more day for the baby to gain weight."

"What will happen if she does go into full-blown labor?"

Dr. Walkerman explained that they would have a team of neonatal specialists in the room. Immediately after it was born the baby would be taken to a holding room to evaluate and stabilize its condition.

"Then the baby would be sent upstairs to NICU. We have babies smaller than that there right now. One that's three pounds would seem big compared to some of them."

Scott asked what problems a premature baby was likely to have. The doctor explained about the steroid injections Mara had already received to help mature the baby's lungs.

"There are other things we can do once the baby is born. Treatment of these preemies has come a long way in the last few years."

She continued, "I've explained all of this to Mara, too, but it will be your job to keep her calm. She needs to know that everything is under control and you'll have to keep reminding her of that. If there are no more questions, I'll check on her and then you can go back in."

Later in the evening while Mara dozed, all four of them congregated in the visitors' room. It was here that Del first observed the change in Scott and Alyssa. They were talking civilly to each other, and that alone was quite an improvement. Also, Del noticed, Scott was being attentive toward everyone else's needs. As tired as he must have been, he was the one who would ask if anyone would like a cup of coffee or some water.

Alyssa, for her part, while not acting overtly friendly toward her former husband, was at least polite. Del was grateful that a truce, even if springing only from the present emergency, seemed to have been declared.

Around ten o'clock Eva announced that, since nothing seemed to be happening, she wanted to get home to her family. Scott and Alyssa returned to Mara's room and Del began to put on her coat, figuring that she still had time to make it to Midnight Mass.

But that was not to be.

42

Special Delivery

Alyssa came running into the visitors' room.

"Her water broke!"

Del rushed out to the hall where she could see medical personnel running to Mara's room. In a moment Scott joined the two women. Hearts in their throats and worry etched on their faces, they watched as Mara was being wheeled from her room and down the hall to a waiting elevator.

The three of them scurried after the gurney, only to be told that there was no room for them and they would have to take the visitors' elevator. By the time they arrived at the birthing area, Mara was already being prepped for delivery. With so much going on and no one having time to give them answers, they finally found seats in the waiting area.

When Dr. Walkerman arrived, Alyssa asked if she could be in the delivery room. The doctor looked compassionately at her but said no, that there were too many medical personnel in there. Del thought that seemed a bit strange – not allowing Mara to have her mother with her at this critical time. It was only much later that she found out from Eva, whom Dr. Walkerman confided in, that Mara had in fact requested to have *Del* there. At that critical decision point, in order to head off any problems, the doctor simply told Mara that there was no room for anyone else.

"But Mara won't be without a labor coach," she smiled, beckoning to someone, dressed in scrubs, who was approaching. Del was astonished.

"Ann!" she cried. "What are you doing here?"

"I came in a short while ago to see how things were going and the floor nurses sent me down here. I've known Elena

Walkerman for years. When she saw me, she recruited me. Don't worry," Ann said to Alyssa, noticing the strained expression on the mother's face. "I'll be with her the whole time. Everything will be fine."

"But, Ann," Del interjected. "It's Christmas Eve. What about your family?"

The younger woman laughed.

"Oh, the kids went to bed early so Santa could come. Richard's going to try to assemble a doll house and a bicycle, and I'd just be in the way anyway. Tomorrow my mother-in-law is cooking – so I can nap all day if I want!"

Somehow, Del didn't think that was going to happen, but she smiled in appreciation of Ann's generosity.

"I have to go in now," said Ann. "I'll keep you informed."

The three of them resigned themselves to settling in for an anxious wait. They talked a little, flipped unseeing through magazines and stared at the out-of-focus TV as it droned on. Every so often, Ann came in to give a report.

At one point Del borrowed Scott's cell phone to let Eva know what was happening. Shortly after that Ann came one last time to inform them that it wouldn't be much longer.

"Mara's doing great," she said. "She's a real trooper."

Del thought to check the time. It was after eleven!

Oh my gosh! I forgot all about Midnight Mass!

She borrowed the phone again and caught Mae Beth just as she was walking out the door.

"Please ask the choir to pray," Del begged. "There's no better prayer in the whole world than the Holy Mass!"

Del was distressed that she wouldn't be there, as Midnight Mass was always so beautiful. *Oh, no,* it suddenly occurred to her. *I'll miss Trish's debut!*

Swallowing her acute disappointment, she turned to prayer. *This Christmas is chock full of disappointments. Lord, I'm not complaining. Really! The most important thing right now is what's going on in that delivery room. Please bring them both safely through this...*

The waiting seemed interminable. Christmas music drifted down from the ceiling speakers as the three of them kept their watch by night. It was half past midnight when they saw a young nurse hastening down the hall toward them. At the doorway she paused.

"Mr. and Mrs. Ramsey?" she said, looking around with uncertainty. All three jumped up and rushed over to her.

"Congratulations!" she said, beaming. "It's a girl! Three pounds, five ounces – fifteen inches long."

They all began talking at once.

"Is the baby okay?" "How's Mara?" "Where's Ann?"

The young woman held up her hands.

"Whoa!" she smiled. "One thing at a time. Ann Spencer is still holding Mara's hand while the doctor finishes up. She asked me to tell you so you wouldn't be in suspense any longer. The baby seems fine! She's small, but she's pink and crying loudly. Mara's doing great. She's not in pain – well, at least she won't be until the epidural wears off!

And now..." She paused for dramatic effect. "I suppose the grandparents would like to see the baby!"

No one moved. In their fatigue, they stared wordlessly at the nurse. After a long moment, Alyssa awakened from her stupor with a start.

"That's me!" she said, wonder spreading across her face. "I'm the grandmother!" Tears sprang to her eyes as she turned to Scott.

"And I guess that makes you the grandfather!"

Scott's eyes were shadowed with exhaustion, but a silly grin turned up the corners of his mouth and he exclaimed, "Well, what d'you know!"

"Come on!" urged the nurse. "They need to take the baby upstairs to NICU. You'll have just a few minutes."

No one thought to invite her but Del trotted after them anyway. They met up with the neonatologist and his team of specialists in the hallway, pushing an incubator. The team paused long enough for the newcomers to take a peek.

Concern furrowed their brows as they caught their first glimpse.

"She's so little!" murmured Alyssa. The baby lay on her side with not even a diaper on, her tiny ribcage moving rhythmically up and down. Her dark eyes, in a head which seemed too large for the rest of her, were wide open. Her arms and legs were like skinny sticks stuck on a scrawny red body. It seemed like there were tubes and wires going everywhere.

While they all peered down at her, she suddenly squirmed and her fist landed squarely on the side of her face. One diminutive finger poked out and pressed into her cheek. Del was tickled, recognizing the identical gesture which Mara used when deep in thought. She was just about to point it out to the others, when the doctor, noting the worry on their faces, cut in, "It's not as bad as it looks. She's a pretty good size. Much of the paraphernalia you see here is just precautionary.

"This Isolette," he went on, indicating with his hand, "is a warming bed, designed to regulate the baby's temperature. And these meters monitor her heartbeat and how much oxygen is in her blood."

"But what about the tubes?" asked Scott.

"That's pretty routine for a preemie. We're giving her oxygen since her lungs aren't fully developed yet. But she's doing very well." He smiled at them.

"You'll be able to see her again. Right now we need to get her upstairs."

As they wheeled the infant away, Del noticed that someone had gotten into the spirit of Christmas. Plastic holly and ivy leaves festooned the outside of the incubator where the newborn baby lay.

43

Christmas Day

In the brightness of morning, Del watched the snow fall steadily. She was hoping it wouldn't get any worse.

John had left a message the previous evening that he and Natalie were still planning to come on Christmas. As she prepared the turkey for the oven, Del worried about them driving in the snow. She also hoped the roads in her own town were still clear. She needed to get to church today as there was much to pray about.

The previous evening they had a few minutes to see Mara before she was taken to her room. Then Scott returned to his motel and Alyssa headed out to pick up Stephie from the neighbor's.

"Even if it *is* the middle of the night," she had said. "I want her to wake up Christmas morning in her own bed."

Del spent a few minutes with the girl, assuring her that the specialist team knew what they were doing, and promising to call sometime in the afternoon. Mara, looking utterly exhausted, started to doze off even as she was being wheeled away.

Still weary from the midnight escapade, Del placed the turkey in the oven and headed out into the snow for noon Mass. As she drove, a twinge of anxiety shot through her.

Please, please, please, Lord, I beg you – give perfect health to that little one!

The small church was filling rapidly on this holy day. It looked so festive. Bright red poinsettias adorned the sanctuary and a large crèche nestled among potted evergreens in front of the altar. Del joined the other parishioners who knelt briefly before the figure of the Christ Child.

Amazing! God himself – becoming a helpless human baby!

For a moment she contemplated the figure of the Infant in the manger before her. He stretched his little arms out widely as if to include the whole world in his embrace.

And then, my Jesus, you stretched out your arms again on Calvary. First on the wood of the manger, then on the wood of the cross. What an amazing love!

The straw that had been placed in the manger spilled out onto the floor of the stable. *Straw – from wheat. Wheat to make the finest bread. First God takes on the nature of human flesh to redeem us, then he takes on the nature of bread to nourish us. Truly, what an amazing love!*

Del touched the feet of the infant Jesus with grateful devotion before climbing to the loft. The other choir members crowded around to ask about Mara.

"The baby arrived just after midnight last night," she announced. "A little girl, three pounds, five ounces."

"A Christmas baby! Imagine that!"

"What's her name?"

"How's Mara doing?"

"Is she keeping the baby?"

"Is the baby going to be all right?"

Del held up her hands to stem the flow of questions. She explained that the baby was on oxygen but seemed okay, she didn't know the name yet, Mara was tired but fine and no, Del didn't know what her plans were yet.

"After all," she exclaimed, "no one expected the baby to arrive this early!"

Laurie called them to order so that the musical prelude could begin. Trish reprised her solo of the previous evening, thrilling Del to no end. She closed her eyes to savor the beautiful voice and timeless words.

The world will be saved through beauty. As the phrase drifted into her mind, she opened her eyes and looked down over the crowded pews below to the manger where the Christ Child lay.

His coming into the world was a miracle – a miracle of beauty. And the weary world rejoices...

When Del arrived home that afternoon there was a car in the driveway.

John! she thought with delight as she quickly entered the house. The smell of turkey cooking already permeated the air. Her guests were waiting in the living room and John jumped up to give his mother a hug.

"Merry Christmas, Ma!" he said, lifting her off her feet with his embrace. Laughing as he put her down, she exclaimed, "Oh, John, I'm so glad to see you! I hope the driving wasn't too awful."

"Well, it took longer than we had planned. But we're here now."

Natalie greeted Del, receiving a hug also. Del noticed that the bright red color in her hair was gone. Her hair was still spiked – and bleached – and the earrings were still in place. Yet it was an improvement.

The first topic of conversation was disappointment over Robert's family being unable to make it.

"But what can you do?" asked Del, philosophically. "At least they promised to call today to wish us a merry Christmas."

The afternoon wore on as they visited, yet Robert never called. Del was thinking that she'd give *him* a ring when she suddenly realized she needed to get the potatoes started for dinner. As John lent a hand peeling and Natalie cut up fruit for the ambrosia salad, Del finally remembered she had been planning to make a phone call. She just forgot whom it was going to be *to*. She trotted to her bedroom and dialed Mara's room at the hospital.

Scott answered the phone and put Mara on. In response to Del's query, the girl replied that she felt all right even though she was in some pain. But she was animated as she related how she had gotten to hold the baby.

"This morning I actually got to take a shower and then my dad came and he took me to the nursery. We both had to put on these *awful* green gowns and then scrub our arms and hands with some red soap...Hey, I just thought about it – red and green for Christmas!"

As Mara rattled on, Del grinned.

"One of the nurses had put a Santa hat on the baby! Then I sat in a rocking chair and they put her in my arms. There were still tubes and wires all over and I had to be real careful. But Del, she stopped fussing as soon as I held her! She seemed to know my voice. I rocked her and I sang 'Jingle Bells' real quiet and she liked it! My dad even got to hold her for a few minutes."

Mara's tone of voice dropped a bit. "But they've had to turn the oxygen up. She's having some difficulty breathing."

Del was alarmed and asked if she should come to the hospital. Mara said no, her mom was coming in a little while and Eva would come that evening.

"Besides, it's Christmas, and you have your own family."

At that Del smiled, thinking that Mara, now a mother herself, was indeed growing up.

"But can you come tomorrow?" the girl asked eagerly.

Del replied that, of course, she could.

"By the way, does the baby have a name yet?"

"I'm still thinking about it."

Del returned to the kitchen where she found the pot of potatoes ready to boil over. *Never leave a man in charge of food!* she huffed to herself while sending her son to get the tablecloth and good silverware. She asked Natalie, finished with the fruit, to get the plates out of the cupboard while she herself set about mixing dough for biscuits.

There was a knock on the front door, and Del, spoon in hand, hurried to answer it.

44

Surprises All Around

She threw open the door to see Robert – and Emily and the children! Her jaw dropped and so did the batter-covered spoon.

"Surprise!" Robert shouted, hugging his mother as his family crowded through the front door. John and Natalie rushed into the living room, adding to the happy commotion.

"What are you *doing* here?" Del asked, tears of happiness in her eyes. Overjoyed, she held her son away from her and looked him up and down. His build was shorter and rounder than his brother – *like me,* thought Del with a grin – and his face was a masculine reflection of her own. He seemed to have a perpetual twinkle in his dark eyes.

"What about the snowstorm?" she demanded.

"Well, we found out that the snow wasn't as bad south of us. While the Denver area was still plowing out this morning, down in Pueblo the planes were on schedule again. We were fortunate to get tickets – a lot of other people had the same idea!"

"But, Robert, the roads must have still been bad," Del scolded. "You shouldn't have tried it!"

Secretly, Del was glad they did, but the mother in her needed to say something.

Robert chuckled. "There were a few times we thought so too, as we skidded a few times. But on the bright side, there wasn't much traffic!"

Emily, brushing snow from her hair, hugged Del and instructed the children to give their grandmother a kiss. Susan, a petite four-year-old with straight-as-a-poker dark hair, did so right away, but little Theresa hung back. Her honey-blond waves fell over her eyes as she clung to her mother's leg, thumb planted firmly in her mouth.

"Go on," urged Emily. "Give Grandma Del a kiss."

Theresa removed her thumb long enough to declare, "Farmer Del!"

"'Farmer Del'?" asked Del, puzzled. Everyone else laughed.

"I do believe," explained Emily with a broad smile, "that she has you mixed up with a certain nursery rhyme!"

Over dinner that evening there was animated talk and high spirits. Just before Del brought out the traditional "Happy Birthday to Jesus" cake, John announced he had something to say.

"I already mentioned this to Ma," he said as an aside and then continued, "Natalie and I are engaged!"

In the split second it took for Robert and Emily to assimilate the news, Del noticed her daughter-in-law eyeing Natalie's hair. However, sincere-sounding congratulations were quickly offered. Smiles were broad while everyone tried to imagine this *interesting* young woman as part of the family.

The children finished eating and ran off to play while the adults sat around the table drinking coffee and herbal tea. Emily glanced over at Robert and then addressed Del.

"We have some news, too," she declared. "We're having another baby!"

Del was excited and thrilled at this unexpected news, but it got even better.

"Also," Robert added, "My company is transferring me. We're going to be moving to Toledo."

"Toledo!" shouted Del with joy. "You're moving to Toledo? That's practically next door!"

The high spirits continued as they proceeded to the living room to open gifts. At the very last, John reached behind the couch and brought out a large package which was gift-wrapped attractively in foil and blue ribbons.

"This is for you, Ma. Merry Christmas!"

What could be so big? wondered Del. She tore off the paper, reached into the box and pulled out – a coat!

No, it wasn't purple. But it *was* a lovely deep, rich burgundy.

"Try it on," urged Natalie.

Del proceeded to do so. Knee-length, soft and cozily lined, the coat fit her perfectly.

"It's beautiful," she cried, and meant it. It may not have been purple but she loved it.

"Natalie picked it out," said John proudly.

Del looked over at the young woman.

"Why, Natalie, you have *wonderful* taste!" And she meant that, too.

The hour was late and John and Natalie needed to get going. As Del kissed them both goodbye, she reflected that there was a side to Natalie that she would like to know better.

At least, Del reflected gratefully, *she mentioned that she lives with her parents. Thank God! And that was definitely a cross around her neck. Maybe we'll have more in common than I thought.*

Later that night, after Robert and his family had turned in, Del sat praying quietly at the kitchen table. The house lights were off but the Christmas tree lights were still bathing the house in softly-gleaming radiance. The sky had cleared and the moon illuminated the snowy landscape. She could see a few white stars twinkling alongside the reflection of the colored tree lights in the window.

Silent night, she mused gratefully. *Holy night. Can it get any better than this?*

45

Crisis

Tuckered out from the previous day's festivities, they all slept late the morning after Christmas. For brunch Del whipped up some of her fabulous French toast and served it with the last of her homemade maple syrup. While eating, Del told them about Mara and the baby. She said she would like to go to the hospital to visit them, but she hated to leave her company by themselves.

"That's not a problem," responded Robert. "I was hoping to go see Greg today. Remember my old buddy from high school? He's here visiting his folks for Christmas and asked if we could drop by. But I don't like to see you drive to the city by yourself. Maybe I should go too."

Del had to chuckle to herself.

And how have I been doing it all this time? I can manage quite nicely, thank you.

"That's so kind of you, but really, I'll be fine. You and Emily enjoy your visit with Greg. And say hi for me!"

Upon arriving at the hospital, Del found Alyssa helping Mara pack her things in order to check out.

"They won't let me stay any longer," said the girl.

"Actually, it's the insurance company's policy," explained Alyssa. "One day and you're out. Mara's going to stay with her dad at the motel so she'll be close by."

As Del complimented Mara on how nice she looked in her new turquoise sweater, Scott walked in.

"Ready to go, babe?" he asked, picking up the bag with her few belongings.

Before leaving, they stopped at the NICU. As they approached the nursery, the neonatal specialist who had spoken to them before caught sight of them.

"Oh, good," he exclaimed, coming over to them. "I was just going to call you."

He looked at Mara. "I'm afraid there's been a slight setback."

Her face went white as the doctor explained quickly.

"The baby has developed a low-grade fever. We're not sure what this means yet. We've started her on intravenous antibiotics and have increased her oxygen a bit. She should be fine, but right now all we can do is wait and see. I don't think there's anything to worry about."

They were asked to wait in the visitors' room until Mara was given clearance to see the baby. To distract the girl from her worries, Del told her about everything that had happened at her house lately. Mara listened politely but inattentively. Every time someone went into the nursery, the girl's eyes would follow. Then Alyssa described Stephie's delight in opening her presents, and Scott chimed in with his own comic tale of trying to find a fast food restaurant open on Christmas day.

After an hour ticked by slowly, they all fell silent, lost in their own thoughts. Del took her rosary from her purse and sat quietly meditating on the third Joyful Mystery, the birth of Jesus. When she was finished, she looked up to find Scott's eyes on her. He leaned closer to her.

"One of my grandmothers used to pray the Rosary. I never understood what the fascination was with repeating the same prayers over and over."

Del explained how one was to meditate on the life of Christ while saying the Rosary prayers.

"But I meditate while reading Scripture," objected Scott.

"That's wonderful!" Del replied. "In fact, I do that too. But my rosary is always with me and my Bible isn't. So I simply pray through the life of Christ on these beads.

"I look at it this way," she continued in a confidential tone of voice. "Who knows him better than his own mother? When I say the Rosary I'm praying in union with Mary, and it helps me to see Jesus through her eyes..."

Their conversation was interrupted by a nurse telling Mara that she could go into the nursery for a few minutes. The others stood outside the large nursery window, watching the girl get scrubbed and gowned. After all that, she was only allowed to reach in to the incubator and stroke the baby's tiny arms and legs. They could see her talking to someone.

Returning to the hallway she said, "Her temperature hasn't gone down – but it hasn't gotten any worse, either. They suggested I leave and get some rest and they'd call if there was any change. I gave them Dad's cell phone number."

"I have to get going, honey," said her mother. "I need to pick up Stephie. It sure is lucky she likes it at the neighbor's place!"

"Mom, Dad, I need to talk to you about something first."

Mara's tired face was flooded with sadness. She said in a soft voice, "I just don't know if the baby is going to make it."

They tried to reassure her but she brushed off their remarks, continuing, "She's so little and she's got an uphill battle ahead of her. I want to do everything I can for her. So I've decided that I want to have her baptized."

Whatever it was they thought she was going to say, one could tell by the looks on their faces that that wasn't it. There was uncertain silence for a moment before Alyssa finally spoke.

"But, honey, we don't baptize infants."

Mara answered, "Some churches do."

"But we believe that a person should be old enough to make that decision for herself," Scott argued, shifting the bag he held to his other arm. "Maybe what you mean is you'd like to dedicate the baby to God. That would be a good idea."

Mara shook her head decisively.

"No. I want to get the baby baptized. Baptism isn't meant to be something that *we* do, but something God does for us. By being baptized we become part of the Christian family – and that's what I want for my baby."

Scott turned to look questioningly at Del. She threw up her hands.

"Don't look at me! I didn't tell her that!"

Mara explained that she had researched the subject on the internet and had decided a while ago that she wanted to do this. Clearly, Alyssa and Scott were uncomfortable, but in the end they both agreed that it was Mara's decision to make.

"Who would you get to baptize her?" asked Alyssa, bewildered.

"I called Amy this morning and asked if her father could do it. She's going to ask him."

Mara's parents were speechless, so Del asked, "Have you decided yet what to name the baby?"

Mara nodded.

"I'm going to name her Gianna." She pulled a folded, well-worn prayer card from her purse. "I've been asking St. Gianna to pray for me and the baby, and I like her name."

With a glance at Del she added quietly, "It's Gianna Christine."

After Alyssa left and Scott went to get the car, Del and Mara waited in the discharge area. The late afternoon sun, reflecting off the snow, dazzled blindingly through the glass doors. As a steady stream of people brushed past them, Del glanced at Mara, thinking, *She looks a little lost.*

"Are you all right?" she asked.

Tears sprang to the girl's eyes.

"It's just that everything has changed so much from when I first got here." A tear trickled down her face.

"Now I'm a mother. You know, Del, the baby is the only good thing to come out of all this. And I can't help it, I'm just so worried."

Del looked with compassion at the girl.

"Mara, you've been brave so far. You have to keep up your courage. Look at me."

Mara turned reddened eyes toward her.

"Child," the woman asked gently, "do you know what sets Christians apart from others?"

Mara shook her head and a shank of blond hair came loose from her ponytail. She seemed too tired to even think.

"Well, it's not faith," Del answered her own question. "It's true that we believe in Jesus. But everyone believes in *something.* And it's not love, since anyone can love.

"Mara – it's *hope.* Hope is what makes us different. Even when everything seems to be going wrong, it's hope that keeps our eyes on God, believing that he has a plan for our lives. You could say that hope is like an anchor. Storms may come along and rock the boat, but as long as it's anchored it won't drift away. God is our sure anchor. No matter what happens, we have to cling to hope in him."

Seeing Scott pull up in the old beater, they walked out to meet him. Mara asked Del if she was coming the next day.

"I'm sorry, honey. Robert and Emily will be leaving sometime tomorrow. But call me and let me know how little Gianna's doing and when the baptism will be. Okay?"

As Mara left with her dad, Del prayed, *She's come so far already, Lord, but she still has so far to go. Please be with her. And that little baby – so helpless, so sick – please bring healing to that child, Lord. I just don't know what it would do to Mara if she was to lose the baby after all this.*

46

Bearing Gifts We Traverse Afar

Del was feeling uneasy about the baby's condition from the moment she got up the next morning. However, she tried to take her mind off everything else and simply enjoy her limited time with her loved ones. Her family left in the afternoon to catch their flight home. Del was sad to see them go, but her feelings were tempered by the joy in knowing that soon they would be settling closer to her.

And another grandchild to look forward to! I am so blessed!

However, it wasn't long after their rental car pulled out of the driveway that Del found agitation once again growing in her.

A fine talker I am! she scolded herself fruitlessly. *Telling Mara to stop worrying – and all I've been doing since yesterday is worry!*

A phone call from Mara didn't help. Gianna's temperature had gone up a degree during the day. The doctor was going to let the baby be christened the next afternoon, but the only persons he would allow in the nursery were Mara and the minister.

While straightening the house, doing laundry and mopping floors, Del prayed continually. Making a light supper for herself, she prayed. Driving to church that evening for the choir's Christmas party, she prayed some more. As she climbed the steps to the church loft, she wondered if she had any energy left to celebrate with her friends.

However, the other choir members did not exhibit any lack of Christmas spirit. Munching on goodies and drinking punch, they were busy congratulating Laurie and Trish on the wonderful job they had done on the music. Trish, for her part, seemed more at ease with the others and was introducing her husband, Adrian, to everyone. Del shook his hand, impressed with his friendly attitude and blond good looks.

"You'll have to come to Mass," she invited, "to hear your wife sing."

He grinned. "Oh, I was here on Christmas Eve. That was the first time she's sung publicly in a long time and I wasn't about to miss it."

Del excused herself when she realized that Ernestine was waiting to speak with her.

"How are Mara and the baby doing?" the older woman, with a grandmotherly concern for the girl, asked.

Mae Beth overheard the question and she came over with Harriet tagging along. Del gave them the latest news, ending with, "Please pray that the baby pulls through this crisis." She could feel a knot of fear in her stomach. "In any case, she still has a long way to go 'til she can be released."

Mae Beth spoke up.

"You know, I was thinking...We all know that that little baby is going to be in the hospital for several months at least. And Del, you mentioned how insurance might not cover everything. Well, what if we were to donate the cookbook money toward helping to cover the medical expenses?"

By now, the rest of the choir had gathered around and heard Mae Beth's suggestion. Murmurs began to arise from the assembly. Some expressed support for this new, generous idea, while others were against it and a few were asking questions. Laurie didn't say anything and Del also stayed out of the debate, feeling that she was too intimately involved to be adding her two cents.

As the discussion got louder, Laurie had to ask them all to keep their voices down. Then she directed a question to Mae Beth.

"What are you thinking about, Mae Beth? Using some of the money, or all of it, or what?"

Mae Beth shrugged.

"Whatever we decide on as a group. I would vote for all of the money. We can get by on the piano we have for now. Helping someone in need like this – well, it would certainly be the right thing to do."

"I don't know about that," objected Franklin. "It seems to me that the people of this parish bought those cookbooks thinking that the money was going for a new piano. I'm not sure it would be right to divert those funds to someone most of them don't even know."

It would be nice to report that the dialogue continued after that with charitable hearts and cool heads prevailing. However, it only goes to show that reason tends to go out the window where emotions are concerned.

I wonder if someone put something in that punch? Del was thinking as she escaped from the rancor in the choir loft. She left the problem in the hands of the choir and its director, and only much later did she find out what was finally resolved. They did end up putting the cookbook money into a new piano. But in the spring, with that kind of small-town generosity which takes care of its own, a rummage and bake sale would be held. A joint venture with the Presbyterian church down the street, its proceeds would go toward paying off the baby's outstanding medical bills.

However, at the time Del knew nothing of all this. She just knelt in prayer before the tabernacle, hearing the buzz of voices for some time before the party dispersed. She prayed for peace and harmony for all her friends before turning to the more pressing needs troubling her heart.

There was, of course, still the matter of George and his proposal. She sought earnestly to understand God's will in the matter. She didn't trust her emotions, as one day she was ready to say yes to George and the next day she wasn't so sure. She prayed for a clear answer, but there seemed to be only silence in return. Finally, she wearily left this particular need in the hands of God, trusting that he would help her to know in his own good time.

Trust was a little harder to come by in her prayers for Gianna.

O, my Lord Jesus Christ, savior and compassionate healer, I beg you to spare the life of this child. You must have a plan for this little one, even if we don't know what it is. Please help her to gain strength and fight off this infection. And Lord, I'm worried about Mara. She has gone through so much...Hang it all, why don't I ever have a tissue when I need it?

Tears streamed down her cheeks while she searched in vain through her pockets. Images of death and "what if's" kept floating through her mind, agitating her and causing a fresh bout of worry. She wasn't finding any comfort in prayer this day, no whisper to her agonizing soul that everything would be all right.

192

At last, worn out and bleary-eyed, Del brushed away her tears with the back of a hand. At that point she happened to glance at the floor near where she knelt, and for the first time noticed the three kings, in colorful raiment, standing next to their camels. She remembered, during this week before Epiphany, the custom of moving them little by little closer to where the Christ Child lay in the manger. To take her mind off her problems for a few minutes, she decided that this would be a good time to pray a favorite Christmas mediation, one which had become a yearly tradition for her.

Taking several deep breaths to clear her mind, she made a valiant attempt to focus on the king who was bringing gold. Del contemplated how much "treasure" she possessed in material blessings – enough to eat, a nice house, *and don't forget Windmill Gardens,* she reminded herself. She presented them all as a gift to the Baby Jesus.

You gave them to me, and they are all yours, Lord.

Next she reflected on the second king, bringing frankincense – *a token of our praise and thanksgiving which rises to the throne of God.* For a few moments she gave unto the Lord all the honor and glory and gratitude she could muster, even though, to her, it seemed so small an offering.

From the last king there was myrrh, that bitter perfume given to the Child, foreshadowing the torment the Man would endure for the salvation of all.

And my sorrows also, Lord, I give over to you. The difficulties in my heart, my bitterly sad soul and my helplessness in the face of suffering...

Her attention returned abruptly to the plight of baby Gianna. As she knelt staring at the three kings, there was a nagging little thought which kept running around the edges of her mind. At first she was unable to identify it. Then, as she searched the depths of her heart to find the cause, Del realized that her prayers of recent days were bordering on desperation. With a profound feeling of disquiet, she began to understand that she had become so intimately caught up in the lives of Mara and her baby that she was unable to bear the thought of losing either one. With sudden clarity, she could see the fear which had been stalking her relentlessly and she came to know it was born out of her own tragedy of losing her daughter so many years ago.

That moment of insight brought on a raging mental and spiritual battle in Del. She felt the overwhelming desire in her to keep holding her newly-found beloved ones closely to her, to grasp them so tightly that her own ferocious affection would allow nothing dreadful to happen to them.

Yet, she knew in her heart of hearts that she needed to let them go – to open the prison of her love and release them – and leave them entirely to God's providence and his design. She struggled mightily to make this one final oblation. Pain settled into the depths of her being and she felt as if her very heart was being torn from her in her reluctance to give up her hold on them.

Finally, it was only when she joined her prayers to those of Mary – *'Fiat,' may it be done according to your word* – that Del found the courage she so desperately needed to place her offering, like that of the kings, at the foot of the manger.

Her head cradled in her hands, she cried again, but now the tears were of liberation and acceptance. In refusing to cling any longer, there was peace.

God's will be done – whatever may happen.

47

Christening

On the following day, Del headed out for the baptismal ceremony. Driving to the hospital, she thought about the previous evening. After she had completed her prayers, even though spent from the anguished mental wrestling, she had taken a few moments to tidy the bouquets around the altar. Branches of barberry, bare except for their red pendant berries, had been tucked the previous week amongst the greenery. And now she noticed there were new, tiny green leaves sprouting from the branches between the thorns.

That always happens, she reminded herself, *once you place them in water.*

However, in her current frame of mind, it seemed to be a hopeful sign – new life springing forth. And as she reached the NICU, Mara reported that Gianna's temperature was nearly normal. That was good news, certainly, even though the baby was still on a higher level of oxygen.

Others were arriving for the baptism and the hospital corridor was taking on an air of celebration. Besides Mara's parents, Eva was there with her daughters Risa and Megan. After a little while, a tall black man with grey hair and a winsome smile strode in. Spying Scott, he walked over to shake hands and Scott introduced his friend Marshall to everyone. Del was pleased to meet him. She knew that he was a man of prayer, and many prayers were going to be needed in the coming months.

The last of the guests to arrive were Reverend Symon, his wife and daughters. The girls were hugging Mara when the neonatologist came in with Dr. Walkerman. The two MD's conferred briefly before calling Mara over.

"Mara, you and the reverend can start scrubbing and suiting up. And we've decided that since the baby's temperature is down, your parents can go in with you also."

When Del heard Mara ask, "Could my grandma come in too?" she looked around, puzzled.

Her grandma? Is her grandmother here somewhere?

Del saw Dr. Walkerman smiling furtively at her.

Del cast her gaze at the floor but her mouth twitched. *I guess I've been elevated to honorary grandma,* she thought in delight, but was disappointed to hear the other doctor say too many visitors in the nursery would not be a good idea.

So Del joined the rest of the group which would watch the proceedings through the nursery window. Eva held Stephie in her arms and showed her the incubators in the room.

"Baby! Baby! Baby!" said Stephie, pointing. "Lotsa babies!"

Laughing, Eva tried to direct the child's attention to where baby Gianna's Isolette stood. It was difficult to follow what was happening. As Mara and her parents had their heads bowed, it seemed like the pastor was starting with prayer.

The solemn moment was suddenly shattered by a shriek from another monitor in the nursery. Several nurses converged on a nearby incubator to check on an infant. Satisfied that it was a false alarm, they turned it off and the ceremony continued.

Reverend Symon looked around and one of the nurses handed him a small cup.

"The water for the christening," murmured Marshall. As the reverend reached into the incubator, out in the hallway Marshall continued speaking in his sonorous voice, repeating the words of baptism for all to hear.

"Gianna Christine, I baptize thee in the name of the Father and of the Son and of the Holy Spirit."

Together, all the watchers outside the window replied, "Amen!"

From the start of the ceremony, Del noticed that Mara's parents were standing next to each other. Now she saw Alyssa slip her hand through Scott's arm. Marshall apparently saw it, too. He glanced over at Del and winked.

With a broad smile, Del repeated the "Amen" in her heart. *And alleluia!* she added.

48

What Gladsome Tidings Be

The assembly managed to commandeer the visitors' room for a celebration. A few streamers were quickly hung between the doorway and windows. Brightly colored balloons were taped to the walls, intriguing Stephie who was determined to have one of them as her own. Alyssa kept impatiently shooing the child off the chair where she was climbing in order to reach them. Scott, laughing at the little girl's exuberance, finally plucked a big pink balloon for her.

Eva brought decorated cookies and the pastor's wife had baked a lovely cake. The caring staff of the NICU had been invited also, and nurses and specialists wandered in and out on their breaks to enjoy a sweet or two. Eva's girls ladled out the punch into pink plastic cups while Alyssa cut the cake and Scott handed out the pieces.

Everyone's here except the guest of honor, mused Del. *Well, I guess punch and cookies wouldn't do her much good.*

She looked through the window of the room to where the nursery was. *Sleep in heavenly peace, beloved child of God,* she prayed. *Sleep and grow strong.*

She looked but didn't see Mara anywhere. While everyone else was conversing in groups of twos and threes, Del walked around the large room's perimeter until she spied the girl. Mara was sitting by herself, half hidden by a towering potted ficus plant.

"What are you doing back here all by yourself?"

"Just thinking."

As she sat in a nearby chair, Del noticed how the girl's blue eyes were dark-circled with fatigue.

"What about?" she inquired compassionately.

197

Mara stared at the floor.

"I've been thinking about all kinds of things," she answered quietly, "and praying too. Del, you know what?" She looked up again.

"I just don't think I can do it."

"Do what?"

"Be the kind of mother that my baby needs."

The girl's eyes glistened with tears as she continued, "She might have lots of medical problems because she came so early. And even if she doesn't..." Mara stopped and gulped, then took a deep breath.

"Oh, what do I know about being a mother?" she wailed softly.

Del reached over and took the girl's hand.

"Mara, what are you trying to say?"

The girl wiped her wet face with her free hand.

"Ever since you told me about St. Gianna, I've been praying for her help. I want to have the kind of courage that she had, to do the best thing for my baby.

"Del, I haven't told anyone else yet, but I decided this morning..."

She looked up, her eyes big pools of tears.

"...that I'm going to ask Trish if she and her husband will adopt Gianna."

"Trish?" Del asked, astonished.

The girl nodded. Then Del remembered the time she had first seen the two of them together in the choir loft, when she wondered if they already knew each other.

"How is it that you know Trish?"

"I met her and Adrian at Thanksgiving."

"Thanksgiving?" Del was bewildered.

"Yes." Mara stared at her uncomprehending expression.

"Del, don't you know who Trish is?"

Still confused, Del simply shook her head.

"She's Eva's daughter."

"Trish?" Del's jaw dropped and then suddenly the light dawned. *Patricia!*

"For heaven's sakes!" she exclaimed. "That explains her face. She was in that horrible accident!"

Mara nodded. "She was also injured internally and can't have children. She and her husband have already applied for a foster-care license because they were hoping to adopt a child."

Del had to take a moment so her head could catch up with her emotions. Finally she asked, "Did Eva suggest this?"

The girl shook her head.

"She told me about her daughter when I saw a picture of her on Eva's desk at the center, but she never tried to influence me as to what I should do. Anyway, I didn't really decide until I was praying this morning."

Although Mara was still weeping quietly, it was clear that she had made up her mind. There was a new sense of determination and serenity about her.

Del sat thinking quietly for a moment. Then she said softly, "Child, you've discovered the secret of real love. That's to love your baby so much that you're willing to sacrifice your own desires for her sake."

Suddenly, another thought popped into Del's mind and a revelation hit her like a ton of bricks. In retrospect, she knew that this insight had been with her all along, but until now she had refused to take a good look at it.

George! she thought with an ache in her heart. *Would he want me to give up my home? How could I continue to have my beautiful garden? He would probably want to travel – and who knows what other changes I'd have to make in my life. I'm a fine one to talk about sacrifices! I realize now that I don't have the kind of love for George which would put him first in my life.*

Sadness engulfed her and she was weeping too.

It would never work out...

Mara was saying, "I want the best for Gianna. I want my little girl to have a mother and a father who both love her."

She pushed back the hair which had fallen into her eyes and wiped her wet face on her sleeve. Del needed a tissue herself, but her pockets were empty. So she opened her roomy purse and, pulling out a roll of toilet paper, tore off a generous piece for Mara.

"Here. Use this."

The girl reached out and took it with the barest hint of a smile breaking through the tears.

"Del, why do you have that in your purse?"

"What? This?"

Del held up the toilet paper roll and explained in a confidential whisper, "It's because the last time I used the restroom here, they were out."

She tried to rip off a piece to dry her own tears but somehow lost her grip on the roll. It flew into the air and went reeling off down the tiled floor where it bumped to a stop against Scott's shoe. He looked down, and then Alyssa and the others noticed it. In a twinkle everyone was staring at Del, still holding one end of the long trail of toilet paper in her hand.

Mara giggled through her tears. Del shrugged and rolled her eyes in dismay.

This one, she figured, *is going to be awfully hard to live down.*

Epilogue

On February fifth, two weeks before her original due date, little Gianna Christine went home from the hospital in the loving arms of her new parents, Trish and Adrian Allbright. Mara went on to finish her senior year of high school, making plans to join Peter at college in the fall. Scott and Alyssa began to phone each other frequently – "just to talk." George eventually moved to California to be closer to his daughter's family.

And Del? Well, that spring she would often stand at her kitchen window, admiring the flowers as they awakened from their winter's sleep. She'd reflect on the strange twists and turns of life which took away people she cared about and brought into her heart new ones to love. She prayed unceasingly for Mara, that desperate soul whose footsteps the Lord had guided to Windmill Gardens. And for little Gianna, a child conceived in violence and thrust all too soon into the world, she prayed for an overflowing cup of blessings all her days.

"And a little child shall lead them..." Isaiah 11:6

Endnotes

For further reading on the beauty and holiness of marriage as taught
by the Catholic Church:
Humanae Vitae (Of Human Life), encyclical of Pope Paul VI, 1968.
www.vatican.va (proceed to "Site Map")

Good News About Sex and Marriage: Answers to Your Honest Questions
about Catholic Teaching, Christopher West, Servant Books, St. Anthony
Messenger Press, Cincinnati, Ohio, 2004.

Chapter 4: "Jelly and Deli"
The rule about abstaining from meat...
 The Code of Canon Law states that Fridays of the whole year
are to be days of penance, and that the bishops of any particular country
may determine the particular ways in which fast and abstinence are to be
observed. (Canons 1250, 1251, 1253) In 1966, the U.S. bishops, in their
Complementary Norms on Penance and Abstinence wrote, "Friday
should be in each week something of what Lent is in the entire year. For
this reason we urge all to prepare for that weekly Easter that comes with
each Sunday by freely making of every Friday a day of self-denial and
mortification in prayerful remembrance of the passion of Jesus
Christ...We give first place to abstinence from flesh meat. We do so in
the hope that the Catholic community will ordinarily continue to abstain
from meat by free choice as formerly we did in obedience to Church
law."

...abortion is legal in the U.S. even up through the ninth month...
 For further information on the background of Doe v. Bolton, the
Supreme Court case which allows abortion even in the last months of
pregnancy, go to www.priestsforlife.org/testimony/ffsandracano.html.

Chapter 7: "Choir Rehearsal"
...she picked up her scapular...
 The brown scapular is not a magical charm nor an automatic
guarantee of salvation. Rather, it is an outward sign of one's commitment
to live like Mary – being totally open to God's will and living a Christ-
centered life. www.carmelnet.org/scapular/scapular.htm

Chapter 9: *"Fruits and Nuts"*
"By their fruits you shall know them."
From Matthew 7:16-17: "You shall know them by their fruits. Do men gather grapes of thorns, or figs of thistles? Even so every good tree brings forth good fruit, but a corrupt tree brings forth evil fruit."

Chapter 12: *"Whoever Welcomes the Least of These"*
"...the pill acts as an abortifacient..."
For more information on how the birth control pill can cause an early abortion, go to http://epm.org/articles/bcp3300.html.

"Children are a heritage from the Lord; blessed the man whose quiver is full of them."
Psalm 127:3-5: "Lo, children are a heritage of the Lord: and the fruit of the womb is his reward. As arrows are in the hand of a mighty man; so are children of the youth. Happy is the man that has his quiver full of them..."

For more information on the ethical problems of contraception and the joy of following God's plan for marriage, see *Open Embrace: A Protestant Couple Rethinks Contraception* by Sam and Bethany Torode, William B. Eerdmans Publishing Company, Grand Rapids, Michigan, 2002.   www.openembrace.com

These organizations have information on Natural Family Planning:
Billings Ovulation Method: www.boma-usa.org
Couple to Couple League   www.ccli.org
One More Soul   www.omsoul.com

"...Christ gave himself entirely..."
Ephesians 5:25: "Husbands, love your wives, even as Christ also loved the church, and gave himself for it..."

Chapter 13: *"The Singer"*
...the power of beauty to lay hold of our souls."
"...human beings by nature desire the beautiful."
St. Basil the Great
"In his essence, man is created with a hunger for the beautiful; he is that very hunger."
Paul Evdokimov, Orthodox theologian

Chapter 15: "Interlude"
Didn't Dostoyevsky say something about...
"Only beauty is absolutely indispensable, for without beauty there is nothing left in the world worth doing."
> Fyodor Dostoyevsky (1821-1881)

Chapter 17: "To Have and To Hold"
Sacrifice is always tedious and irksome. Love makes it bearable; perfect love makes it a joy.
> The Exhortation before Marriage, found in *Collectio Rituum pro Dioecesibus Civitatum Foederatarum Americae Septentrionalis.* Washington, D.C.: Benziger Brothers, Inc., 1964.

Chapter 19: "Market Day"
"...God's promise that he will give us all we need."
Matthew 6: 32-33: "...Your heavenly Father knows that you have need of all these things. But seek first the kingdom of God, and his righteousness; and all these things shall be added unto you."

"...a morning offering..."
A "morning offering" is a prayer consecrating the entire day, and all our works, to the glory of God and the advancement of his kingdom. Our own wording is acceptable, but many use a prayer such as the following:
"Oh, my Jesus, through the Immaculate Heart of Mary, I offer you all my prayers, works, joys and sufferings of this day, in union with the Holy Sacrifice of the Mass being offered around the world, in reparation for sin and for the intentions of the Blessed Mother and of the Holy Father."

"...he [Jesus] changes us to be more like him."
John 6:56: "He that eats my flesh and drinks my blood, dwells in me, and I in him."

Chapter 20: "Del Explains All"
"...what the aftereffects of abortion are..."
To find out more about the aftereffects of abortion, go to www.hopeafterabortion.com.

Chapter 23: "The Sunday Before Thanksgiving"
"If a couple lives together before marriage..."
Alfred DeMario and K Vaninadha Rao, in their article "Premarital Cohabitation and Marital Instability in the United States: A Reassessment" *(Journal of Marriage and the Family* 54, 1992) say those who are willing to cohabitate before marriage tend to view relationships

as temporary. This mentality fosters in them an attitude that is more conducive to divorce.

Alan Booth and David Johnson ("Premarital Cohabitation and Marital Success," *Journal of Family Issues* 9, 1988) found that cohabitation is related to lower levels of marital interaction, higher levels of marital disagreement, and marital instability.

www.jknirp.com/cohab/htm

Chapter 26: "Birthday Party"
He [Jesus] had no earthly possessions to leave us...

Taken from a homily by St. Peter Julian Eymard (1811-1868), who was known for his passionate love for Jesus Christ in the Holy Eucharist.

"...a wandering sheep who had come back to the fold..."

1Peter 2:25: "For you were as sheep going astray; but are now returned to the Shepherd and Bishop of your souls."

"Let your mercy be on us, O Lord, as we place our trust in you."

Taken from Psalm 33:22

Chapter 28: "Heart to Heart"

St. Gianna Beretta Molla was born in Italy in 1922. From her childhood she had a strong faith in God. As a young woman she composed a prayer which she said regularly. It began, "O Jesus, I promise to submit myself to all that you permit to befall me; make me only know your will..." She became a pediatrician, and was known for her charity towards mothers and their children, the elderly and the poor. She married Pietro Molla in 1955, and when the doctors suggested she abort her fourth child in order to save her own life, she steadfastly refused. Her daughter was born on Holy Saturday, 1962, and Gianna died a week later.   www.gianna.org

"Why don't you ask her to pray for you, too?"

Those who have finished their earthly lives and live in perfect union with God in heaven are powerful intercessors for us who are still on earth. "Since all the faithful form one body, the good of each is communicated to the others..."   St. Thomas Aquinas.

"Being more closely united to Christ, those who dwell in heaven fix the whole Church more firmly in holiness...They do not cease to intercede with the Father for us, as they proffer the merits which they acquired on earth through the one mediator between God and men, Christ Jesus...So by their fraternal concern is our weakness greatly helped."

Catechism of the Catholic Church, par. 956

Chapter 30: "Invitations"
...the Feast of the Immaculate Conception.

The feast of the Immaculate Conception honors the unique privilege given Mary of being the mother of the Son of God. It was fitting that she who was to give flesh to the second Person of the Trinity would be preserved from the stain of original sin in her own flesh. "The Most Blessed Virgin Mary was, from the first moment of her conception, by a singular grace and privilege of almighty God and by virtue of the merits of Jesus Christ, Savior of the human race, preserved immune from all stain of original sin." Pope Pius IX, *Ineffabilis Deus,* 1854.

Chapter 31: "The Presence"
"...you could say that God is everywhere..."

"God is everywhere, in the very air I breathe, yes, everywhere, but in His Sacrament of the Altar he is as present actually and really as my soul within my body." St. Elizabeth Ann Seton

"I will be with you always..."
Matthew 28:20b

Chapter 40: "O Tannenbaum"
"In those days a decree went out from Caesar Augustus..."
Luke 2:1-17

Chapter 43: "Christmas Day"
...he [Jesus] takes on the nature of bread to nourish us...

The Council of Trent (1551) stated: "Because Christ our Redeemer said that it was truly his body that he was offering under the species of bread, it has always been the conviction of the Church of God, and this holy Council now declares again, that by the consecration of the bread and wine there takes place a change of the whole substance of the bread into the substance of the body of Christ our Lord and of the whole substance of the wine into the substance of his blood."

The world will be saved through beauty.

"...the world will be saved through beauty. There is only one absolutely beautiful thing in the world whose apparition is a miracle of beauty: Christ." Fyodor Dostoyevsky, author

Chapter 45: _"Crisis"_
"Baptism isn't meant to be something we do..."
"Born with a fallen nature and tainted by original sin, children also have need of the new birth in Baptism to be freed from the power of darkness and brought into the realm of the freedom of the children of God, to which all men are called. The sheer gratuitousness of the grace of salvation is particularly manifest in infant Baptism...The practice of infant Baptism is an immemorial tradition of the Church. There is explicit testimony to this practice from the second century on, and it is quite possible that, from the beginning of the apostolic preaching, when whole 'households' received baptism, infants may also have been baptized."

Catechism of the Catholic Church, par. #1250, 1252.

For more information, go to
www.catholic.com/library/Infant_Baptism.asp

Chapter 46: _"Bearing Gifts We Traverse Afar"_
'Fiat,' may it be done according to your word.
From Luke 1:38

For more information on the Catholic Faith:
Catechism of the Catholic Church, 1997, Libreria Editrice Vaticana.
(available in bookstores or online at
www.nccbuscc.org/catechism/text/index.htm)

Also see:
www.jimmyakin.com
www.catholicoutlook.com

Reflection/Discussion Questions

1. According to Catholic teaching, a Christian marriage is to be based on the concept of total self-giving, the way Christ gave himself totally for his Bride, the Church. How does that idea differ from what the world tells us a marriage should be?

2. Have you ever been touched by something so beautiful that it was hard to find words to express what you were feeling? In what way does beauty leads us to search more fervently for God?

3. Sacramentals, such as the scapular, can help us to develop a deeper prayer life by being constant reminders of God. Do you have any sacramentals on your person or in your home which help you keep your focus on the Lord?

4. Del believes that receiving the Eucharist and regular confession are the "Golden Keys" which enable one to receive all the graces that God wants us to have in our particular vocation. In what ways do you think these "keys" are instrumental in this?

5. The "Three Kings Prayer" helps Del to lay all at the feet of her Lord and Savior. Is there a prayer that is especially meaningful to you, which helps you to surrender everything in your life to God? Is this prayer difficult to pray at times?

<u>**A READER'S GUIDE TO**</u>

Windmill Gardens

AND

The Christmas Baby

Carol Ann Tardiff

Interview with the author

Before writing *Windmill Gardens,* you'd never written fiction before. How did it come about?

The idea to write a novel came to me one day out of the blue. I kept pushing the thought aside as my interest and training has been in the visual arts, not the literary arts. But the idea would not go away. It was difficult for me to believe that this was really an inspiration from God since the idea was so preposterous. I kept saying, "I don't have time to do this. I don't know how to write. I don't even like to write letters!"

Still, the thought wouldn't leave, even when I was praying. Finally, in frustration I said, "Okay, Lord, if this is from you, then what would I write about?" I figured that would get me off the hook, as one always hears that authors should write from their experience – and I couldn't think of anything in my whole life that would be interesting enough to write about! However, a story started running through my mind, almost like a movie, about a runaway girl who stumbles upon a beautiful garden and a woman who extends mercy and compassion to the hurting teenager. From there flowed the idea of using the Divine Mercy message as an underlying theme for the story.

What about the flowers in the garden and the wild plants? Where did all that come from?

The storyline was rather bare-bones in the beginning, but as it kept playing over and over in my head it seemed like God was showing me that I *did* have experience with a few things. I love flowers and have long had an interest in wild plants. I also grew up on a farm which had a windmill. Somehow, it all started to work into the story. In addition, I have been involved in the pro-life movement for many years, so that, too, became part of the plot.

But why a Catholic novel?

I knew right from the very start that this was supposed to be a Catholic novel. My relationship to Jesus Christ and to his Church is the most important thing in my life. It became intriguing to see if it was possible to impart faithfully the true teachings of the Church while also maintaining a respect for others' religious beliefs, all within the context of an interesting story.

Is the character of Del modeled after anyone you know?

Del was created from bits and pieces of many, many people I know and love! But mostly she's modeled after saints whose biographies I have read. Often we tend to think of "saints" as people who lived a long time ago and did heroic things which we ourselves don't feel capable of emulating. Yet as followers of Christ we are *all* called to live holy lives in the midst of our everyday activities, by making God the center of and reason for our lives. When we attempt to do that, depending entirely on God's grace – no matter how feeble our efforts seem – we will find compassion towards others and joy spilling out of our hearts. Just like Del.

Are there any books you've read which have influenced the writing of *Windmill Gardens* and *The Christmas Baby?*

Whenever I have time to read fiction, which isn't very often, I like a book that is uplifting and one from which I can learn something, even if it is just a novel. Most novels being written today are either embarrassing or depressing in subject matter, or they are so unbelievable as to be ridiculous. Why would anyone want to waste their time reading that kind of stuff? However, there was one novel I really enjoyed, *The Keeper of the Bees* by Gene Stratton-Porter, originally published in the 1920's. The book was about a seriously ill man who found healing in a beautiful garden, and I'm sure it had an influence on *Windmill Gardens.*

Why the theme of marriage for *The Christmas Baby?*

Quite simply because the Catholic Church's teachings on sexuality and marriage are the best-kept secret in the Church, and in society, today. A book like Christopher West's *Good News About Sex and Marriage* (recommended in the Endnotes) lays out these teachings in a sensitive and compelling way. Authentic Catholic thought on love, marriage and sexuality, and indeed life itself, are the most *integrated* and profoundly beautiful a person will find anywhere. It may be only upon living them that one discovers the treasure that they are.

You say that the story of *Windmill Gardens* kept playing through your head like a movie. Was *The Christmas Baby* just as easy to write?

I don't want to give the impression that God "dictated" *Windmill Gardens* to me! I wish it had been that easy! While the idea of the story certainly seemed to come from Him, I still had the hard work of figuring out *how* to write down what was in my head. Yet it's true the story line was strongly present to me right from the beginning. *The Christmas Baby* was totally different. The title popped into my mind, even before the first book was finished, but I had no idea if this was supposed to be a second book or if it was just a random thought. Strangely enough, the funny episode about Del's pants came to me first, and then a possible beginning and a vague notion of how the story could end. Since that's all I had, I did a lot of praying about it, wondering if this was really the start of another book. Finally I decided to write down what I had so far. I figured if this was from God then He would guide me to the next step, and if nothing happened, I would give it up.

So what happened?

The first thing I did was write what seemed to be a good beginning for the book. Then, having no idea what to do next, I wrote the "Fruits and Nuts" chapter. After that the second chapter came to me, and from there on I wrote it straight through. However, I never knew where a chapter was going when I sat down at the computer. I just started each time with a prayer for guidance. What was strange to me was how writing this book was so different from the first one. Yet isn't that how God often works? When He first asks you to do something that seems totally outside your field of competence, His guidance is strong and certain. Then it often feels as if He pulls away, leaving you to stumble along on your own while you pray and search for His will. He is still there, still leading you, but now He is asking you to trust Him, to go ahead and take that next step into the unknown. When we do that, who knows what exciting paths we'll find ourselves on?

Any more books in the future?

Only God knows!

Acknowledgments

I would like to thank my husband Dan and our children for their support for another of "Mom's projects." Also, special thanks are due to friends Cynthia and Tony Yanik, my excellent proofreader Eleanor Burley and my pastor, Fr. John Riccardo. I couldn't have done it without all of you.

Windmill Gardens
by the author of *The Christmas Baby*

A contemporary novel of Divine Mercy for adults and teens
Paperbound   195 pages $14.95

Looking out the kitchen window at her beautiful garden, the woman is startled to see a teenage girl emerge from the woods and slip into the old work shed. She tries to help the runaway, yet the girl's past remains a mystery. The gardener has a few secrets of her own, which may explain why she acts a bit eccentric at times. But she intercedes for her young guest with a heart that has come to know God's love and forgiveness, and so is able to extend mercy to another.

Praise for *Windmill Gardens*

"Carol's descriptive writing draws the reader in very quickly but softly. Right away you will feel as if you are living in the middle of, or down the road from, Del's house and the Windmill Gardens. This book is a beautiful way to escape our fast-paced world and a wonderful tool to help us get closer to the Lord and learn even more about loving and giving...It's like taking a retreat in your own home."
Teresa Tomeo, talk show host, Ave Maria Radio, Detroit

"Excellent!"   Fr. John Riccardo, pastor, St. Anastasia parish, Troy, MI

"A wonderful story and characters made it very enjoyable, and I find myself praying more during the Lenten season because of the 'lady gardener'."
Marilyn Grodi, wife of Marcus Grodi ("Coming Home Network")

"It was a thoroughly enjoyable read...It will certainly bolster your faith."
Mary Jo Johnson, librarian, Our Lady Queen of Martyrs parish

"I found this book to be very inspirational. I had a hard time putting it down and read it in two days. Carol's knowledge of gardening is a bonus and a delight for those of us without a 'green thumb'."
Eleanor Burley, editor, *Marian Observer*

www.BuyBooksOnTheWeb.com
or call 1-877-BUY BOOK

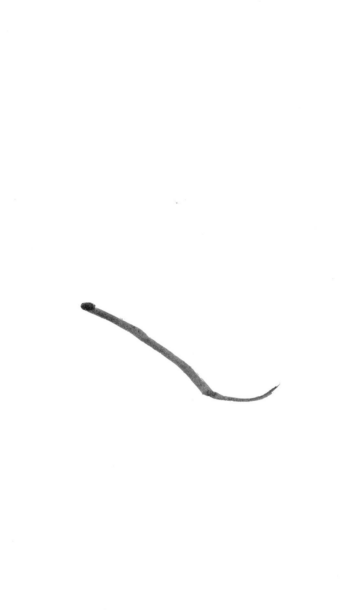